BRING A WARM COAT

Bring a Warm Coat

M.E. Hardiman

Copyright © 2022 by M.E. Hardiman.

Library of Congress Control Number:		2022917411
ISBN:	Hardcover	978-1-6641-0822-6
	Softcover	978-1-6641-0821-9
	eBook	978-1-6641-0820-2

All rights reserved. No part of this book may be reproduced or transmitted in any form or by any means, electronic or mechanical, including photocopying, recording, or by any information storage and retrieval system, without permission in writing from the copyright owner.

This is a work of fiction. Names, characters, places and incidents either are the product of the author's imagination or are used fictitiously, and any resemblance to any actual persons, living or dead, events, or locales is entirely coincidental.

Any people depicted in stock imagery provided by Getty Images are models, and such images are being used for illustrative purposes only.
Certain stock imagery © Getty Images.

Print information available on the last page.

Rev. date: 09/16/2022

To order additional copies of this book, contact:
Xlibris
NZ TFN: 0800 008 756 (Toll Free inside the NZ)
NZ Local: 9-801 1905 (+64 9801 1905 from outside New Zealand)
www.Xlibris.co.nz
Orders@Xlibris.co.nz

845476

Chapter 1

A lot of negative adjectives ran through her head: *bleak, dismal, wretched*. She was looking out the tiny excuse for a window at the village below her attic room, not quite close enough to London to be exciting but near enough for the need to have black-out curtains – another reason she felt hemmed in and cut off, curfews with no action. *If it wasn't for the weather,* she thought, *it might be fine.* She might feel better. *The weather is so constant though*, she thought flatly. How had she become so dejected feeling? *The weather excuse can only go so far.*

She shook her head, struck her cheeks firmly. *Pull yourself together.* She could hear her grandmother's voice. *Ruth, you are too insular, too in your own head.*

Grandma Hetty, short for Henrietta, was the complete opposite. There were family legends of her tangled up in espionage in the First World War, legends she never confirmed or denied, but Ruth was sure they were true. She admired her grandmother.

'A lady before her time,' people said.

The bright clothes and outspoken personality as well as the attitude that she could and did do anything she pleased were, for most people, including Ruth's mother, too much. Ruth aspired, in her own 'insular' way, to be like her grandma, to be a little bit adventurous, at least just in thought. In reality, she stuck to what her mother proudly stated as a solid profession – teaching.

She turned her back on the window, facing the tall wardrobe and dressing table. The furniture was far too large for the room, but her landlady had forbidden her to keep the wardrobe on the landing. There was plenty of room, but it was forbidden. Of course, she could have had a sensibly sized wardrobe, but that would have meant letting go of her vast variety of clothes. She had not inherited her grandmother's gusto, but she had indeed instilled a love of fashion in Ruth. The wardrobe had fit perfectly in her bedroom at home, in fact made for the space, matching the architraves and doors, and before the war, it gave her great pleasure to fill it full of items. She would not give these up lightly, even if it meant squeezing in through the door that only opened halfway – a small price.

Absently, she twitched the wardrobe door open. The sleeve of her green felt jacket was poking out. She remembered the day she had bought it, her grandmother had 'business' in London and thought Ruth might like to accompany her. It seemed a lifetime ago now, and she supposed it really was. She had always liked the idea of the hustle and bustle of the London streets. However, it was too much for her when it came to actually being in the crowds, mixed with the sights and smells. On this particular occasion, her grandmother left her at the top of Oxford Street with a sweeping gesture and a passing comment of 'Buy something I would be proud of' before stepping into the throng of people and leaving her to her own devices. Ruth remembered the bewildering feeling and shuddered.

Looking back down at the jacket sleeve in her hand, she could see her grandmother disappearing into the crowd. She stood out for a long time in her bright plum-coloured hat. Ruth had been spurred on by the London women in flowing skirts, fitted jackets, and angled hats, with shoes to match. She stepped off the curb and, without aim, went with the flow of people. She remembered pushing back the panic and the urge to stop as she made her way to the side of the footpath with the shopfronts. There was an inset door which had given her relief from the crowd and, in the window, the exact jacket that would make grandma proud.

On the train, her grandmother had slipped her some notes. Ruth had been shocked at the amount, but money had never seemed to be an issue for her grandmother. From all accounts, she had never worked, and her grandfather had died young, killed in an accident at work on a building site. Grandma had always spoke fondly of him and said he would have loved his little granddaughter.

Ruth's mother always shook her head at her own mother, treating her with the huff and puff of a bothersome child, and never really had time to tell Ruth much about her. Nonetheless, Ruth had got along splendidly with her grandmother. At the time, the green jacket with matching green check-patterned dress felt like slipping into it meant slipping into another life where she was brave, vibrant, and admired, just like Grandma Hetty.

From top to toe, it was all she wanted. The green stiff felt hat was a style she hadn't seen before – a round top and scooping over the ears and a round brim arching elegantly back above the brow. The dress was the perfect, modern length, stopping to swish just past mid-shin and with a long flowing scarf-tie neck. Little white gloves poked out at the end of the jacket sleeves. *That green jacket.* She sucked in her breath; she could still see the shop lady smiling primly and beckoning her inside.

The shop lady had said, 'I believe you'd like this outfit in an eighteen. Is that right?'

Ruth had been embarrassingly dumbstruck. She had been acutely aware of what the beautiful shop lady must have thought of her flat shoes and her stiff skirt. The lady set about fussing with arranging everything and instructing Ruth on how to tie and zip and fold, and before she knew it, she was running her gloved hands over the beautiful folds and angles of the jacket, and the lady finished off the look by tying the belt at a jaunty angle on her hip.

'I really don't think you should leave without shoes.' The lady had been pushy, looking back. 'Double A, narrow?'

Remembering the shame she had felt at not knowing her own shoe size, Ruth squeezed harder on the door of the wardrobe. After that day, she never went without fashion; it seemed to be the way she could think as herself but be someone completely different on the outside, so different that day that she had to call to her grandmother outside the underground as she had walked straight past Ruth. Her grandmother's response to her new look was everything Ruth had wanted. Grandma Hetty had approved, and that green jacket was the start of a grand love of fashion.

A loud crashing, followed by women shouting, jolted her out of her thoughts. She shut the wardrobe door and squeezed past it onto the landing. More negative adjectives ran through her head: *bossy, pinched, lonely. Don't be so mean,* she told herself. It wasn't that she didn't like her landlady, but Trudi did make life so unnecessarily difficult for herself. She was always so cross. She could hear the argument clearer from the landing, and she stayed, listening to see if she should go down and mediate. It sounded like Alice had tripped and knocked things in the kitchen over; she couldn't quite follow as Alice's voice had got quite shrill.

It seemed to Ruth that Trudi wasn't as mean as she made out to be, but she hadn't quite tapped into what might bring out her softer side. She seemed always on edge, and things needed to be just so. Ruth wondered what had happened in her life to make her this way. There was never any mention of a husband, but she wore a thin gold band on her wedding finger. There were no photographs in the house to give any clues either. Though Ruth had not been in her bedroom, she imagined it to be just as stiff and neat as the best room at the front, with its large gold-framed landscapes and overstuffed furniture nobody sat on.

Ruth's mother had known Trudi from when she was a nurse in the county hospital. She had looked after Trudi's father, and they had got close. Ruth suspected it was their shared passion for order and proper behaviour. When it came time, in Ruth's mother's opinion, for Ruth to get a job and move out of home, Trudi offered room and board. She already had Alice in the back bedroom, so Ruth was happy with the attic room. It was away from the rest of the house, which she liked, and it had its own fireplace, which was snug. In the summer, it was too hot, but Ruth tried never to be there much, except to sleep.

She could still hear the two women arguing, so she started down the stairs to help. Just as she got to the bottom step, she saw Alice running out the door, followed by a clatter of a metal dish, propelled through the open door.

Alice stomped down the hall, and as she got to the front door, she yelled at Ruth, 'That woman has gone completely mad this time!' and slammed the door behind her.

Ruth stood blinking in the dim hall as the complete silence became worrying. She was unsure of what to do. She didn't want to go after Alice – she wasn't dressed for the outside world of a Saturday morning – though the thought of what was behind the kitchen door made her stomach clench. After what seemed like hours, she heard the tap go on, and normal kitchen noises resumed. She realised she had been holding her breath, and she let out an audible sigh. For now, there was nothing she needed to do, though she was dreading supper. She walked back up to her room to make herself Saturday ready. Where would she go?

The short walk to the village lifted her out of herself, and Ruth began to feel a little less dreary. However, she had chosen an outfit to match the dreary day – a grey overcoat and sensible shoes, for her. She had decided to go and meet Helen in her father's shop. She might be able to get a couple of hours off, and they could look in shop windows and gossip.

Helen taught in the senior classes at the school, and Ruth had loved her from the start. Helen was poised and professional at work, but as they got to know each other, Ruth was drawn to how exciting Helen could be. Once, after a long day in front of the class, where her feet ached and all she wanted to do was climb into bed, Helen had knocked on her classroom door with a mischievous grin on her face.

'Leave all that,' she said briskly, waving her hand at the papers in front of Ruth. 'I have something,' she beckoned, still grinning.

Ruth followed her into the cloakroom, where Helen proudly produced the top of a small metal bottle. Ruth hadn't known what a hip flask was until that day.

'Can we go to your room, Ruth, please, please?' Helen pleaded. 'My father is home, and my little sister is a terrible snoop.'

Helen was about a year younger than Ruth, and her sister was much younger, about 11, Ruth guessed. Ruth had nodded, not really knowing what she was agreeing to, but hadn't wanted to show how naive she was. Somehow they managed to sneak past Trudi and spent the early evening and on into the night sipping from the flask and gossiping. Ruth didn't ask how Helen had got home or managed to sneak back into the house, but the next day at school, it was like it had never happened except for a sly wink and a smirk from Helen when she passed Ruth in the hall. That was the first but definitely not the last time.

She arrived outside the provisions shop, and Helen immediately spotted her and waved excitedly and then lowered her arm, smiling, when she saw her father's stern look. Ruth liked Mr Masters; he was all bark and no bite and had even been known to crack a joke. He was mostly quite serious, and today he seemed extra so, and Ruth thought that he would most likely say he needed Helen in the shop.

Ruth went in anyway, and Mr Masters acknowledged her with a nod and then said, 'Helen is needed until after lunch, Ruth, but then the afternoon is yours.'

'Thank you, Mr Masters,' she said, pleased.

He actually smiled and replied, 'Young lady, please call me Douglas.'

She could never do that, but she agreed with a polite smile.

Helen said, 'Go through to the kitchen, and Cook will fix you a drink while you wait. I won't be long.' She looked at her father. 'I think I can get this done before lunch, Daddy.'

'Very well,' he replied, not looking up from the window boxes.

The shop was a lot more sparse than previous years; the locally grown produce was barely stretching past the front boxes. She felt sad. The war was being fought in far-off countries, and her little village was being greatly affected. Her own cousins were fighting in Egypt – she couldn't fathom that far away. Helen's brother was somewhere on the frontline as well. She didn't like to keep thinking about it. She turned away and walked down the hall to see Cook in the little kitchen.

Cook was the most pleasing and satisfying person, like a children's storybook character of a cook in a large house who looked after everyone. She cooed, 'Oh, Ms Ruth, hello. Do sit, do sit.'

Ruth sat at the small table with her back to the window.

'Cup of tea, Ms Ruth? Now mind, I have no sugar to spare. I'm counting you as family, and you can do without. You can absolutely do without. It's a compliment, mind. You can do without?' Her voice lifted at the end as if she realised she might have offended, but Ruth was not worried.

'I'll have it black, Cook. How's that?'

'Very good, Ms Ruth. How is your mother?'

Ruth sighed inwardly, not really wanting to talk, but she replied, 'Oh, she's fine, thank you, Cook. She seems a lot busier now than when she was working. War effort and all.'

Cook nodded. 'Mm-hm, mm-hm, very good.'

Ruth sipped her tea and watched Cook busy about. Cook chatted, and Ruth listened. She was comfortable and warm and quite content.

Helen broke the peace with a bang of the door and jolted Ruth out of her cosy comfort. *Had she been asleep?* 'Come on, let's go. Get your coat, and let's go.' Helen was chomping at the bit, almost childlike in her anxiousness to get out.

'Thank you, Cook!' Ruth exclaimed as Helen bustled her back through the shop and out into the street.

Helen put her arm through Ruth's and marched down towards the high street. It wasn't busy, and as they neared the shop windows, Ruth was disappointed to see that the display in Iris's had not changed. Helen shrugged and marched on. She seemed to have direction and wasn't going to stop.

Just as Ruth had got used to the pace, Helen stopped and pointed across the road. Ruth followed her gaze towards a bridal shop. The window was dressed in lace and flowers, so much so that Ruth couldn't really make out any clear features. Helen suddenly darted in front of cars and people and pressed her nose against the shop window. When Ruth arrived at her side, she was slightly out of breath and less than impressed with Helen's mad dash.

'There, Ruth, look. It's the most beautiful dress, and it's going to be mine. It's all sorted, Ruth. Oh, I can't breathe.'

Helen had been seeing Elliot since they were very young, childhood sweethearts. Ruth had met him a few times before he enlisted and had thought him perfectly nice. He was quiet and not much influence on reigning Helen in but nice nonetheless.

'The next time he's on leave, he's coming home to marry me!' she almost screeched, loud enough for glass to shatter.

'Hush,' Ruth said, smiling but still quite embarrassed by the scene she was making.

Ruth was pleased for Helen – it was lovely news – but a part of her was entirely envious. She let that part take over as she walked home. She had no sweetheart, and now that there was a war on, what hope was there? She realised she had her hands clenched and was stomping up the hill. She paused and took in the view back down to the village. Alice was coming up the hill behind her, and she waited. She hoped that Alice had cooled off and wouldn't be in need of an ear. Alice puffed up the hill and grinned at her. She had a pretty face, and it was all flushed with the effort.

'That was good timing,' she said. 'I called out to you, but you didn't hear, so I tried running.' She made a kind of grunting puff noise mixed with a wheeze. 'Perhaps I shouldn't have given chase. You didn't hear me?'

Ruth was amused. Alice was very good-natured and a great chum to have in the house with her. She was mostly oblivious to her own oddities and their effect on people – hence the blow-up that morning, Ruth supposed.

'I've been in town with Helen. She's getting married the next time Elliot is on leave.' She tried to make her voice happy.

Alice grunted. Was it still with the effort of walking up the hill or indignation? Ruth couldn't tell. Helen never really acknowledged Alice. She was never nasty to her or about her, just didn't seem to see her. The only thing they had in common was Ruth. Alice worked as a receptionist for a dentist. She didn't talk about work. She liked talking books and art. As far as Ruth could tell, Alice was paid to read; she couldn't imagine a dentist receptionist being run off her feet. Envy almost took over again. They walked in silence until the lane where Alice tensed.

'Come on. I'm here. You'll be OK. Whatever it was is past now, I'm sure.' Ruth wasn't so sure, but she tried to reassure Alice.

They went in through the front hall and paused to take off coats and hats, listening. Was Trudi in? It was four o'clock, an hour before supper. Perhaps they would be OK; there was no noise coming from the kitchen.

'I'll see you at supper,' Alice whispered.

She clomped down the hall, undoing all the stealth with every step. Ruth smiled to herself.

In the end, supper was very uneventful. Trudi had laid out a pretty decent spread on the kitchen table and left them to it.

Chapter 2

Monday morning was still dreary weather. The pages of Ruth's binder were curling, damp too. The children were not due for another few moments; she could hear them playing outside. There were a lot more children than the class could hold – but needs be as they had many of the evacuees from London in the village. They hadn't gone out as far as the countryside like some, their parents believing school was still important. Ruth ran her eye over the week's agenda. The headmistress had set lessons for the primary classes, and she was grateful she didn't have to use too much brainpower. The handbell clanged, and the children filed in.

Ruth didn't have a lot of strict rules, and she very rarely used her strap, so the children didn't exactly meet the school guidelines of walking sensibly into the classroom. However, she did seem to have good rapport with them, which lifted her grades enough that the headmistress, mostly, turned a blind eye to the madness. Every now and then she would pop up unexpectedly and give the children what for. Ruth appreciated this as it meant she wasn't the bad, disciplinary teacher and could get on with actual teaching.

Today seemed exceptionally hectic, and then she remembered there had been more children evacuated over the weekend. She heard from the women at church, who had friends and family in London, that the air raid warnings were more and more frequent. The children didn't want to talk about anything other than what it was like in London. The village children were asking a lot of questions, and if Ruth was honest, she would rather hear the answers herself. She let them talk for the best part of the morning.

With a heavy sigh, Ruth turned the handle of the big front door and walked into the small entrance hall – so familiar to her yet so unwelcoming. Her parents were not the problem, but Ruth just felt even more suffocated and stuck, thinking that she had only moved down the road from where she grew up.

She peered around the front room door. Her father was in the easy chair; she could hear the radio tuned to the London news. She let him sit for the time being; she would say hello later. Even before the war, the radio news was his favourite pastime. He was very good to Ruth, and she had fond childhood memories of them together.

She went down to the kitchen, but her mother wasn't there. She went out the back door and found her in the wash house.

'Hello,' she said brightly.

Her mother harrumphed and looked up. 'Can you give me a hand with this, Ruth? Then we can go in for a cup of tea.'

They heaved the sodden sheet from the tub, and her mother spun the old wringer wheel while Ruth fed the sheet through.

'Go and put the kettle on. Call your father. I'll hang this.'

Ruth walked back up the short path and did as her mother had asked.

Her father came strolling in. 'Hello, little friend. Nice to see you,' he said, smiling.

Ruth never felt like an adult when she was with her parents, and pet names like that made it worse. 'Nice to see you too, Dad. Cup of tea?'

He nodded. There were some plain biscuits in the tin and sugar – a real treat. Her mother came in and immediately started asking questions and making 'You really should' statements. Ruth only half-listened and nodded every now and then. She had had a long week and wasn't in the mood.

Sunday afternoons were spent in this way since she had moved out. Ruth wondered how she would really cope if she moved out of the village on her own like she had always daydreamed about. She knew she wouldn't. She was not as courageous as Helen, not as stoic as her mother, and definitely not the lady her grandma Hetty would be proud of. What was stopping her? She could go to all the fashionable cities and style fancy ladies and see the world. *Don't be silly. There's a war on. The last thing on anyone's mind is fashion.*

However, it would be a good distraction. Her mother was big on the war effort at home. Organising and problem solving was her thing; she was in her element. There were lots of families at church who needed her help and support. Ruth knew some of them well, and it saddened her to think of the young boys' lives cut short. A boy she had liked since the primmas was lost in action and assumed captured. It was too much for her to think about. For the time being, her cousins were not seeing any action, and she was slightly removed from the real suffering, being an only child.

Sitting in the kitchen with her parents and sipping tea wasn't a bad way to spend an afternoon. She thought of school the next day, and her brow was furrowed. She might go past the provisions shop, find some sort of treat for supper, and invite Helen. She knew Alice would be pleased with a treat, and Trudi would probably turn her nose up at the extravagance and leave them to it – she hoped.

Ruth thanked her parents and said good night earlier than normal. She made the excuse of work in the morning but then made the detour to see Helen. The shop lights were off, but Ruth went around the back and, to her surprise, found Helen in the alleyway. Helen giggled at being found out and put the hip flask in the inside pocket of her big coat.

'I came to see if you wanted to come up for a nightcap, but I see you've already started.' Ruth was giggling too.

'Sure. Give me a moment to tell the olds where I'm going.'

They hurried back up the hill, giggling for no apparent reason for most of the way. Alice greeted them warmly when they came into the kitchen, but Ruth could see she was disappointed that Helen had come. She did, however, brighten up considerably when Helen produced some very squashed and very small tarts.

'Cook's special,' Helen said proudly.

Alice just shook her head at the crumbs and mess on the table and put the tarts on a plate. They did actually spend quite a nice evening together, and Helen went home at a reasonable hour. She brushed off Alice's attempts to call the neighbour to walk her home.

'I'm a big girl,' Helen said indignantly.

Ruth's heart raced. Waking up suddenly from a deep sleep, she heard voices. As she woke up more, she realised they were shouting in the street outside. What had awoken her? It wasn't the shouting. She heard it again, coming louder. Was it a plane? She put her gown on and went downstairs. Alice was in the front entrance; even in the dark, Ruth could see she was white as a sheet.

'Trudi is out talking to Mr Matthews. He thinks it was an Allied plane, but Trudi is swearing black and blue that the engine noise was wrong. Oh, Ruth, are we under attack?'

Ruth was in a blind panic herself, but her calm voice surprised her. 'It's OK, Alice. It's OK. Trudi only thinks that because her father flew planes. You know she thinks she knows everything. I'm sure Mr Matthews is right. I'm sure.'

She was hoping too. She knew nothing about the air raids in London except that they happened almost every night. Did the planes bomb every night? She had gleaned bits and pieces of information from the children in her class, their young years far more worldly than herself – seen more, experienced more.

'Evening, ladies.' Mr Matthews was at the door. 'I want to reassure you that those planes were Allied fighters, heading to London. I'm sure of it.'

Ruth couldn't quite see the fine details of his expression but felt that it didn't match his words. She went back to bed with a sick feeling in the pit of her stomach. It was still there in the morning. At breakfast, Alice said nothing; it was so unusual, and it worried Ruth.

Naturally, the children could talk of nothing else. Again, Ruth let them talk. She was beyond lessons and was sure they were learning enough through robust discussion. She certainly was. She also liked hearing what other people had said to the children to explain the planes. There were many different theories from the families they were staying with. Most of the little boys were adamant the planes were being flown by their fathers, superheroes on their way to save London and the world. She was glad her own father was too old and safe at home with his radio and books.

Helen caught her in the hall and pulled her by the arm into the staff offices. She was not at all bothered by the planes, her wedding plans always taking presidency in her mind of late. 'Ruth!' Her cheeks were flush with excitement. 'He's got leave!'

Ruth's stomach was knotted, but she felt her face smiling. Was it shared excitement or jealousy? 'When?' she asked.

'In a month, in a month, in a month. There's so much to do. Of course, it will be longer than a month as he will come home on a ship,' Helen said with a crestfallen face.

Ruth replied cheerily, 'The time will fly by, what with planning and all.'

Helen hugged her and jumped up and down on the spot, still pinning Ruth's arm to her side. Then she flattened her blouse and skirt, shook herself straight, and walked off primly. Ruth could tell she was still beaming. She wondered what it must be like to have someone else to think about. Elliot only had a much older, already married brother in Scotland.

In the afternoon, Helen came into her class. Ruth looked up. Had she actually been reading? She couldn't even start to think. Her body was on automatic, and her brain was elsewhere.

She sat down at a desk and sighed quietly. 'Are the children in your class scared, Ruth?'

'They don't seem to be, actually. Most of them are pretty excited and used to it, I think.'

'Are you scared, Ruth?'

She paused, thinking of how to answer. She was terrified yet thrilled at the same time. 'It's hard to say. There's still so much unknown.'

Helen looked up from scratching her fingernail into the desk. 'I'm quite scared, Ruth.'

She was taken aback; had she heard right?

Helen continued. 'What if they aren't Allied planes?'

Ruth didn't know enough about anything, and she hated it; she felt out of control. The person she was relying on for distraction and hope was coming to her. 'They have to be. What is here to bomb?'

'Us,' replied Helen.

Ruth stared at the floor.

Alice was making supper when Ruth came home. It was later than she had wanted to be out, but Helen had taken a lot of talking down. She wanted to unpack every detail. They were going around in circles, and Ruth's head was pounding. Alice smiled at her – no words. Had she become a mute? *What is wrong with her?* Ruth thought crossly. What was wrong with everyone? *Dry sandwiches and black tea – you couldn't do better?* Ruth thought, fuming.

They ate and drank in silence. Alice was staring at the window. Suddenly, she jumped up and flicked the light off.

Ruth understood; she didn't react. 'Are you going to be OK, Alice?'

She nodded – no words.

'I'm going to bed. Thank you for supper.'

She left her sitting in the dark, but what else could she do? She got along splendidly with Alice, but mute Alice was different. She tucked herself into bed but didn't go to sleep.

They didn't come again, and that made everyone relax a little bit and Trudi say, 'I told you so,' over her tea and toast. Alice wasn't up before Ruth left. She had half-expected her to be still sitting where Ruth had left her. She was glad she wasn't, but then she started fretting that she might have wandered off into the night in her dumb state. She walked down the hall and knocked on Alice's door, just to check – no answer. Ruth didn't know whom she should contact if anything should happen to Alice. She realised she knew very little about her. She certainly knew now that she could not be relied upon in a crisis. Then she felt bad for thinking so ill of her. She had made supper, even in a trance. She could be relied upon for sustenance at least.

Rather than fret all day, Ruth went via the dentist office. It wasn't open, but the window shades were up, so she cupped her eyes and pressed her nose to see in.

'Can I help you?'

A face right in her face made her jump back in shock.

The dentist opened the door. 'I'm afraid I am fully booked today, and my receptionist is not in at the moment to take your details.'

Ruth stared blankly back.

He half-said to himself, 'I was expecting her at half past.'

Ruth nodded and mumbled something about coming back and walked away, embarrassed. *No Alice.* She was worried. It was too late to go home again.

'I'm worried about Alice,' she told Helen when she saw her at lunch.

'Oh, blow Alice. Whatever are you worried about?' Helen retorted.

'She—'

'I've found the perfect pair of gloves to match my shoes,' Helen interrupted.

Over her panic then, Ruth thought. *Over anyone else, except herself.* She switched out and stared at the magazine on the table without seeing it. She really was worried about Alice, and she really was growing tired of wedding talk. When she was small, her grandmother had talked a lot about her wedding day and Ruth's parents' wedding. She had seen the lace gowns folded into the large flat boxes in the attic but never been able to try them on. She longed to, and she longed to have her own. She knew she was envious, but she couldn't help it. She would be pleased when it was all over.

Ruth walked home quickly and wasn't bothered by the rain and wind. Her mind had been elsewhere this morning, and she had barely remembered to put a coat on. She clutched it around her and put her head down, into the wind. She was only slightly bothered that she had grabbed the oldest and most worn-out coat she had. She made a mental note to put it right at the back of her wardrobe. Helen wasn't worried, but Ruth hadn't been able to get Alice out of her mind all day.

She went straight to the kitchen. Trudi didn't even look up from the sink. *No Alice.* She walked to the back bedroom and paused. She felt her heart beating; she sucked in her breath and knocked on Alice's door. She had only been into her room once. It was neat as a pin and so stylish. There was silence. She knocked again – nothing. Dare she open the door? She stood with her hand on the knob. Alice could be asleep.

She decided to call through the door first, announce herself. 'Alice, I'm coming in.'

Nothing. She shut her eyes and wished, breathed in, and opened the door.

The room was neat and empty. Her heart started beating faster again. What was she going to do? If Helen wasn't worried, she knew Trudi definitely wouldn't be. Who was there? Her. There was no need to go back out looking like a tramp, however. She went to change and put on more appropriate clothes for the weather.

Her mind was racing. She didn't even know where to start to look for Alice. She had visions of her alone and in a ditch – or wandering totally away, gone. Why did Ruth just leave her sitting there? What was she thinking? She called behind her as she went out the front door, but Trudi didn't answer.

Where would you look for someone who'd wandered off in a stupor? She decided to go down towards the village. Should she call out? It seemed a bit silly. She felt ill. Would it all fall on her if Alice was dead? She was only responsible for herself; she didn't know how to be responsible for anyone else. The children in her class were only reliant on her to fill their minds and grow their learning; no lives were at stake. She was well looked out for, but who did Alice have? Why didn't she know more about her?

Her emotion took over. Her chest seized up, and she had to lean hard on a lamp post. She was a bad friend, leaving her there in the dark, scared. Ruth's head was in her elbow, soaking wet and near hysteria. It had been too many hours, too long. Alice would have walked miles away by now.

Her head felt like it had been in a vice, her ears were ringing, her chest hurt, and there was a strange thudding feeling on her collarbone. Was she having a heart attack? She couldn't focus; there was only white, blurred. She was cold. She needed to get out of the rain. If only she could stop the thudding. She reached up.

'Ruth? Ruth? Is she coming around?'

'Ruth, it's Helen. She needs a doctor. We can't lift her. I will stay with her. You go.'

The thudding stopped; it was a relief, but there was still only white. She needed to get up, keep looking for her friend.

'No, no, hush. Don't move. Stay here.'

What was stopping her? *Come on, Ruth. Pull yourself together*, she thought. It was all just white. Alice needed her; maybe the dentist office was a good place to go back to, retrace familiar steps.

'Stay here. Helen's here. I've got you.'

White, black. Murmuring voices. She stirred, realised she was in her bed, and sat bolt upright. The door opened and hit the wardrobe.

'Damn thing,' an annoyed, hushed voiced. Helen poked her head around the door. 'Oh, you're awake!' she said.

Ruth noted the sheer relief in her voice. Ruth's face must have shown her confusion.

'Don't pull that face. You'll get wrinkles,' Helen said with a wink. 'I'm so pleased to see you awake.' She hugged her.

Ruth wasn't expecting it and ended up with her arms pinned to her side. Helen squeezed the air out of her, and she made a squeaking sound. Ruth was embarrassed and very confused.

'It's OK. You're OK now. Alice and I found you slumped on the footpath near the village last night—'

'Alice!'

She made Helen jump. 'Yes, we were walking home from the town hall and found you.'

'Alice?' Ruth grabbed Helen's shoulders and shook her.

'What's wrong? Do you need the doctor again?' Helen looked frightened and called out, 'Mrs Simpson!'

Her mum came in. What on earth was going on? Why was her mum here?

'Calm down. Whatever has got into you?' She sat on the edge of the bed and stared, sternly but caring, straight at her.

Nothing like your mum to see you straight. Ruth swallowed hard. 'I'm sorry. I don't know what's going on. Did you find Alice? I am so sorry I left her alone in the dark.' The panic was rising again.

'Ruth dear, Alice was the one who found you. Her and Helen.'

Helen sat down, plopped on the floor. 'Oh, Ruth,' she said with a heavy sigh. 'I've never been so worried in all my life. Alice ran back to the village and managed to get Dr Harold. He said you had a panic attack. What were you doing out in the pouring rain at that time?'

Ruth stared at her. She didn't know what was real and what seemed to be a bad dream. 'Is Alice alive? Where did you find her?'

'She wasn't lost. She's here. Don't worry. She has gone to work.' Helen was still slumped on the floor.

'Work!' Ruth said.

'Oh, goodness me,' her mum said in her strict, no-nonsense tone. 'Your headmistress will understand. The both of you need a rest. Calm down.' She walked out.

Chapter 3

The planes came again. There was no mistaking them this time. They all heard them; some people saw them, and London was flattened. The headmistress was standing at the gate to tell everyone to go home and keep safe. The bombs were still falling on London.

Helen walked home with Alice and Ruth. She even talked to Alice and about things other than weddings. 'Where are you from, Alice?'

Ruth was taken aback but also curious. She hadn't asked, and for all Alice talked, she hadn't offered anything up either.

'I lived in London most of my childhood but moved out here when my grandfather died. To look after my gran. And then I never left.'

She sounded wistful. They would rather talk about anything than the obvious. Ruth was scared out of her mind. The other two seemed calm, but she supposed the same things were running through their heads.

They got to the top of the hill, and Ruth was surprised to see her parents pulled up in their car. They never really bothered with the car except on 'high days and holidays', as her grandmother used to say. Also, Ruth remembered the time when it was an emergency and her father speeding with her mother down the road. Grandma Hetty sat with her. She just remembered the dark kitchen, the soft humming, and the total relief to see her father back in the morning and learn her mother was OK. She also remembered her mother being annoyed at having to recover from appendix surgery in the hospital where she worked. Nobody was up to scratch, and she made her feelings very clear.

'Ruth dear. Pack up a suitcase and come with us.'

Ruth stared at her mother.

'This is not a drill. We are heading down south to your aunt in Devon.'

Ruth stood in the lane, and Helen and Alice seemed to have disappeared into the hedge behind her. They were not going to argue with Ruth's mother and were probably mentally packing a suitcase to go themselves.

'I can't just pack one suitcase.'

'Oh, for heaven's sake, Ruth. Really? Your precious clothes?'

She was not leaving things to get bombed to smithereens. Alice came forward and tentatively suggested she could help her refine things. Helen agreed. Any excuse to try on her clothes, Ruth thought angrily.

'I can't just up and leave,' she said in a calmer voice than what was in her head. She could understand why they were so panicked and anxious to leave. Being so close to London was frightening her too, but this was so sudden. *What had they done with the house? Just left everything?*

'Can you at least come in for a cup of tea and talk this through?'

They agreed.

Trudi was mercifully nowhere to be seen. Ruth wondered what it was that she really did all day but was always pleased when she wasn't about. Alice put the kettle on. Helen leant against the bench, and her parents sat at the table. She felt strangely out of place and started rummaging in the pantry.

'Don't bother about food, Ruth dear.'

She stood awkwardly in the door of the pantry. None of them spoke, and then Helen cleared her throat. She didn't say anything. She opened her mouth and then shut it again with a little *hmm*.

'You know, I've actually been organising something . . .' She tailed off.

'What's that, Helen dear?' asked Ruth's dad.

'Well, since the first planes flew over, I've been frightened.'

'We all have,' said Alice quietly.

Ruth thought that Helen hadn't been herself but had put it down to wedding madness.

'I've been using some contacts I have overseas, and I've managed to sort out a mass evacuation for the village children.' Helen continued, 'It has been a bit difficult with the post, the time differences, and obviously, the phone line is especially tricky.'

'I have been helping to organise and using some contacts I have in London as well,' Alice explained.

'The only thing is timing,' Helen said.

'Timing for what?' Ruth asked, confused. Helen's words were jumbling in her head.

'Explain what you want us to do before we go, Helen dear. What do you need?' her father asked.

'Oh no, nothing like that, Mr Simpson. I just . . . It's just that . . . Well, things aren't organised quite yet, but we would be ready to leave in about two weeks.'

'It won't take me that long to pack,' Ruth retorted.

'Ha! It might!' said Alice, who clapped her hand over her mouth as soon as she said it.

The stress level made everyone fall about laughing. Her father slapped his leg, head back, tears rolling down his face.

When they had calmed down, Helen became rather serious. It was sobering, which made the war and its effects hit home in a way that they hadn't before. She had been tricking herself, really, just getting up and going to work and going to the shops, her little week routine, her quiet village. Pushing the feelings down made it worse when they actually surfaced. *Don't have another panic attack standing in the pantry*, she thought. She breathed in through her nose and let the air out slowly and silently while Helen explained further.

'In two weeks, Alice and I will be taking a group of children to London to board a boat bound for New Zealand. We need more than two adults, and I thought Ruth would be ideal as she will know most of the younger children from her class.'

'New Zealand?' Her mother questioned.

'Yes, it's not being bombed,' Alice said, adding, 'I don't think people know where it is, and that's a good thing. Very far away.'

Ruth's parents and her friends had just decided her fate around her. Had she been talking? She felt like she was in a haze. Her parents agreed to stay the night and say a proper goodbye in the morning. Alice kindly gave up her room and bunked in with Ruth. It was like a sleepover when she was little, and it made Ruth feel nostalgic for midnight snacks and giggling well into the night. Helen stayed under the guise of planning and logistics, but really, she had other ideas in the form of a little tin bottle.

Ruth was still not sure what she had signed up for. 'What is happening?' she asked – a broad, all-encompassing question that Helen and Alice didn't answer.

Alice changed the subject slightly. 'Shall we just sort out some packing now?'

Ruth agreed. It wasn't about the packing; it was about her clothes, but she didn't really mind.

Her father hugged her tight. 'Make sure you write to us, little friend. We want to know all that you're up to while we are in dull Devon.'

Her mother gave him a look. She kissed Ruth on both cheeks, held her by the shoulders. 'Go well, Ruth dear. It's an adventure. We will keep in touch.' She smiled.

Watching their car squeeze down the lane, she welled up inside as tears streamed down her face. She tried not to chase after the car. *Take me with you. Come back.* Her father's arm came out the window and waved jauntily all the way to the end of the road. Oddly, it comforted her and made her feel calmer about what was ahead. *Just wave.*

Chapter 4

Elliot came out of the front door and stood on the top step, looking lost. Ruth was pleased she had managed to convince him to wear a suit rather than his military dress. Helen had asked her to find the best suit in town for him, and she had done just that. It wasn't high fashion by any stretch of the imagination, and for that, Ruth was disappointed – but hard times. Nonetheless, he looked very smart in the dark pants and one-button jacket, which cut handsomely down to his lower waist.

'We will be late. You look great,' she said with a big grin.

Elliot half-smiled back and followed her beckoning. She had managed to convince Trudi that borrowing her car was a matter of life and death. She silently chauffeured him to the church and left him with Helen's father. *Surely, he can hold his own*, she thought. *Too bad if he can't. It's a taste of the rest of his life. Too mean, Ruth.* He stared after her like a scared puppy. *Oh dear.* She didn't have any wise words for him. Perhaps she should have been giving him a pep talk on the way. She smiled and waved enthusiastically, hoping he read the gesture as a 'Chin up, best day of your life' and all that.

The Masters place was in a twitter. Helen was fussing with her veil.

'Ruth!' she exclaimed. 'Oh help! Alice is no help, and I can't fit this veil.'

Ruth glanced at Alice, who rolled her eyes and waved her hand down angrily. 'Blow you, Helen. I was only trying to help.'

'You were going to put a hole in it!' screeched Helen.

'Girls,' came a calming voice. 'Girls, girls, girls. Helen, shh, hush. Right. I've got this. Turn around and sit here, Ms Helen. Trust your old Cook.'

Helen sat, quiet. Cook passed her the mirror and placed the veil, pinned it in a flash, and arranged it perfectly. For all Cook was, Ruth had not picked her to know anything about fashion, let alone bridal fashion.

'Just a trick I learned by and by.' Cook smiled in the mirror at Ruth and winked.

Alice sat in the front, and Helen and her mother sat in the back. Ruth drove around the block, and Helen made a noise, but Alice piped up.

'You'll need to be late. It's tradition.'

Helen rolled her eyes. Ruth felt sorry for Alice; it would have made more sense for her to drive and Ruth to help, but she couldn't drive. Even just talking about it made her twitch something chronic. Ruth was slightly amused. She remembered her grandma Hetty teaching her. It was rather hectic and almost too much for her, but after a while, she just clicked, and she was proud to say she could drive. She was pleased her grandmother had patience.

'Ruth, you're hopeless in the extreme! Why are you not getting this? If an old lady like me can do it, you can damn well do it!'

She remembered how red her grandmother's face had got. It was a happy memory, really. She missed her grandmother terribly, and teaching her to drive was one of the last things she had done for Ruth – a lasting impression and impact in her life.

Helen looked lovely; she just beamed from ear to ear. Her parents seemed very happy for her too. It was a sweet ceremony and then a reception in the small church hall. There were a lot of people whom Ruth didn't really know, and Alice had gone home with a headache. Ruth thought, *I wish I could get away with going home*. She felt sour and needed to snap out of it.

She glanced over the table to where Helen and Elliot were sitting; they did not let go of each other all this time. She looked back down at the table. *Come on, Ruth. It's a happy day*. She went to the drinks trolley and poured herself a small nip of brandy. She wasn't really in the mood to drink it but thought the warmth might warm her mood up. She looked out at everyone from her corner. The evening slipped away.

The next day, Ruth's heart broke for Helen. She tried not to watch the tearful farewell at the train station. She knew she needed to be there for Helen, but all of her was consumed by the effort of staying put. She gave them as much time as she could, but the train was gearing up, and the conductor was blowing hard on his whistle. The noise suddenly seemed deafening, and there was an ear-piercing screeching. She had to rip Helen away from Elliot. If it wasn't for the fact that Ruth knew Helen well, she would have written this off as melodrama. It was very hard to be part of it, and she caught herself feeling almost glad that she didn't have anyone, didn't have to suffer the loss. Elliot was paralysed with his sorrow and didn't give much back, but he remained standing in the door until the train was out of sight. Helen sat down right where she was and dragged Ruth with her. She awkwardly fell on her elbow. *What now?* she thought. *How do we move on from here?*

'A cup of tea?' she quietly posed.

Helen didn't respond, but she got up off the ground and slowly walked back through the station. Ruth tailed behind; her elbow ached.

Ruth was packing furiously. She caught the hem of her wool blend cardigan on the metal suitcase catch. As she pulled the thread, more came apart, and so did her emotions. She ended up on the floor in front of the wardrobe. What was she thinking? *It would be easier to pack and go to Devon. New Zealand? What do you pack for a ship voyage? What do you pack for a different country on the other side of the world? How does Helen know people on the other side of the world?* Two weeks had gone so fast, and the next day loomed over her. She tried to channel her grandmother; she must be in her somewhere. *The genes are there. Take courage. Go.*

She put all her effort and energy into packing as much as she could as efficiently as she could. If she was going to do this, she was going to have the right outfit handy for any possible encounter, her green felt jacket right on the top. Yes, that would bring forth her grandmother's courage and sense of adventure. Her elbow still ached, and the pit of her stomach sank even lower.

She forced herself to have supper, took it up to her room, and sat looking out her window. The colours changed and turned black, but she sat a long while, crackers still in her hand. She must have put herself to bed, and she must have slept, but she felt drained and anxious in the morning and not at all well.

Trance-like, Ruth took her luggage down to the hall. She walked down to the gate to prop it open and just kept on walking. It didn't take her long to get to her parents' house. She stepped into the hall – dark and silent, somehow not the same without life in the house. She walked past the front room, dared to peek in – furniture covered in dust sheets and pictures off their hooks. She sat down at the kitchen table. Her parents were well in Devon and said that there were a lot of people from the village there, and her mother had joined the war effort down there too. She had said it was more about tea, biscuits, and gossip but an effort nonetheless. Ruth sat, still and quiet, already feeling a million miles removed from here.

'Where have you been?'

Helen was in a panic, and Alice literally looked like she'd been to hell and back.

'I'll just go and say a quick goodbye to Trudi.'

'You'll do no such thing!' Helen shrieked. 'We are late as it is.' She threw Ruth's rucksack at her. 'Get in and drive,' she ordered.

Ruth felt like a naughty child in her class; next, Helen would have the cane out.

They drove in silence, but Ruth could feel Helen's anger seething from the back seat. Alice was silent again. Ruth parked in the far corner of the station park like Trudi had asked her and put the keys on the back left tyre. It seemed strange to think that Trudi would go on as normal while they shipped off into the sunset. It was safer for the children, and they'd be back in no time. However, the thought had even crossed her mind that it was all a little pointless as it took so long to get there and back that the war would be over. She didn't keep up with the war news; it got too harrowing.

If they didn't know where to go, they could have followed the chatter and noise from the children. It was actually chaos. Ruth left Helen and Alice to do the organising and found a group of her class to talk to. They were all naturally excited and talked to her all at once, asking questions she couldn't answer.

'I know as much as you, I'm afraid. It's a mystery we can solve on the way,' she suggested. She liked the idea herself, actually. *Find out as much as you can about New Zealand from the people on the ship.* The idea seemed to steady her, and she felt better as they boarded the ship.

They stayed on deck to wave at everyone. It was a big deal. She felt famous. It was a real rush. Alice and Helen seemed to be feeling it too as they stood next to her, waving furiously and blowing kisses. Ruth thought that was a bit extreme but, in the end, couldn't help herself. As she was caught up in the fanfare, there was no time to think about the reality of leaving home for the first time. Helen's parents became coloured dots in the blur and then went completely out of sight.

The next hour or so, they milled around on deck. The horizon was blue in front of them, and the land was getting hazy. Was it still land? Had it changed sides? Her sense of direction was shot at the best of times. If she didn't have much authority in the classroom, she sure didn't have any on the ship. She felt her cheeks flush as a group of children almost bowled over an older couple. They glared at her and shook their heads at her lacklustre approach to disciplining them. They ran back in the other direction, whooping. She felt ill. What had she got into?

She decided to find her cabin, get settled, maybe write to her parents.

She went down a flight of stairs and immediately felt claustrophobic. She turned around and went back to the deck. She stood over the railing and breathed in deep. *Now is not the time to panic*, she told herself sternly. She looked down at her feet, willing them to move.

'You look comical. What on earth are you doing?' It was a stranger's voice.

She stood up and turned around. Unable to think of anything witty, she admitted the truth. 'I'm trying to make my feet walk down those stairs.' Her voice sounded strained and unfamiliar. She swallowed hard, and when she went to speak again, she bit her tongue hard. With a wincing smile, she said, 'Don't worry about me.'

He stayed standing in front of her, smiled widely, and asked, 'Do you know your cabin number?'

She didn't react.

He blinked at her, made to wave his hand in front of her face, and thought better of it, scratched his nose. 'See here?'

She followed his finger to the door frame.

'The numbers go in the direction of the floor and cabin number. Have a nice day, miss. Might see you around. I hope.' He winked and walked away.

The stairs went to a dead-end corridor that did not seem to be cabins or anything else. She needed to orientate herself, find a visual prompt. Her bags had already been taken, and Helen and Alice had gone down before her while she still looked out over the water. She couldn't bring herself to take her eyes off the haze that was home. The chatter and disruption of the children fell on her deaf ears – and the coaxing from Alice too. She just felt emotionless except for the fact that she felt every emotion possible.

She heard a familiar, jovial voice and turned the corner to see Helen laughing and joking with a group of men. Alice was standing a few steps away, looking on. She stood at her elbow, and Alice made a gesture towards Helen with a *tsk* and a sigh. Ruth laughed. She couldn't help herself.

Alice glared at Helen and then with a questioning, disapproving tone said to Ruth, 'What? You think it's OK for her to be behaving like this? A married woman?'

'Oh, Alice! She loves Elliot. You know that. She's Helen. She's having fun.' Ruth squirmed inside. She was envious of the way that Helen could behave any which way and get away with it. *It's just Helen.*

There were three other women in charge of their group of children.

Ruth had expected a bedroom to herself, so when faced with all five people, including three strangers, she felt like she might bunk up on a deck chair.

'It's going to be so much fun, us all in together! I'm Isabella.' She enthusiastically put out a dainty hand at Ruth and shook hard, a huge grin on her face.

Oh dear, Ruth thought.

'My uncle is the headmaster at the boys' school . . .' She paused. 'Back home . . .' She tailed off.

Ruth felt bad; she had prejudged the poor girl's enthusiastic manner and realised she was just as unsure as her. Ruth put her hand on Isabella's arm and squeezed. She smiled at her, but tears were still in her eyes. Ruth felt her eyes welling too, and suddenly, they were both blubbering and awkwardly laughing. *Perhaps it would be OK all in together. Perhaps.*

Chapter 5

'They call it getting your sea legs,' Helen said. She looked as green as Ruth felt.

Alice was slummed in a deck chair. 'At least the weather is nice for heaving over the side,' she said from under her hat.

'Don't talk about it,' Ruth said. She was not at all well and believed herself to be actually dying. She didn't voice these fears. She never really voiced anything apart from banal reassurances to everyone. Now land was completely out of sight; she was homesick as well as seasick.

She felt silly for feeling like this. Hadn't she longed for adventure? Hadn't she willed some action to happen? Now it was here. She fancied a cup of tea in her attic room, looking out over a stable, unchanging view. She wandered down the deck, in search of something but not really sure what. She drummed her fingers along the rail. She was so deep in thought, she almost walked into a man.

'I see you got your legs working.'

'Excuse me?'

'Your legs? Working? Never mind.'

She realised who he was and what he meant and flushed.

'I'm Geoffrey Taylor, air chief marshal, Royal Air Force. At your service, ma'am.'

'Air chief marshal?' She didn't know much, but she knew someone as young as him and as scraggly looking as he couldn't be that highly ranked.

She made a face at him, and he laughed.

'No, not, but doesn't it sound good? Someday.' He hadn't really said that to her, just near her.

He stayed in her way, and she didn't move either.

'Well, to tell you the truth, I'm a lowly aircraftman, not even a pilot.'

Ruth hadn't got a word in yet, but she had heard all about his family in London, his family in New Zealand, and his life plan. She remembered the quest she had set her children and asked, 'What is it like in New Zealand?'

He stopped mid-sentence and looked at her. 'Well, I don't know. It's my first time. I was downed in a training exercise, and our air commodore . . .'

She stopped listening. *How do you get out of a conversation you never started in the first place?* It was a running joke in her family that they all had the knack of attracting unwarranted chitchat with strangers. Her mum had once even been offered a biscuit, right out of the packet, from a homeless man in London. When she politely declined, he kept on insisting, so she took a biscuit and said thank you. Ruth looked past Geoffrey, over his shoulder, trying to see an out. Where was Helen when you needed her? The children were all over the place, causing havoc, except for now.

Alice, at last. 'Alice, this is Geoffrey. He's in the RAF. Geoffrey, this is Alice, who's with us escorting the evacuees.'

'Pleased to meet you.' He shook her hand but was still looking at Ruth. She blushed again.

'Ruth, we need you on the lower deck, please,' Alice said in her most official, prim, and proper voice.

'Good day, ladies.' Then to Ruth, he said, 'I hope to talk again soon.' She smiled politely.

Alice looped her arm in hers and bustled her quickly away. When they were out of earshot, she hissed, 'Oh my goodness, Ruth, who is he? He's delightful.'

Internally, she rolled her eyes. Weren't they too old for whispering behind their hands about boys? They got to the lower deck, and Ruth realised it had been a ruse. The rest of the girls were sitting in deck chairs, living it up. Alice was pleased to pull up next to them and have gossip.

'Ruth has a handsome stranger,' she blurted and then giggled with the delight of the juiciest gossip she'd ever been privy to.

Ruth was red, flushed, and if she explained that she had literally just bumped into him, they'd all say she was protesting too much.

'Oooo, Alice, do tell us more,' said Isabella. She was just as thrilled.

'He's in the RAF.'

There was a complete circle of *oooo* with that tidbit.

'His name is Geoffrey.' Ruth didn't engage.

'Come on, Ruth. You looked so deep in conversation, I practically had to rip you from his grasp.'

Ruth said nothing and looked out to sea, half-smiling.

'We will find out soon enough,' Helen said mischievously.

Isabella giggled with glee again. The shortage of men was making women go weak at the knees over any old pair of trousers walking past, and his were less than desirable, grey slacks. She had noticed some of the other female passages and their attire. She was taking careful note of what was worn when and where and tried to mix and match as she went from her now-uninspiring pile of clothes. There was nowhere to hang anything, and most of her things were so wrinkled, they made prunes look smooth. There was a limit to what she could fold, and the close living quarters were wearing her down. She put some skirts flat under their mattresses. When she asked Isabella if she could put a couple under hers too, naturally, she wanted to see everything, try everything on. Ruth obliged but felt selfish about it, didn't want to share. Isabella offered up her own suitcases, and Ruth was surprised to see some very nice pieces.

'Why don't you wear any of this?'

'Well, I just don't feel like I fit in with all you London ladies.'

'We are far from London ladies.' She said *London ladies* with a posh accent that made Isabella laugh.

She was a sweet girl, younger than them but not by much. She was a nanny for two of the children and had decided to escort them. Like Ruth, she had no real control over the group of children. Though she was too quiet, Ruth was too lazy. She knew it.

Lessons were meant to be every weekday from nine o'clock to three o'clock. Even Helen didn't run much of a strict schedule but thought it best to keep up appearances. Ruth was in the small room set aside off the main dining hall. She thought it was more of a cleared-out broom cupboard, but it did have a porthole at least. It was also equipped with a chalkboard and basic classroom objects, including a world map. She was studying it closely.

It was poor form; she couldn't pick out New Zealand, and she was looking hard for it before the children came in. She could barely pick out England, and that was something she would never admit. She almost fell backwards when she finally spotted New Zealand. She traced her finger over the waters. Were they going up and over or down and around? She thought it best to simply hypothesise with the children. *No need to have the answer for them – they can think for themselves.*

The door opened, and in they all came. There were no desks, but she had managed to drag a low coffee table into the room, which she set on the floor behind, and they sat on the floor in front. It was quite comical on days with rolling seas.

The evening on deck was quite pleasant. Ruth had been down in the cabin trying to sort and tidy. It was near impossible, and she'd given up in frustration and stomped up to the deck. She knew her way around now. She was quite pleased with herself. She had laid out a visual cues map in her head and could trace her steps very well. The rest of the ship was a different story. The days seemed endless, and the water seemed endless. She thought it hadn't been possible, but now after weeks at sea, she had her sea legs. The homesickness was ever present, however. Some days, it consumed her, and she stayed in bed.

She breathed hard in through her nose. *So much for fresh air.* The smell of salt was quite overpowering. Would she ever get the smell out of her clothes? She had admired a woman's dress one evening at supper and got a terrible scowl for her troubles. Alice had grabbed her by the elbow and hustled her along, making apologetic noises.

'Why are you saying sorry for me? I'd done nothing wrong.'

'She honestly looked like she was about to launch at us,' Alice had said; her voice sounded genuinely frightened.

Now Helen walked up beside her. It was good to see her. Ruth felt like she hadn't spoken to her properly in days.

'How are you, Helen?'

She looked wistful. She smiled at Ruth and nodded slowly. 'I'm homesick.' She just said it flatly.

Ruth could feel tears pricking in her eyes. 'Me too,' she replied.

Helen looped her arm in hers and hugged in close, leaning on the railing. She put her head on Ruth's shoulder. 'It's going to be fine though. Still a good adventure. I will honestly be glad to be rid of the children.'

She wasn't being horrible about them, but Ruth understood. It was one thing to teach all week and have a home to go back to but quite another being in charge and responsible all day every day. She needed to be stronger, be there for the children, jolly them up. She thought about what she could do in her next class. Nobody would know. They were so far from anything normal. How had she not realised this before?

Isabella helped her with a big pile of sacking. From behind her huge armload, she asked, 'What on earth are we doing with these?' She coughed. She sneezed. She giggled as more flour blew into the air. 'It's like a snow dusting. Oh my goodness, look at you. Your lovely clothes are covered.'

Ruth looked down. For once, she didn't mind. She pointed at Isabella. 'If this is snow, then you're the abominable snowman.'

They were both in hysterics when Alice came in.

'I can hear you across the dining room.' She was laughing but warning them to keep it down too.

Ruth had a plan to tear up the sacks and decorate the room. Some of them could be opened out, and perhaps they could do a collaborative piece of art. It was just something to do, really, something to take their minds off home. The children would be pleased enough to not worry about lessons.

Helen came in beaming. She had scoured the ship and passengers top to bottom and proudly held out a box with a small tin of white paint, two builder's pencils, a tiny tube of red oil paint, charcoal, and – best of all – a whole tray of watercolours.

'Helen!'

She was still beaming. 'I know.' It was a pleased-as-punch tone. Helen had done well.

Ruth's hands were red raw from ripping up sacking all day, her back ached from kneeling on the floor all day, her clothes were a wreck, and she was exhausted, but she couldn't wipe the smile off her face. The children had done their own scavenger hunting over the weeks on the boat. When they realised what they were doing, they had produced even more art supplies – loot from their escapades. She wondered how much of it had been pilfered, probably the lot, but she wasn't about to pull them up for it. There were too many wonderful things to use.

She had always loved art. Her father was a good painter and had a corner of the wash house set up as a studio, just a corner. She remembered one day, when she was about 10, he let her choose a small-sized canvas, and they had gone out to the edge of the moorland to paint the heather. Sitting and painting next to her father on the picnic blanket was a very clear memory, and she could hear him explaining how to divide the canvas into the foreground, mid-ground, and background.

'You're the artist. You choose what's important for your picture. What you want to look at the most – and paint that.'

Their canvas now was stunning, and they had all been able to forget for a while. *Success*. There were still more materials as well. She hoped that the children would be just as enthused tomorrow; she knew she was.

She stood looking over the work. It wasn't of anything; it was definitely abstract, but it had a whimsical, appealing vibe. She went and got a chair from the dining room and stood with a bird's eye view. She was so engrossed in thought that she didn't hear the door open or anyone walk in. It wasn't until Geoffrey walked into her field of vision that she jumped a little.

'I didn't mean to frighten you, Ms Ruth, but I saw the top of your head through the window and . . .' He looked at the floor, scuffed his foot. 'Well, I thought the worst, Miss Ruth.'

'The worst?' she questioned.

He looked ashen. 'I thought you were swinging from the roof, done yourself in.'

She gasped and gulped, shook her head and hands furiously. 'No, no, no. Why ever did you think that?' she exclaimed.

He didn't answer. She was now shaking and gingerly stepped off the chair. They stood staring for a moment, silent.

Ruth changed the subject. Blithering, she said, 'We made this today from art supplies we scavenged from passengers and crew. Stunning, don't you think?'

'Wonderful, Ms Ruth. Just wonderful.' He smiled, but the shock hadn't quite gone from his expression.

Ruth felt awkward. She walked behind Geoffrey, out to the dining room, and closed the classroom door firmly. She wanted to get to Helen or Alice or even Isabella. Geoffrey muttered something about needing to meet his crew and hurried out one door. Ruth purposely chose the opposite door and started walking down the corridor. It was unfamiliar, but as long as it was in the other direction from awkward and uncomfortable, she didn't mind. She came to the end, turned around, and went back again. It had taken her a good few minutes to get down the end, and she hoped it was enough time. She hurried back to the deck and was so pleased to see Alice on a deck chair, she almost fell in her lap.

'What's the matter?'

Alice was always on tender hooks around Ruth after her panic attack, and with any slight change in temperament, Alice switched to crisis mode. It was good, in a way. This was different; it was an awkward social interaction that Alice was, herself, afflicted with but not aware of – probably not the best person to talk it through, but Ruth was desperate. She relayed what had happened in the classroom.

'He must have had some kind of past experience.'

She pondered. Ruth hadn't thought of that.

'I wouldn't worry. I wonder what's for dinner tonight. Shall we go and find the menu?'

Alice had befriended the staff in the kitchen, so she was privy to the menu. They often chose to go or not to go and hold out to supper if dinner didn't appeal, which was more often than not. She would wait to speak to Helen.

'The question is why was he coming to your classroom at all?' Helen said excitedly. 'He's sweet on you, you lucky goose.'

'Helen, you're married. Elliot, remember?' Alice said from under her covers.

Her back was to them, and Helen rolled her eyes and smirked. 'Oh, blow you Alice. I'm excited for Ruth.'

She wasn't harsh, but Alice bit back again. 'You carry on so.'

Helen frowned, her voice pitched. 'I am—'

'Don't squabble,' Ruth said quickly.

'You're hard to listen to.' Alice rolled over. 'You're hard to watch.' She was almost in tears.

'Alice? What's the matter? What's it to you?' Helen was concerned now.

Ruth went and sat on the edge of Alice's bunk. She started crying, big plopping tears. Ruth didn't say anything, just hugged her. Helen left the room and banged the door behind her. Alice jumped a little and cried even harder. It wasn't the time to ask questions, but Ruth mused. She wondered if it was part jealousy, that Alice didn't have a sniff of a suitor and it came so easily to Helen. Perhaps Alice was more aware of her social awkwardness than Ruth had thought. *She is so pretty and stylish, always so neatly put together.* Ruth wondered why she wasn't married.

She knew why she herself wasn't. Teaching took up too much of her time, too much of her head space, and too much energy. She had worked hard at studying and didn't have time to even think about the word *man*, let alone try a relationship. Then it seemed it was too late; nobody was interested anymore. Then war broke out.

Her mum was fond of saying, 'You attract men like flies, but who wants men like flies?'

She had thought it would just come easily for her when she was ready, and now if Geoffrey was interested like Helen had suggested, she didn't know what to do, how to behave.

Alice sniffed and hauled herself up. She looked a wreck. 'I'm sorry,' she whispered. 'I don't actually know what got into me.'

'It's OK. Helen is Helen. She's loyal to Elliot. You've seen the letters she writes. She loves him. She just gets carried away.' Ruth was a little bit fed up with defending her, but she knew it to be right.

Their door opened, and Helen proudly pranced in with Isabella in tow. She had a half-full brandy bottle in her hand. 'This is what we need,' she stated. She took a swig and shoved it at Alice.

Alice looked at Ruth, and she put her hands up. *Up to you.* Helen shook it in Alice's face. She didn't move. Ruth took it instead and took a swig. It ran warm and sharp down her throat – nasty, but as Helen meant, it would do the trick, calm the tension.

Isabella sat down, unaware of the simmering feelings. She looked at Alice. 'Are you ill? You look a fright!'

Alice looked away. Her shoulders shook, but then they realised she was in hysterics.

'Blow you, Alice. I can't keep up with your emotions!' Helen was cross. 'Drink this. Go on.' She grabbed the bottle from Ruth's lap and thrust it even harder at Alice.

'All right, all right. Don't get your knickers in a twist.'

'I'll tell you something for free. Sea air, strangers, cramped quarters, dull food, weather that's like none I know, all the children – it's enough to drive anyone round the bend. I'll be pleased to be on dry land and off this wretched ship and . . .' It was Isabella's turn to cry.

Helen was visibly fed up, and to keep the peace, Ruth suggested fresh air. 'Such as it is – but air nonetheless. A walk around the deck. Then back.'

They walked in silence, and then Helen surprised Ruth and took Alice and Isabella arm in arm. 'It's OK. There aren't many more days left on this wretched boat. We will be off in no time. You'll see.' She even managed a genuine smile.

Ruth lay in bed thinking about what was to come. Her feet and her head touched the walls, and she was happy she wasn't any taller. The others were asleep, but things were whirring in her head. It really was just a matter of days until they were in a foreign land. She felt very far from home, very far from anything that she really knew. She was somehow able to keep it together as the others all fell apart, but then internally and when she was alone, the emotions flowed over her, rolling and pitching with the ship. In a way, she would be sorry to say goodbye to the children. They had given her purpose, given her the excuse to set foot out of her comfort zone – but then what?

It wasn't very late in the afternoon, but it was getting dark, and black clouds had gathered. They had been through a couple of storms on their journey, but this seemed different. Ruth tried not to notice the wind picking up, tried to remain positive that they were a day out from shore and dry land. *Dry land.* She repeated it over and over in her head, willing it to come faster. She was leaning out over the railings as if to crane to see the land approaching. Someone tapped her elbow, and she jerked back.

'Dry land!' she gasped.

'What? You really are a funny one,' Geoffrey said. He had a big grin on his face. 'Can you see land, Ms Ruth?' He laughed.

She flushed red. Why was she always in the most odd or awkward situation when he was around? She was angry with herself but tried to reply sensibly. 'I am worried about those dark clouds.'

'Oh, don't be.' He sort of brushed her off, and when he noticed her distressed look, he softened. 'It's OK. I was concerned too. I had a word to the crew on the top deck. They assured me it is typical weather patterns this close to New Zealand.' He went on. 'We have to study weather as part of training. I'm not up to speed with Southern Hemisphere conditions, I'm afraid, but I'm sure it will be covered.'

She was only half-listening as he continued to talk about cloud formations and high winds, adding in big words like *atmospheric*. She had become distracted by his mouth and face, and his voice lulled her into a daydream. She thought about what Ruth and the other girls had teased her about. Over the weeks, she had really grown fond of Geoffrey. He was jovial, and even though he talked non-stop, she had stopped worrying about thinking of what to reply with as she never got a word in anyway. He even answered his own questions without taking a breath. She smiled. It was nice just to be next to him.

They skipped dinner. Alice relayed the menu while pulling a face, and even Isabella, who normally ate anything going, said, 'Ew. Ugh. It's like they've run out of everything this close to land and they've decided to serve the scraps from the last few weeks. No, thanks!' She put her arm over her brow and collapsed onto the bottom bunk in a heap of giggles.

'Where are you going to go when we get there, Isabella?' Ruth asked. She actually felt rather bad for not knowing that. They had got quite close, and she would like to keep in touch if she could.

'I'll stay with the children's relatives at first. They said they would help me find accommodation, but I will go back on the next ship too.' She looked sad. 'Will you be on the next ship back?'

Ruth nodded, and Alice said, 'To be honest, one day on dry land, a proper bath, and some new clothes would set me right to just turn around and go home.'

Helen just sighed loudly and said, 'Home!'

None of them really knew what to expect on dry land.

Chapter 6

'Terra firma.' Geoffrey laughed. 'Still just as wet.'

The rain was pouring over the brim of his hat, and his long jacket was sodden almost to the ground. He still managed to be upbeat as he lifted their luggage and hauled each piece to where they were standing at the terminal.

Somehow she had been left with all the children. She was grateful for the fenced area and largely turned her back. Ruth was uncomfortable and clammy. It was an odd sensation, and she put it down to exhaustion. Things would be different after a rest. Where and when would they rest? The children were running amok, but she had other things on her mind, barely heard them or cared.

Geoffrey stood awkwardly in front of her. She didn't want him to leave. He was quickly a familiar comfort she was not ready to give up. The rain had gone down her back; she was so uncomfortable, and she started to squirm. She was trying to be polite, but suddenly, she felt quite faint. She fidgeted with her sleeves, took her jacket off.

'Everything OK, Ms Ruth?'

'Just so hot,' she flustered.

'Are your legs working?' He grinned again. His eyes flashed.

She heard herself laugh, but there was a ringing in her ears. Why was it so damn hot? She tugged at her clothes again.

'Ms Ruth?' Geoffrey seemed coy. 'I would very much like us to keep in touch.'

She smiled, relieved she didn't have to admit she felt the same way.

'Can I give you my barracks accommodation and my RAF number? Then you could write to me?' He actually had flush in his cheeks; she liked it, wanted to reach out and touch his face.

'I would like that,' she said, 'very much.'

He grinned again. Was she faint with exhaustion or faint with excitement? She was so damp and uncomfortable, she couldn't tell. It was hard watching him walk away. He turned and waved a couple of times. Then he was swallowed up by his crewmates, and they blurred into one.

The children were suddenly a lot louder in her ears, and she turned and snapped, 'Be quiet!' and started to cry.

Helen and Alice came back after what seemed like months. Ruth was sitting on her upturned case with her chin in her hands. The children had calmed down in their penned state and were milling around. It was a bit of a sorry sight. Dirt and exhaustion had taken over.

'We managed to get us all into the sailors' barracks tonight as we are a day earlier than expected.' Helen sounded low and distant, and she looked how Ruth felt.

Ruth hoped she didn't look such a fright as Alice, but she supposed she did. It had been a long, hard journey. She pondered the heavy jacket in her hands. Had she actually, after all, packed too much? It was still raining, but the thought of putting the jacket on again made her feel ill.

'File through and pair up!' Helen screeched out over the children's heads. 'Follow us!' she boomed again. Then to Ruth, she said, 'Stay here and wait for the last one out. You be at the back.' Helen, good old Helen, always got the job done before collapsing in a heap. 'Go! Fall out! Quick march!'

They trudged – it was the only word for it – shoulders down, rain beating their heads even lower, along the road, with the harbour on their left and the rise of the inner-city buildings on the other side. She wasn't looking at anything, just her feet on the pavement. She had never felt anything like this: extreme tiredness, hollow in her heart – sad. Ruth was so sad, and she felt it fold in around her as she walked.

In a blur, they organised the children, and they organised themselves, and the people at the barracks were very nice to them. She was surprised to find that they were mostly women, and even in her blurry state, she was appalled at their uniform. *So masculine.* She put her head on the flat pillow, pulled the scratchy blanket to her chin, and murmured something to the others, and everything went black. Her body still rolled with the motion of the ship. How was it possible to have a harder bed than the one on the ship? The last thing on her mind, a flash just before sleep consumed her, was Geoffrey – his flushed cheeks and grin.

She was drenched in sweat and breathing hard. The pitch darkness frightened her. As she lay on her back, the room started coming into focus – Helen breathing softly in the bunk next to her and the bunk above her head too close for comfort. *How many miles away from home?* Why was it so hot? *This close to the end of the year, surely, it should be cold.* She untangled herself from the blanket and carefully unfurled her legs to stand up. The gap between the bunks was just a slice, narrower than the ship. Manoeuvring around in the dark in tiny spaces had become second nature to her, but she still felt giddy and ill. The end of the bunk caught her toe, and she yelped. Isabella stirred. She held her breath, but nobody woke. The hallway was dark too, but there was a window at the end. She walked down without aim. It was mercifully cooler, and she put her cheek on the cold glass. There was another building opposite and a courtyard below. Her window in the attic came to mind. There was nothing to be sad about, but misery weighed her down. *In the daylight, things will be different*, she told herself. She didn't go back to the stuffy room.

The chatter and excitement in the dining area was deafening. She hung her head, held her breath for a moment, and went in. Isabella waved at her excitedly and beckoned her over. Her smile instantly made Ruth feel much, much better. She was very pretty, and today she had chosen an outfit that Ruth hadn't seen on the ship.

'Don't you just love it?' she said when Ruth remarked on her dress. 'The colour and the fit are like a dream. I was saving it for best, but what else would be better than finally getting off that ship?' She grinned and grinned.

Ruth agreed and wished she'd kept something different to wear too. Maybe there would be some shops she could get to. If the war felt far away at home, it seemed it was in a different world now. Helen plonked down and shoved a scone and a cup of tea under her nose. Alice was talking to a woman in uniform. She looked decidedly better than she had in a long time. Ruth began to feel hopeful and even slightly excited. What was going to happen once the children had been billeted? They would be free to do what they wanted.

'What are you smiling about?' Helen questioned, laughing. 'You look like you're up to mischief.'

Ruth looked at her and winked. 'Perhaps I am. You're a bad influence on me.'

'Me?' Helen mocked shock and laughed. They were going to be fine.

It was actually quite sad to say farewell to Isabella. She was cheery as she got on the bus with the two children in tow. They waved her off and then stood for a moment in silence. They'd see her again on the ship home in two weeks' time, but for some reason, it felt like they were losing a member of the family.

It was late morning, and the street was quite busy. None of them were used to the mass of trams and cars that seemed ceaseless, and it was still hot. Ruth had put on too many clothes again. She was eager to look at the shops and get an outfit to match the weather, envious of Isabella's peacock blue dress.

'Come on.' Alice pulled her elbow. 'I know you're dying to look in shops.'

Helen said, 'You can help us with a new outfit each.'

Ruth grinned at the prospect. She was beginning to relax and have fun. This was the start of the adventure she had longed for. They were at the bottom of the main road. It was a gentle rise up from the port and so busy. London was, of course, busier but at least familiar. They didn't know how to navigate the flow; there didn't really feel like there was order. People, cars, trams, and even horses pulling loads just swarmed around them. They walked up the edge of the buildings. Ruth saw the shopfront sign like a beacon – Smith and Caugheys. It had brass double doors and floor-to-ceiling display windows. This was where she belonged.

There wasn't a peacock blue dress, but there was a ruby red dress with a plunging, scalloped neckline and puffed shoulders, nipped in at the waist with a wide sash and a flowing skirt, loose round the hips. Ruth had seen it almost immediately but refrained. Was it too extreme for her? They browsed a long time, but her eye kept wandering back to it.

Her grandmother's voice was in her head, loud and clear. 'Go on, girl. That colour is too wonderful to be stuck on the rack. Liberate it.'

She smiled. However, she still felt the stress of exponential liberty squeeze in her chest and distracted herself with Helen and Alice, who were hopelessly in fits of laughter over Alice's undergarments.

'See here when I put my arm down. It all just flows down the sides and spills into my pantyhose.'

She was crying with laughter, and Helen was near rolling about, hooting. The dignified shop ladies and customers were looking sideways at them. Ruth flushed red. She shushed them but admitted to herself that it was actually nice to see them getting along.

'Well, I'm going to get this little number.' Helen cheekily held a black pencil skirt twin set-up with one finger on the hanger.

She hadn't taken any of the advice she asked Ruth for. *Typical Helen.* Still, Ruth knew she would still look amazing.

She turned to Alice. 'How about you, Batwings McGee?'

Alice's brow furrowed; the laugh at her expense had obviously soured.

To quickly keep the peace, Ruth said, 'I think you should go for the green. Your hair is the perfect colour, and your skin is flawless. It will show off that alabaster.'

Alice smiled again.

'That's us, Ruth, but you? Then we can take our new outfits on the town tonight. Sailors galore!' She swooned backwards over the fitting room chair.

Alice rolled her eyes.

Ruth replied, 'I am still deciding. There's a red—'

'Get it!' Helen, over the top of her, repeated, 'Get it, get it, get it.'

For fear of her continued taunting, Ruth relented. There was hope for freedom yet.

Helen was true to her word – or was it a threat? She pulled out the hairpins, the makeup, and the sheer pantyhose and started getting them ready to 'go out and colour that town red. Ruth, you're halfway there'.

Ruth was apprehensive. She remembered the night before they left on the ship where Helen had done the same thing. She felt like she still had the bruises from stumbling around in the blackout and downstairs into what seemed like smoke-filled dungeons. It wasn't fun, and she didn't know how Helen had thought it was. Alice had just seemed like she was along for the ride, not minding either way. Ruth had hated it and was sad that one of her favourite outfits was now marred with the smell of smoke and stale alcohol.

'Do we really have to, Helen? Wouldn't it be nicer to just stay in and have a few nips together?' She sounded like she was pleading for her life, so she added lightly, 'You know we always have fun, and we don't have to worry about how we look.'

Helen just shook her head vigorously and grinned. 'You're not weaselling out of this, Ms Ruth.'

Her name said like that jarred her, and her heart twinged. Geoffrey seemed to have made his presence known, even if just in the back of her mind. *Don't collapse in a heap over a man, Ruth. Don't do it.* Her heart was still heavy, and she started to daydream about seeing him again, talking to him – rather, listening to him, not a word in edgewise. After the awkward encounter in her classroom, they had actually had a wonderful conversation about art. She now sat on the edge of the bunk, and the room dissolved into a loft apartment, Paris, full of light and air, Geoffrey set up with a sketch book, her with an easel, coffee and cakes between them.

Tick, tick, tick. 'Time to go.' Helen was clicking her fingers in her face. 'Alice, she's away with a million fairies.'

'Not fairies,' Alice said with a twinge of mockery in her voice. 'Geoffrey.'

Ruth held back tears. 'Let's go then. It will be fun.' Maybe just saying it, she might believe it.

It was eight o'clock at night and still light like late afternoon. Ruth felt odd dressed up for the night and walking down the road. They followed a group of sailors in their white shore leave uniforms. Alice was *tsk*ing at Helen the whole way. Ruth ignored her. Her feet already hurt – the wrong choice of shoes. She looked down at them – the perfect choice for her new dress, with a slightly pointed toe and the strap over the top, a button too big for function on the side, and a short heel. They rubbed. She winced. The men were chattering loudly and looking back over their shoulders at them. Helen was encouraging them. They went up a lane and piled into a small doorway. Helen went to follow, but Alice pulled her arm.

Helen swung round with a glare. '*What* is your deal?' she screeched in Alice's face.

'It's not proper,' Alice said primly.

Ruth was actually a little bit disappointed. It looked like it could be fun, harmless. 'Come on, Alice, what's the harm?' She nudged her elbow softly and smiled encouragingly. 'There were a couple of handsome sailors looking in your direction. I told you, the green shows off your lovely skin.'

Helen sighed, tapped her foot, and rolled her eyes. 'I'm going in. Blow you two.' She turned and disappeared into the gloom.

Ruth sighed internally. She didn't really want to miss out now, and what better place to let your hair down than in a place far away from anything and anyone they knew?

Chapter 7

By the time she convinced Alice to go in, Helen was already on her second cocktail. She was a beauty, perched on a barstool, surrounded by laughing men in uniforms, not just sailors. She recognised the RAF uniforms. She took Alice by the hand and slowly dragged, pulled her lead weight over to Helen.

A man with the biggest moustache she had ever seen yelled at the barman, 'A grasshopper for a vision in green and a lady in red for *the* lady in red!'

His friends fell about laughing, and his moustache waggled comically. Ruth couldn't help but laugh too and happily sat down when the man offered an empty barstool with an over-the-top, sweeping arm bow. Alice stood stiffly but accepted the neon green concoction. The sharp taste of her lady in red burned in the back of her throat. Her eyes watered as she was holding back a cough. She didn't want to look a fool. *Play it cool, Ruth Simpson*, she said to herself. *Grandma Hetty is in here somewhere. Pull out the charm.* Again, the smoke was suffocating, and she tried not to think about the night ruining her new dress. She also tried to forget just how much she had actually spent on it. *So frivolous. So far from home.* It didn't count, lost in the ethos of wartime madness.

Madness was a less-than-efficient word to describe the night. The band started, and the dancing was extremely fun. After a couple of grasshoppers, even Alice was having fun. She was actually having fun, and Ruth was pleased. Helen was in her element. She was swinging around and around on the arms of every man in the house, singing the songs and downing the drinks. Ruth was caught up in it all and admired all the other women in the bar too. They all seemed so glamorous and carefree. It was easy to be swept up in it all. The night seemed endless.

Ruth slowed in downing the drinks, even though all the men were eager to replace empty glasses with full ones just as soon as she sipped the last drop. Heady and hot, she went up the stairs to get some air. It was dark now, the wee hours of the night. No blackout was needed at the end of the earth; the streetlamps seemed brighter than day, and she squinted at them, pondering their existence.

Another loud group of uniformed men came up the road – RAF, so easily recognisable to her now. She was feeling bold and waved out at them. They walked past her, waving back and shouting out, wolf-whistling. Why was she feeling so brazen? She model-posed and blew kisses.

Her back was to the street as she turned to go back inside. As she was walking, she was grabbed from behind. A strong arm wrapped around her waist, spun her around, and as she felt herself being dipped back, before she could see a face, a big wet kiss was planted firmly on her lips. Gagging, she pushed back, stood up, and swiftly kicked the man in the shins – the right shoes after all. She went to kick again, thrashed her arms at him.

He caught them round the wrist, yelling, 'Ms Ruth! Ms Ruth, it's me! It's me!'

She stopped, stood gasping. Why was Geoffrey standing in front of her? Why did he just do that? She started crying, screeched at him, 'Why?'

Through tears, she could see him wobbling and realised he was quite full, on the drink all night and inhibitions thrown to the wind. What was this mess in front of her?

'I'm sorry, Ms Ruth.'

'Don't call me that! Only a sweet man named Geoffrey calls me that!'

She was still crying. Why had this upset her so much? She was embarrassed by the way she had behaved; she had encouraged that sort of behaviour, and now she was paying the price.

'I'm sorry, Ms Ruth.'

'Stop calling me that!' she yelled.

She was still yelling, incomprehensible, Helen at her side now and Alice pulling her to leave, Geoffrey standing in front of her, head down. Alice's tugging moved her backwards, and she walked, not turning, eyes on Geoffrey. Helen stood next to him, hand on his arm, warning him, *Don't follow.*

All of what was meant to be fun and happy was smeared on her pillow in the morning. Ruth looked in her little pocket mirror. Her eyes were still puffy and red from crying. Poor Alice – she had cried on her shoulder, literally. She had unloaded on Alice, told her about her debaucherous behaviour. To give her her due, Alice was very reassuring and very nice to her. Where was Helen? She wasn't there for the rest of the night or now, her bed not slept in. Ruth left Alice asleep. She was probably feeling the effects of one too many grasshoppers as well. She went to get them both a cup of tea, smuggle it back to the dorm somehow. *Maybe a scone too.*

The memories of the night still flooded her mind. How could she have been so silly? How could Geoffrey do that to her? What was he thinking? He wasn't. What if that was the last time she would ever see him? She was clenching her fists and digging her nails into her palms. She was not, was *not*, going to cry over a man. She was. She did. She sat down on a bench in the dining area and, head in elbow, sobbed.

There was a tap on her shoulder. She looked up to see a woman from the barracks smiling kindly down at her.

Ruth was still horrified at the uniform and, without thinking, without any formalities, she said so. 'How can you bear to wear that uniform?'

The lady smiled and laughed. She sat down next to Ruth. 'I do so hate it.' She had an Irish accent. 'It comes with the job, and a job is a must, so the clothes are a must. Are you OK? Why are you crying?'

Ruth couldn't bear to hash back over the events of the night. 'A man,' she replied again without thinking.

'Oh, they're not worth those sorts of tears, my lovely.'

Ruth didn't offer any more on the subject, and the woman just sat in companionable silence. Ruth guessed she was about the same age as her mum, though with a few more lines on her face, and the backs of her hands were rough and red – a harder life, much harder.

'I suppose there's a special fellow then?'

She hadn't thought about it, except she had. She had daydreamed about him constantly. 'No,' she said.

'Ah, I see. He's upset you. Really upset you.'

Ruth nodded. A complete stranger knew her thoughts better than her.

'Will you be able to forgive him? There's a war on after all.'

What was that supposed to mean? She didn't want to be rude, but she didn't want to talk either. 'I will . . .' She stammered. 'Rather, I need to get my friend a cup of tea. May I please make an exception to take it back to the dorm? She is unwell.'

'Certainly. Be my guest.' The woman got up and added, 'I hope you will.' *Take the tea or forgive?*

Ruth had been low for a week now. The heavy fog of events was still thick with angst. They'd moved to a boarding house in a suburb called Parnell. It was directly next to the cathedral and in the grounds of the vicarage. She had thought about attending mass that morning, but she had not actually even sat up in bed. It was a stuffy, small room, but at least it was her own. The time away from Helen and Alice had been bliss. So close to them physically for so many months, she was dreading the voyage home.

Her whole body felt limp and lethargic. She hated that she felt like this over a man. She was desperate to see Geoffrey again, forgive him, and see his smile once again. It hurt her heart that the last sight of him was sad and dejected. *If I don't get out of bed, I won't even have the chance of seeing him again. Get up. Get dressed. The short-sleeved blouse with the tie and the yellow trimmed pencil skirt. Do it. Get up.*

Alice and Helen were clearing the breakfast. There were other guests staying at the house. In all, there were about twelve, women. She hadn't spoken to them to get to know them, just passing pleasantries in the halls and over meals. She wasn't about to commit to friendship – no real time, all just passing through on their way in and out.

She wandered back into the entrance hall with a view to collecting her coat and going for a walk. She felt she could cope with heat before this country, but it was a different kind of heat, one that clung to your skin and made you sweat even without physical effort. She hated sweating. She never 'glowed' like a lady; she always just went hot pink. She looked in the hall mirror. Even just thinking about the weather had made beads of sweat form under her nose. Her thick brown hair was less hair, more dank fluff, and there was nothing she could do about it. She peered closer; her breath fogged the glass. She barely recognised the face staring back, hooded eyes and pinched mouth. *Smile, for heaven's sake.*

Alice came out of the kitchen, tea towel in hand. 'Are you going out? Have a cup of tea first?' she asked, concern in her voice.

Ruth had her hand on the doorknob. *Push and run. Run far away.* She turned and smiled weakly, nodded, and followed Alice back through to the kitchen. Helen was standing over the bench, and it reminded Ruth of Cook. She wondered what they were all doing at home and then thought, guilty, *I need to write to my parents.* Alice put a teacup and saucer in front of them both and poured the water into the teapot.

'I have something to confess.' Helen sat down opposite her.

She looked back at Helen expectantly.

'Please don't be angry at me.'

When people say that, it can never be promised. Ruth bit the side of her mouth and clenched her jaw. What on earth was Helen going to confess?

Alice awkwardly cleared her throat and shuffled around in the pantry, tidying up tidy things. Helen scratched at the edge of her saucer. Nothing was said. Ruth sighed audibly, making her frustration known. Alice filled the jug again and turned it on. *Silly flapper. You poured the tea already. Don't get angry at poor Alice.*

'It's about Geoffrey.'

The sentence fell between them. Ruth didn't move or take her eyes off Helen. She squirmed under her gaze.

'I had to do something. You were so upset, and he was so upset.'

'I don't care about him,' Ruth lied, deadpan, no emotion – except it wrenched at her throat to say it.

'I know you don't mean that.' Defensive, Helen continued. 'I stayed with him that night. He had had too much to drink, and his mates had ditched him. Some mates.'

Ruth was secretly pleased, but she didn't let on. Hopefully, good old Helen had pulled off another sweet-talking miracle.

'Thank you for looking after him.' She meant it.

Helen relaxed a bit. 'In the morning, he was very regretful, truly heartbroken. I couldn't stand by and do nothing. So I said I'd talk to you.' It was all coming out now. 'The thing is you were so sad and angry, I didn't know how to.'

Ruth listened.

'I have his contact details and a permission pass for the base, but you have to go today.'

Ruth blinked.

'He leaves for Trentham tomorrow.'

She took the pass from Helen – 'Thank you' – giving her nothing.

'Shall we come with you?' Alice asked eagerly.

Helen nodded encouragingly. Ruth shook her head slowly, stood up, and walked out the front door. She heard Helen say, 'No, don't go after her,' to Alice, obviously worried.

She walked down the main road. She had automatically grabbed her handbag and coat. *Stupid girl. That damn coat.* She had half a mind to turn back, but she folded it over her arm and kept walking. She didn't know if she was on the right side of the road, and the place names were so difficult. The bus driver got cross at her. They spoke English here, but written down, the words may as well have been in code.

'Where to, miss?' the driver repeated sharply.

She had to get the pass out and point dumbly. He grunted, the doors crashed shut behind her, and the bus lurched off. She took that to mean she must be on the right bus. For a while, she relaxed into the journey, looking out the window. It was late morning, and the streets were busy. The buildings were an odd mix of familiar mixed into what felt like inner London suburbs in the middle of a field. *Like in a dream when you know where you are but none of it looks right.* These were familiar forms but strangely clad, mostly in wood with tile roofs. How was she going to know when to get off?

Chapter 8

The buildings turned to houses, and then the houses turned to sheds, and then there was nothing but trees and grass. There was also only her and another woman on the bus. It stopped, the driver opened the doors, and the other lady got off. Ruth sat upright.

'Last stop!' the driver bellowed.

She got off, and as the bus trundled off, she began to regret her actions. She just stood at the fence line. There were no signposts, no clues as to where she even was. She felt like she was at the end of the earth. She found herself thinking about a summer holiday they had taken when she was little in the south with her aunt and grandma. The cottage was beautiful, and the places to explore were endless. However, she did not fancy exploring these endless fields. Panic rose, but she needed to find some scrap of know-how in her fogged-up mind. Walking back to the last shed, maybe? Following the road up? Standing alone, the sun beating down, she had to think of something.

Not a single vehicle had gone by in about twenty minutes of Ruth standing there. She hadn't moved, petrified to the spot, and she was beginning to wonder if she really was in a dream, the bus that had brought her here just an apparition, a figment of her imagination, and she would wake up any minute. She waited, pinched her forearm; it hurt. *Not a dream then.* Was Geoffrey worth this? It would be the end of the day soon, anyway, and she would have missed him.

The thought got her legs working, and she decided to walk down the road, back to the last shed, in search of life. The road stretched hot in front of her. Why had she come? Her mind had made itself up, and her body had just followed along. What was she going to do when – or if – she saw him again? Fall in his arms? Swoon? She wasn't that sort of person, but what sort was she? *Now is not the time to have an identity crisis.*

There was a family story of Grandma Hetty lost in the wilderness in a foreign land, the reason for the slight scar above her left eye, but she never elaborated. Ruth liked to think it was from wild animals. Her heart pounded; what kind of wild creatures were out here? Her pace quickened, and she was near running, as well as she could in the silliest shoes she could have chosen for a wilderness excursion. Why did she always dress up? Who was she trying to impress? Who was she trying to fool?

The heat was extreme, and her jog had turned to a shuffle, her arms limp at her sides. She could feel every stone through her shoes.

'Ms Ruth! Ms Ruth!'

Now she was hallucinating, hearing her name.

'Ms Ruth!' It was louder.

Stupid brain. Why are you torturing me with the sound of his voice? The grass was softer on her cheek than she had imagined it might be. It was warm. She sank deeper into it and closed her eyes – a rest, and then on to find her way out. Sleep might stop the voices in her head. Was she going mad? She wished for her bed at home, wondered what Trudi was doing. That was a funny thought; she hadn't really given Trudi any headspace since she left. She was still so damn hot. Why did she think an adventure would be the thing to do?

There hadn't been anyone around, and suddenly, she was being scooped into a car. Typical – now she was being kidnapped. She was too weak to put up much of a fight but managed to kick out at the person, caught them on the shoulder.

'I see you're still in control of your legs.'

Did she imagine that? The laugh too? She opened her eyes more, but everything was blurry. Not a hulking figure – her head was on the lap of dark green pants, and the car bumped along the road.

'Don't worry, Ms Ruth. You need some water and to be out of the sun.'

She didn't imagine it. 'Geoffrey!'

'Sure am!'

The relief washed over her, and she fell back into his lap. Swooning may not be her thing, but she was sure doing a lot of it lately.

Scratchy bed linens seemed to be the norm for ships and military. She was getting used to them. Ruth was alone in a big hall of beds. She felt much better, and there was a breeze coming in from the open double doors at the end of the room. She slowly sipped the water from the tin cup next to her. She was getting used to tin crockery too. Was it crockery if it wasn't made from porcelain?

She was still pondering when she heard footsteps behind her, a familiar gait that made her heart beat. She turned to see Geoffrey's smiling face.

'Sun's a terrible beast of a thing down under, isn't it? What on earth were you doing, Ms Ruth?'

She stared at him. She decided to tell him the truth. What did she have to lose? 'I was looking for you.' Her voice was small. She cleared her throat and made herself sit up from her slummed, defeated position. She smiled at him, put her hand on his cheek as he sat down next to her.

'Well, you found me, but it was a good job we were in the mobile unit coming back from training. We were going to run, but the sun . . .'

He tailed off, stared back at her with questioning eyes. He put both his hands on her face, tilted her head back, and kissed her – soft, scratchy, harder, scratchy . . . *wonderful*. She dropped her head forward and rested on him, forehead to forehead. The air was hot between them.

Geoffrey sighed deeply, put his hand under her chin, and kissed her quick again before drawing back. 'Ms Ruth.'

There were no words to fully explain their feelings.

'Geoffrey.'

There was a stinking war on. She was miles away in a tiny, hot country, and Ruth still couldn't get away from the ripples it made. In fact, it seemed strangely closer than it had at home.

Geoffrey's hand was in hers as they walked, slowly, trying to extend time and stall the inevitable. There was mercifully nobody else at the bus stop. They didn't talk. What do you say when you're about to be torn away from each other, one to war, the other at sea for weeks to the other side of the world? The thoughts were spinning in her head, mixed with her daydreams of their artist's loft. Tears started trailing down her cheeks. She moved closer to Geoffrey.

He put his arm around her waist. 'Ms Ruth.' He was staring straight ahead, and she could tell he was holding back.

They heard the bus and saw the dust cloud before they saw the bus itself. It gave them time to have the last few seconds together. He held her so tightly, it was almost painful. He kissed her and kissed her and kissed her.

'I will . . .' Ruth's words were caught in her throat. There really were none.

'Ms Ruth, my you,' he whispered into her neck.

'Geoffrey, my you.'

The bus driver had seen it all, but his impatience was lost. Both of them were still locked in eye contact as she ran to the back window. Geoffrey jogged after the bus a little way, but his figure was soon lost in the dust.

'Good grief.' Alice was coming out of the front door as Ruth came up the path. 'Good heavens.' Her voice was cracking.

Ruth thought she must look a fright if Alice was the one exclaiming at the sight of her. 'I need to wash and change, that's all,' she said flatly.

'OK, well, I'm going out for some things we need, but go and see Helen.' She had put on her authoritative voice, which made Ruth giggle. 'Why are you laughing? Good gracious.' She huffed away.

'Thank you!' Ruth yelled after her.

Alice didn't turn, but she flicked her hand back in acknowledgement.

Ruth felt oddly happy. She was desperately sad, but the thought of the time she had just spent with Geoffrey made her feel light-headed. Ruth thought back to her school day crushes, when she thought the world would end because the feelings hadn't been reciprocated, the thoughts she had wasted on them as they chose other women, got married, had children. She had an accomplished feeling that these emotions were grown up – a grown-up relationship. The memory of their short time together made her grin as she walked into the kitchen.

'Well, don't you look like the cat who got the cream,' Helen said, a hint of knowing in her voice. 'Is all forgiven? Am I safe to approach?' She was only half-joking.

Ruth nodded. 'Thank you, Helen. Where would I be without you?'

Dryly, she replied, 'Well, still sat here, I'd say.'

Ruth thought she was probably right. Grandma Hetty would approve of Geoffrey; she was certain. Her voice came into her head. 'Perfect for you – actions to go with all the talk.'

The suburb where they had been staying reminded her of their village, a small, compact, wooden version. She was astonished at the wooden houses. They were perfect little replicas of the cottages at home – but wood. She had talked to an old man standing at his letterbox one day when she had walked over the road to the greengrocer. The accent had made her giggle a bit; she'd turned away so as not to offend. From what she had gathered, the house next to him was the oldest wooden building in the city. She stood out the front of it now.

She wished she had brought a camera. She wished she even had a camera. They were leaving the next day, and Ruth felt like she hadn't properly seen the place. If she hadn't been so wound up on the bus ride, she might have enjoyed the views, taken them in a bit more. She decided to see what she could find at the shops to draw with and come back to sketch a couple of drawings, one for memory's sake and one to send Geoffrey. There was a post office not far down the road. She bought two big envelopes. That was all there was to draw on that was plain. There were only fat builder's pencils, no art supplies. She decided to go back to their boarding house and rake out the bottom of the fire. Charcoal would be OK, would save her dwindling cash supply too. That should worry her more than it did at this point in time.

She ruined her lovely cotton skirt despite pulling it up to kneel by the fire grate. She was angry at herself. She loved the light shade of blue, and in this heat, it was lovely and cool. Would there be time to wash it out before they left? She had left what she called her artist's clothes at home, for once making a good decision in the editing process, though she missed them now. It was a lovely big shirt of her father's. It perhaps shouldn't have been commandeered by her at all; the label read Abercrombie and Fitch. She had liked it for its utilitarian, sporting look, and it had a deep front pocket.

'What on earth are you doing?' Alice asked in an exasperated, high-pitched voice.

Ruth had managed to get quite a decent stick of charcoal, and she held it up like a trophy to Alice. The bewildered look on her face was priceless, and Ruth laughed.

'I don't know what you're laughing at, Cinderella. You're the one covered in soot.' She was still confused and probably thinking this was the last end, that Ruth had completely lost the plot now.

'I will explain later. Tell Helen I won't be in for supper and I might be late in. I'm not far away.'

Alice filled the kettle.

Chapter 9

The afternoon was hot, but she found a shady spot. The tree was beautiful, the red flowers glistening in the sun. She wished she had some colours to capture them too. She wrote a note to remind herself when she got home. *A dark ruby red, like wet rubies with a hint of saffron as a halo. Leaves, a mix of gloss green and a matte, dusty finish. Light, mossy bark.* The moss was the only familiar thing about the beautiful tree. She lightly sketched in the building and surroundings.

Cross-legged on the grass, she thought about painting the heather with her father again. She hoped her parents were well and vowed to scribble a quick note to post at the docks tomorrow along with the sketch for Geoffrey. Once she got into the flow of drawing, the other buildings, the cathedral, the street, and even their boarding house became inspiring; she wanted to draw them all.

In the end, she ripped the back off both the envelopes and then folded the other pieces to make four spaces to sketch in. The time disappeared, and the light faded. Walking back up the road, she was struck with an overwhelming sense of dread – the thought of weeks on end in cramped quarters again. She sighed heavily and tried to think of how much she wanted to be home, how she was certain the war would be over by the time they were home.

Alice and Helen were quietly chatting at the kitchen table, a pot of tea between them. Ruth's heart panged for Cook's kitchen. The months on end with no news from home was agonising.

'Can we see what you've drawn?' Alice gestured to the clutch of papers in her hand.

'I want to see the result of your transformation into Cinderella.' Helen bust out laughing and between the sobbing fits of giggles tried to speak. 'Alle . . . Aller . . .' There was more uncontrollable laughter.

Alice and Ruth couldn't help themselves; they were laughing too.

'Allerednic!' Helen finally shouted, tears streaming down her face, the peace of the stuffy kitchen broken by their frenzied outburst.

'What are you talking about?' Alice was still laughing.

Helen replied, 'You know, backwards Cinderella. She goes from rags to a ball gown. Our Ruth goes ball gown to rags . . .'

The laughter didn't stop for a long time. It was a welcome tension release. At least half an hour later, they were still hooting, trying to say their own names backwards, when another house guest rapped very loudly on the door and whistled like a train. They were shocked into silence and then even more silent as looks might kill. They tidied up in silence, still smirking at one another, and went to bed, the last night alone in a room for a while.

'I actually don't want to go home,' Alice said, a flat, reflective statement. She was sitting on the end of Ruth's bed. They were both procrastinating.

Ruth looked at Alice – head down, staring at her toes.

'Perhaps when the war is over, I might come back.' It was as if she was asking Ruth's permission. What had struck her suddenly to say such a thing? 'I am desperate to get home, but at the same time, I would rather not.'

She was wistful. Ruth had been squashing her own feelings, and she knew it. There were a lot of adjectives for the adventure she had so longed to go on. She streamed them through her mind – *exhilarating* but mostly *arduous*. She didn't exactly long to be home – she hadn't come near enough to any action – but she would rather do her travelling in style instead of cooped up with the others.

'I'm looking forward to seeing Isabella.' Her voice was raised at the end, inviting Alice to agree.

Alice beamed in agreement. It was funny how a stranger had managed to become such an integral part of their friendship in such a short time.

Ruth carefully folded the tissue paper from her garment bag over her drawing and folded the envelope ready to post. She wished it to find him healthy and safe. Then she turned back to packing and wished she hadn't bought so many clothes. She decided to wear her Smith and Caugheys dress under a cotton smock with longer sleeves. It wasn't about the look; it was about the space. Had her suitcase shrunk?

The ship didn't sail until the later evening, but they had got down to the wharf early, and there was not a lot to do. Alice was quiet again, but Ruth understood the heavy heart feeling of facing the long journey home. Helen was absentminded and, for some odd reason, was kicking the fence. It was actually a beautiful red wrought-iron fence. It stretched down the road for quite a distance, decorative lampposts at every section. They had walked along here the very first day, but she couldn't recall the fence. She looked at Helen's shoe, the scuff marks on the side from the paint. Then they all jumped.

A gruff voice called out, 'Hey! Don't do that!'

A gatekeeper? He was in uniform and looking angrily at them. They moved on, back towards the bottom of the main road. Who knew how long they would have to wait for Isabella? They decided to find a teahouse.

Ruth still couldn't get over the way the buildings felt like home but somehow inside out. She was disappointed that the veranda shelters obscured the complete view of their facades. She craned her neck out and looked skyward. A tram went by and a bike and a car, all at once and all too close for comfort. She trotted to catch up to the others as they stood looking down a short arcade. The inside roof details and Georgian-style front to the building were magnificent, and the smell of tea and scones wafted out. In they went. Ruth was suddenly very aware she was wearing two dresses and began to giggle. *Hold it in. Don't get us kicked out of a royal arcade, for pity's sake.*

Excited squealing could be heard a mile away, and as it got louder, they realised it was directed at them and coming from the familiar little figure of Isabella. She was running, waving, and squealing. Ruth was slightly embarrassed at the commotion, and both Helen and Alice were purposefully looking in the opposite direction. *If we don't look at her, she won't see us.* Still, in the end, they gave her a great big hug.

She jumped up and down on the spot. 'Isn't it great to be reunited – and no more responsibilities!'

Ruth hadn't thought, but of course, she had been the whole time with her charges and, now relieved of her child-minding duties, had gone completely off the deep end. She smiled. *Fair enough. Perhaps the trip home would be less tedious with Isabella about.*

Ruth looked around and spotted someone she thought she recognised, a woman in a plain black dress and a black hat. *In mourning?* Why did her face look familiar? She awkwardly jerked her head away, looked at the high clouds, when the lady caught her staring. Out of the corner of her eye, Ruth could see her moving towards them. She turned around and realised it was the Irish lady who had been so nice to her at the barracks.

She smiled in recognition. 'Sorry for staring. I couldn't work out why your face was so familiar, but I don't know anyone here.'

The lady smiled.

'I didn't recognise you out of that ghastly uniform,' Ruth continued. She had a small smile, sad eyes.

'I'm Ruth. This is Alice, Helen, and Isabella. We are going back to England. Are you going back to Ireland?'

'My son was killed in Egypt on the front line.'

Tears welled up in her eyes, and Ruth felt a lump in her throat so big, she couldn't talk. She put her hand on the woman's shoulder, patted her folded arm with her other hand.

'I'm Roisin,' she said quietly.

'Are you travelling alone?' Helen asked, concerned.

Roisin nodded.

'You're welcome to join our party.'

'Thank you. The company and the distraction would be good, I think.' She had a thick Irish accent, with a *t'ank* and a *t'ink*.

The noise from the docks swallowed up any more conversation and, mercifully, any more thoughts. Ruth stared at the side of the ship – *Rangitane*, it read. The English in New Zealand was very odd sounding. That wasn't English, was it? She liked the way it sounded in her head.

Settling into cabin life again had been hard. They were only a day and a half out of Auckland, and things seemed even more dire than last time. Alice had got a particularly extreme bout of seasickness and refused to even eat or drink. She spent all day and most of the night on deck. Ruth was worried about her, but the ship's doctor said she just had to ride through it – 'It will pass.'

Ruth was sitting next to her, just thinking, staring out to sea. The horizon was still fuzzy looking and at the stage where she wasn't sure if land was still in sight or not. She had a sudden thought. In a bit of a panic, she stood up and rushed to find Helen. Alice moaned after her, but she was too flustered to listen. She found Helen and Isabella in their cabin, poring over a fashion magazine. Ruth was too overwrought to even want to look at it.

'Will we have to come back to collect the children when the war is over?' she asked, almost at the top of her lungs, Helen with a shocked, confused look on her face. 'I don't want to do this godforsaken ship journey again. Oh, please tell me we don't have to.' She was pleading.

'I actually hadn't thought,' Helen replied, flat and calm. 'If we do, you don't have to come.'

It was said in a way that made Ruth think she absolutely should go – the tone used on her pupils that meant the exact opposite. She felt silly.

'What's the magazine?' Ruth tried to make her voice light and carefree.

'Helen was showing me her wedding dress,' Isabella said. 'Though I'm sure you, as a bride, looked much lovelier than her.' She jabbed at the picture with her finger and giggled. 'Here's another one.'

Isabella handed Ruth the colourful pages, and she almost fell over. She had missed them and didn't even realise until she felt the weight in her hand and the anticipation of thumbing through the fashion pictures. Sometimes there were photos, and she remembered poring over every detail with Grandma Hetty. Towards the end, when she was too sick to get out of bed, they would still critique the styles and trends. Ruth sat on the edge of the cabin bed, tucked her feet up. The memories of her grandmother's prim bedclothes and the smooth sheets on her feet made the blankets feel even scratchier, and *dark* and *dingy* seemed to engulf her thoughts, threatened to suffocate her. She decided to go and join Alice again. Her moaning was at least in the open air.

Since Alice was ill, they didn't have access to the menu like the journey to New Zealand. Turning up for meals had already become an adventure in culinary horrors, and they were only three days in. *What would it be like at the end?* Ruth shuddered to think. Standing in line down the corridor, waiting for dinner, she could smell what she vividly imagined was a pile of wet woollen socks and a side of putrid cabbage. When they got near the front, Ruth snorted with laughter; she wasn't far wrong. Then without words, all three of them turned on their heels and left, hoping for supper to be at least something dry. They found Alice on the deck.

'Poor friend, can we get you anything?' Isabella lay a dainty hand on Alice's knee as she sat down next to her. She patted it again and asked, 'Do you think you might be able to manage a cup of tea?'

Alice tipped the brim of her floppy hat up with one finger, nodded, and smiled weakly. Ruth was shocked at how green she was. If it wasn't for that, she would have passed for a lovely lady of leisure with a wide brimmed hat voyaging to exotic destinations.

'I'll be right back.'

Isabella, with her neat figure and sedate but trendy clothes, could be the much-cherished niece, the companion traveller to a spinster aunt. Too mean, Ruth. What would that make Ruth and Helen in their travelling company? *Two more mad aunts.*

Supper was dry, too dry, but they ate it – rock-hard scones dipped in weak tea. All four of them were on the deck.

'I thought I might find you here.' It was an Irish accent – *t'ought*.

Roisin had kept to herself mostly but had come to join them on occasion, Ruth supposed, when she was feeling most lonely. She came up now and, with a jovial harrumph, plopped down next to them.

'I see you're looking a bit brighter there, wee Alice. Pleased to see it.'

She smiled, and all the lines on her face gathered at the corners of her eyes and cascaded down her cheeks. There was a nice twinkle in her eye, and her company added a relaxed, motherly tone to their group, though Ruth sensed sadness.

'Tell us about your son, Roisin.' It was not a demand, just a gentle suggestion that talking might make her feel a bit better or at least give them something to talk about.

Roisin shut her eyes and sighed, head sinking into her shoulders. Ruth instantly regretted it and tried to change the subject.

'It's too hard.' She had a weak, small voice. 'I will talk about my youngest – your age, I would say,' she said with a brighter voice. 'He's always been the one to up and go, a bit quirky.' She tailed off, looked off into the distance.

'He sounds wonderful,' Isabella said with a chirp. 'Is he in Ireland?' she asked.

Roisin nodded, but it seemed she was divulging nothing else for the time being. They sat in silence; the water sloshing below their feet was peaceful, for once, and the air fresh. Heading home was a good feeling.

It was hot and stuffy in the cabins at night. It wasn't anything that Ruth could get used to, but as she was lying awake now, it wasn't bothering her as much. In fact, this close to the end of the year, it was making her think of Cook in the kitchen, the heat from the range, and the many pots and pans it would take her to make 'a fancy roast with thick gravy and the stuffing inside the bird with a fresh lemon – only the best for our Christmas'. She could hear her voice. It was nice how quickly Helen and her family had become part of their lives and traditions.

She felt her stomach flip in anticipation of being home, seeing her parents, working, even. The days had dragged. She thought about Geoffrey as she drifted off to sleep. It sent out good vibes. She listened to Helen breathing softly. Isabella had taken first shift to sit with Alice on deck. *Sweet girl.* The air was thick, breathing was hard, and she half-thought to go up on deck too, but lying down over sitting in a hard deck chair won, and her mind was clouded in sleep.

'Ruth!' She heard screaming, crying. 'Ruth!'

She screamed back, 'Helen!'

They were in their cabin, next to each other, but over the noise and in the pitch dark, it was as if they were on opposite sides of the world. The ship was pitching, and the noise was unearthly, so loud, and with every bang, the ship shook violently. Helen was still screaming and crying, but Ruth was in stunned silence, unable to move, unable to decipher what Helen was screaming about. Over the utter confusion, she realised Helen was stuck in her bunk; the whole wall had smashed in sideways, and she was pinned down.

In a blind panic, still not knowing what had happened, Ruth scrambled over the rubble to get to her friend. It was so dark, she could have been a hair's breadth away from Helen and still not see her. Helen mercifully had her head and one shoulder free – that arm was easy to pull up – but she was still stuck down one side.

'Are you in pain? What can you feel? I can't see anything. Can you describe?'

Ruth was crying too; what sort of request was 'describe where you are stuck'? She was no good in a crisis at the best of times, but she didn't know which way was up. From what she could feel and pull, it seemed like they might be able to free Helen if she pushed and Ruth pulled. She tugged at something, and Helen screamed in pain. She let go and felt around.

'I can't move. Ruth, get me out, get me out!'

'I'm trying. Oh, Helen, I'm trying. Please don't worry.'

She was worried, and they both knew it. She felt around again, slowed down, breathed slower, and tried to use just her sense of touch. *Breathe.* Under her fingertips was fabric, scratchy. *That's the blanket. See if it moves.* She yanked, hard, and it came free. That was a good sign.

'Just breathe through your nose, Helen. We can do this.'

The crashing and deafening smashes kept coming. Something cracked, and the whole bunk collapsed. They were lucky; Helen was able to manoeuvre free. *Lucky?*

'Where are Alice and Isabella?' whispered Helen.

'Are you hurt?' Ruth asked.

She'd heard the question; she just didn't want to think what had happened. They were still in the cabin; there was lots of shouting. Was that English? What was happening? The shouting was drowned out by the thumping in her ears. Reverberations? Palpitations? She supposed both.

The explosion noises had stopped, the boat was still, and she realised it was silent too. The engines were off. They didn't know what had just happened, but they knew it wasn't good. Ruth thanked goodness the children were all safe on land. Had the war come to the end of the earth? She'd wished it.

Chapter 10

They dared not move for hours. When the German officer came to their cabin, they were still clutching each other tight.

'You! You are English women, yes?' He was shouting.

'Don't shout at us.' There was indignation in Helen's wavering voice.

'Get up! Get out! Schnell! Schnell!' The shouting was louder, more harsh.

They scrambled over the rubble. Ruth stopped. The top of her suitcase was visible through the wood. She stood staring at it.

Helen hissed at her, 'What are you doing?'

'I can reach that,' she replied, looking sideways at the German man in his navy uniform that looked like it should be crisp with sharp edges on his hat and collar but was rather dishevelled and crushed looking.

He stared back at her, eyes not moving from her gaze.

She felt them boring holes in her, but she said, 'I'm taking my suitcase,' in a flat, no-nonsense tone, and he just shrugged.

Quickly, they both pulled at the mess and released the case. She thanked the small living quarters in that moment that there was never enough room to unpack.

They squinted in the daylight, which was somehow brighter when they were standing on the ruins of a ship. There was disorder everywhere, familiar and unfamiliar faces and languages blurring into one. They stood in silence but arm in arm. There were two big ships out in front of them flying German flags. She had seen and read about German raiders from the First World War but had hardly realised they were real – a story made up to tell to children at night, adventures on the high seas, cannons and clashing swords. Grandma Hetty was very fond of such tales, often acting out great scenes. Ruth came back to reality. They had just been attacked and captured; their destiny was waiting on those menacing-looking ships.

Despite the obvious disarray, they were organised into pilot boats and ferried to the waiting German boat pretty quickly. The German navy men yelled in broken English, but they knew what they had to do. That's the thing about the English language – one can butcher it so much and still be understood. Ruth wished she was in her classroom teaching English lessons right now. She would take the humdrum over this fear any day. Helen's face was a picture of how she felt. She assumed she must look the same – dirty face, bloodied, sunken eyes with dread pooling, flush cheeks, and mouth open, wanting to speak but having no words. She looked all around and scanned the other boats, but there was no sign of Alice and Isabella. Her heart was beating fast, but reason told her they must already be over on the ship. Then she felt sudden terror with the realisation that there were two ships; would they be on the same one? She squeezed Helen's hand, tighter than ever, but Helen didn't even respond.

What was Helen staring at? Her neck was slightly craned, and her eyes were angled down but peering wide. Ruth followed her gaze down the line of the pilot boat. The water was littered with shrapnel, so much so that it seemed the whole ocean had drained and they were floating on piles of splintered wood. In the broken shards, she saw blank eyes staring back at her – Roisin. There was a ringing in her ears. Ruth couldn't breathe, and as if it wasn't beating fast already, her heart was pounding. All she could sense was her heartbeat everywhere in her body as she stared at her friend in the water. The shock reality of what was happening swooped down on them, and everything became deafening and blinding. She squeezed her eyes shut; could she make hell go away? Helen buried her head into Ruth's chest in a diagonal embrace, and they held tight to each other. They were winched up the side of the ship in the same position and fell onto the deck. What was to become of them?

The dank, the dark, heavy breathing but no talking, the even heavier press of bodies together . . . Somehow they had made it below deck after being sorted into men's and women's quarters. The word *quarters* was stuck in her head, reserved for posh ladies on cruise ships. She wiggled backwards and managed to sit a bit straighter to get her bearings in the gloom. She blinked hard, remembering a funny fact her grandmother told her about pirates when she was little – 'They wear an eyepatch so that they can see in the dark.' She smiled to herself, the cheeky grin on her grandmother's face flashing in her memory.

'From what I can see, smell, and feel, this isn't a smiling matter,' Helen snapped at her, pulling her back to the situation at hand.

No, no smiles. Thank goodness Helen was there, but what of Alice and Isabella? The ringing in her ears started again. Should she just shout their names?

Murmurings started as the other women started to unravel the events and find friends. They realised they had been lucky; there were some very badly hurt people around them. She and Helen set about trying to help in any way they could, but these wounds were far from the scrapes and bumps of playground fun on children's knees. They were climbing over people, trying to be as careful as possible. They were in some kind of holding, the front of which was open, but the stairs leading up and obviously out were shut and locked with an iron gate door. There was a lady yelling up the stairs for help. Ruth gently lay a hand on her shoulder.

'Take a breath,' she said quietly.

The lady peered at her closely; she was older than Ruth, haggard and hunched, but weren't they all?

'Save your energy.'

They slumped down on the ground together.

Helen came over, grunting to move past people. 'Don't stop.' Then she started yelling and rattling the door.

Ruth and the other lady let her carry on like that for a while, but there seemed to be no point. She backed down too and slumped next to them.

Hours passed, and the rotten mess that was bad before had now become putrid swill at their feet and burned in their noses. Still at the door but standing now, the three of them had little to say. Their eyes had got used to the dark, and their thoughts had turned inwards. Ruth was semi-hatching a plan of attack, especially if that weed of a German boy came down the steps, but quickly abandoned the idea. Her head was pounding; there was a sizeable bump behind her ear that she had no memory of getting. She touched it gingerly. Bladder control was at the forefront of her mind now. Helen moved closer to her and put her head on Ruth's shoulder. A mutual exhaustion hit her. Ruth let her head down to Helen's shoulder, and they stood, waiting.

As if Helen had read her mind, she whispered in her ear, 'Alice? Isabella?'

Ruth had been thinking that too. She couldn't get perspective on the length of time or the time of day, but she knew it had been well over twenty-four hours in the depths of the ship. Her stomach was beyond the point of hunger and just jabbed at her every now and then, making her jolt in pain. Her bladder was now empty.

She whispered back, 'We would have known if they were in here,' she said with a sad, flat tone, the weight of Helen's head on her shoulder and the reality of the situation heavy on her heart.

Not quite believing the circumstances and with a small glimmer of hope, she tilted her head back to look around to see any familiar faces. Her eyes were well accustomed to the dark, but by no means was she feeling as brave as a pirate.

'Guten morgen, schöne damen!'

Ruth screamed and pushed Helen, who was now draped on top of her, semi-slouching in the corner of the gate and wall. Helen screamed too and caught Ruth's hand as she fell backwards. Hugging together in the corner, they saw a man in what looked to be a high-ranking German navy uniform. He pushed by them and parted the press of women like an opposite magnet, repellent in looks and sound, still shouting, 'Welcome to my ship!' Ruth could hear the smug smile in his voice.

'I am Kapitän Ewig.'

Did he say earwig?

'Your stay on board this proud vessel will be as comfortable as you're willing to make it.'

There was a pause here for the twittering to settle and the message to sink in.

'I have buckets and mops. You are to clean up this filth and make yourselves respectable.'

His gruff voice was not quite as authoritative as he thought, his rather limp stature making the command even less threatening. He stood on the bottom step, peering but not making eye contact, and then snapped his heels together and marched up the stairs.

Fortunately, Ruth and Helen managed to get away with not having to clean up. Instead, they busied themselves with helping the wounded up off the ground, cleaning, helping them remove as many soiled layers as possible, and organising swaps and lending for those who ended up in undergarments. Some poor women had nothing as they'd been asleep and were in their nightgowns. Ruth suddenly realised she had lugged that blasted suitcase the whole way to the ship but now had no idea where it had gone. She saw red.

The poor lady she was helping into a blouse was stuck with her arms waving in the air, saying quietly, 'Excuse me. I'm a bit stuck,' but Ruth hadn't heard her. She was marching towards the sap of a guard who had been placed at the bottom of the steps. He eyed her sideways, a young boy, not much older than some in the older classes she had taught. The look on his face read that he wasn't happy about this English woman taking charge and storming towards him but with a shadow of fear. Helen pulled her arm, yanking her to a halt and stepping between her and the guard.

Ruth was yelling, 'Get out of my way!'

Helen hissed, 'What the bloody hell are you doing?'

'I want my suitcase.' She was indignant but paused, at least for now. Looking the boy dead in the eye, Ruth leant over Helen's shoulder, her index finger wagging at him. 'I need my suitcase,' she said, snarling.

The boy puffed his chest out and raised his chin in defiance.

'Leave it. Leave it, Ruth, for heaven's sake. What's the matter with you?'

She didn't really know. She had just seen red and knew she had clothes which could have helped at least a few people. She picked up a discarded skirt on the floor and started making a pile. In her mind, it was a washing pile, but who knew, really? Most of the women had now got themselves together as best they could. Ruth looked at Helen. Did she look like her? A battered and bruised face, grimy and grim – she supposed she did. They waited. The initial spark of energy, fuelled by the hope of getting out, was gone, and all they could do was sit. Ruth hunched; the pain in her stomach was like nothing she had ever felt before. A room full of women should be full of chatter and laughing. Instead, there was heavy breathing and the occasional whimper.

They waited until it was really quite late at night. The order to 'Move! Move! Schnell! Schnell!' came from a faceless silhouette in the gloom. It wasn't His Majesty the Earwig. She liked the idea of giving him a nickname, one that was in relation to a scurrying little being, dehumanising. She tried to tell Helen, but the frightened women were all pushing up the steps, out into the night. It was cold after being in the airless fug below deck. They stood shivering, huddled together.

'I realise I have been a poor host. You have not had the pleasure of a tour of this grand vessel you are aboard.' His Majesty the Earwig's English was good, heavy with the throaty snarl of someone trying to make their voice deeper in a public announcement.

She held Helen's hand. She didn't want a tour; she wanted to go home. She wanted to wake up from this adventure now, be in her little attic room, thinking about how she had hated the heat and claustrophobic feeling in the summer evenings, now wishing for it more than she had ever wished in her life. *Take stock, Ruth. You are alive. You're not wounded. Helen is here.* Her thoughts tailed off, stopping before she could list off all the negatives, including where the bloody hell Alice and Isabella were. As she was heaving in a big breath, her whole body shook, and the darkness went darker.

Helen hissed in her ear, 'Stand up. Stand up. I can't hold you!' It was urgent now, with more panic. 'Ruth, stop. Come back. Jesus, girl, stop.'

There was surging pain in her upper arm, a stinging, bone-shaking slap to the face. Her eyes were wide open now, darkness flickering with tears. The boy guard from below had her by the arm and, with the other hand, had given her the slap.

'Stand up!' he yelled in her face.

She stood, shaking uncontrollably, but with all her might, she stood.

They watched daybreak standing on the deck of the raider. In any other parallel universe, this would have been awe-inspiring and peaceful. Earwig had told them they were on board a proud German raider and had listed off their conquests over the past months at sea, their latest being the *Rangitane*. He had explained that their living quarters would be below deck, but they did have free range over the outside deck during the day.

'We have the pleasure of you fine people aboard our ship, but we have the displeasure of being at war with each other.'

They were shown back down below by a different young sailor who had such a baby face, Ruth had to resist the urge to pinch his cheeks, an absurd thought which made her giggle out loud. The sharp look from Helen switched her back to reality. They had one blanket each, and lines had been painted on the floor in rows to square off their sleeping arrangements. The boy left them to it. There was murmuring, talking, and even a woman humming as they arranged their new home. She and Helen were in the corner, farthest from the exit. She swallowed the lump of panic in her throat.

Chapter 11

Life below deck was miserable, cramped, and stinking. Life on deck was made up of snatching some decent sun out of the persistent wind. In the confusion of the sinking and their following capture, Ruth had neglected to even register that the ship's female staff were with them too. She was sitting with one of them on deck, chatting to pass time rather than have them really get to know each other, but it was nice to talk. Ruth had always been interested in languages and other cultures. They were sitting in the pale sunshine on the deck, crouching behind a stack of some description, sheltering from the wind, and trying to pretend they were lounging, back on the deck of the *Rangitane*.

Ruth gasped when her imagination started playing tricks with her. There was the young Polish staff man who had brought them drinks, just strolling past her. She rubbed her eyes, called out to him – 'Hello!' – and he turned. Her mind was a mess, but she managed to stop herself from reaching out to check if he was real.

'Ah, hello, miss. I am pleased to see you well and . . . they say . . . the English . . . in one piece?'

She smiled; he was genuinely pleased to see her well. He was one of quite a few Polish men and women who were working on the *Rangitane*. She asked after his friends and colleagues. He was happy to say there were only a few fatalities, but most were alive and as well as they could be.

'I have been to see the people in the hospital. You are very lucky to not know people in there, miss. Some are very bad.'

She reeled towards him, grabbed him by the shoulders. '*Hospital?*' She hissed it urgently at him.

'Yes . . .'

She shook him. 'Take me, quick!'

'Yes, miss.' He took her elbow, picking up her urgency and guiding her quickly back down below where he had come.

As a ship's crew member, he seemed to have extra power to roam. He bypassed three German sailors with a tip salute and no questions asked. They went further down, and Ruth was lost. Her mind was on Alice and Isabella. How could she not have realised there might be an infirmary?

Well, she had never been a POW on a German raider before either, so there was the rub. She put her hand to the cheek the officer had slapped; it was still quite swollen and hot. *How could you forget your place?*

They reached a metal door with a desk outside, right at the end of a corridor. She was completely lost, and the officer sitting outside was not impressed by their presence.

'It is not zee time to be visiting.'

The young Polish man introduced himself. 'I am Filip Dabrowski, gentleman's bar steward of the *Rangitane*. This is Ms . . .' He darted a look at her that said, 'Introduce yourself.'

'Ms Ruth Simpson, teacher escort of English child evacuees.' It was not so grand sounding; she tried a smile to soften the formalities.

It didn't seem to have worked, but the officer barked back, 'And who are you here to see?'

Ruth's mouth was dry, and fear was knotted in her stomach. Why hadn't she gone to get Helen first? She would know what to do and what to say. She took in an audible breath and breathed out. 'Ms Alice . . . and Ms Isabella . . .' *Oh dear. Oh heck, what was Isabella's surname?*

It didn't matter; the officer stood up, clicked his heels together, and opened the door for them. 'No! Halt!'

She froze.

'One only!'

Filip stood aside, bowed his head to her, and put his arm out to gesture her inside.

'Thank you,' she whispered at him.

'You're welcome, Ruth Simpson. My pleaser.'

She smiled at the small error and walked through the thick metal doorway into an unexpectedly bright, white room. Another officer was standing just inside, and the desk officer yelled something in German. The second one clicked his heels and pushed Ruth along in front of him. She tripped along, small taps from the officer behind making her feet catch the bolts in the floor.

'Here!' He pushed open another door to a room full of hospital beds and turned and left her.

She stepped in, tentative. The woman in the bed by the door groaned and rolled away from the hall light. There was only breathing, no talking.

'Alice . . .' she croaked. She cleared her throat and said, louder, 'Alice? Isabella?'

There was nothing. She started to walk down the dim row of beds, looking, squinting at the women.

'Alice?'

'Ruth?'

'Yes!'

She tripped over the bed legs in her excitement and fell into an awkward hug on top of Alice. Alice, dear, sweet Alice – she thought she'd never see her again. There was relief – then the horror that her friend was in a hospital bed in the depths of a German raider in the middle of the ocean, a wounded POW. The sobbing started. Both of them were sobbing.

'Isabella?' Ruth questioned Alice, trying to put the pieces together of their time apart and working out the timeline, but Isabella was a silent detail hanging between them.

Alice's eyes welled with tears again. She put her hand on Ruth's, cool and smooth. She looked down at the bed. 'She's dead, Ruth.' It was quiet but said.

Ruth's blood ran cold. There was ringing in her ears, uncontrollable crying, tears streaming down her face and onto the sheets.

'I am sorry, Ruth. It was instant.' She was quiet, tears choking her. 'I thought the worst about you and Helen. I thought I was all alone.'

They hugged.

'They look after me well enough here, but gosh, the food is just dreadful, just dreadful!'

Ruth sat up. Was she laughing? They laughed and choked on tears at the same time.

'Gosh, we'd give anything for that mush we had on the passenger liner, wouldn't we?'

Ruth was just about to summon the courage to ask about the details. She needed to know – *Poor Isabella* – but the door at the end of the room slammed open, and stiff clomping shoes came towards them. The officer from the entry was standing over the end of the bed.

'Enough now! Back to your quarters.' The tone was harsh but with no malice, really – just serving orders from orders.

Ruth kissed the top of Alice's head and promised to get Helen in as soon as possible. She felt emotions like no other – one friend found, one friend gone forever.

Helen was standing, leaning over the deck rail. Ruth could see she was talking to someone lower down, craning to shout and hear the replies. *Who could it be?* She had a strange feeling of not wanting to interrupt, wanting to run at her and sob in her arms, wanting to run and tell her that Alice was fine, but Isabella . . . Instead, she stood watching her. She wore a scrappy, torn scarf round her neck and half over her head, her hair in flyaway pieces like a halo, a grubby blouse and skirt, no stockings, slouching socks, and odd shoes.

Odd shoes! Ruth's emotions were so skew-whiff that she burst out laughing, laughing at the sight that was Helen. She knew she probably looked the same, if not worse, but a boot on one foot and a slip-on court shoe with a kitten heel on the other was comical. She had another giggle to herself when she thought about the fashion ads where graceful ladies posed in boating fashion stood or lay on deck furniture in glorious luxury. *This is the height of POW fashion – new season's stock coming soon.* Who was Helen talking to?

Helen caught her out of the corner of her eye and beckoned her eagerly. Ruth stood back. How could she break the news? It was too hard. She couldn't fathom it herself – Alice not fine but more fine than Isabella. *Who tells her family in a situation like this?* She thought of Roisin's face, bobbing in the debris, grey, swollen.

She sank to the ground, one hand on the railings to try and save the fall, the other hand over her sobs. There was the sudden thought of Geoffrey. Who would tell Geoffrey if she died? Who would tell her if anything happened to him? She sat and cried; the tears were ugly and brutal, heaving sobs worse than before – despair.

She heard hard boots on the deck behind her and buried her head further into her knees, sinking into the railings, hoping to blend in – no success.

'Miss, this is no place for sitting. This is no place to enjoy the air,' he said, as if she were taking a Sunday stroll.

She lifted her head. It was an older navy officer. She noted the extra stripes on his sleeve and lapels. *Not Captain Earwig – but possibly second in command?* She realised she knew nothing about the navy or its ranks. She narrowed her eyes at him, not moving.

'Move along now, miss, before I have to help you along.'

She winced at the memory of the slap. Shaking, she pulled herself up and leant over the side, pretending to look for someone.

'Good girl.' It was thick English; you could almost see the words like mud slopped onto the deck. He walked on.

She could see who Helen had been talking to, his face peering up at her – Filip and the rest of the Polish crew. It was nice to see them all, but she still had to tell Helen.

Filip put his hand up in a gesture, saying, 'Wait there. I'm coming to you,' and he pointed at Helen. 'Ms Helen, if I may?'

Filip took her by the elbow and linked his arm through hers and then put his arm around Ruth and guided them both back to the more open end of the deck, where they could perch on piled crates, out of the way.

'Do you want me to stay?'

He was looking at Ruth with such concern, arm still around her. She wanted to sink into his embrace. She wanted him to make all the sadness go.

Helen had realised that something was bad. 'It's Alice?' she said, voice quivering.

Ruth nodded. Filip tightened his hug round her shoulders, holding her upright.

'Dead?' Helen whispered.

Ruth shook her head. 'Isabella . . .' It was a husk of a word. She choked on sobs again.

Helen was crying now. There were no words. Helen put her head on Ruth's lap. Ruth hugged her. She hadn't noticed Filip leave and join the others on the far side, watching, protecting, waiting.

It was hard to get up. The crate was digging into the back of her knees. She was stiff and sore and sad beyond anything she had ever known. She had only known the death of Grandma Hetty, and that was from old age. She remembered the day that her mother told her. She was getting ready to go to work.

Her mother's no-nonsense voice could be heard through the bathroom door 'Ruth? Grandma died last night.'

There were no initial feelings, just the words and a stopping of time. She remembered not being able to stop crying at her funeral and her mother getting cross at her for being overly sentimental. The sadness she felt now was also weighted with terror and the unknown. Ruth felt out of control.

Helen was still clutching her. Ruth patted her shoulder in a way she hoped said, 'Time to move. It's OK.' Filip moved towards them again. He was about to speak when Helen demanded he take her down to the hospital to see Alice.

Ruth was shocked at how rude she was, but all Filip said was 'Certainly, Ms Helen,' and he walked briskly back down the deck side.

Helen meekly followed, perhaps a bit sorry for the way she had talked, but Ruth supposed not.

Ruth was sitting on the sacking they had for beds in the space below deck when Helen came back. She had been thinking about the time when the three of them – Alice, Helen, and she – had been at the village May Day picnic. Brushing her hand down her dress in a vain attempt to rid it of sacking debris, she thought about the cotton dress she had worn that day. Flowers and little birds were printed on it. The fabric had been cheap because the colours had missed the outline of the pattern. Her mother was a basic sewer, but it was a nice dress.

The memory confused her already addled brain. It wasn't a particularly fond memory – it had just popped into her mind because Helen had been so rude to Alice that day – but now it was a very different story. She had already partly warmed up towards Alice, and now, bound by experience, they were forever friends.

It was one thing to have Helen on side and another to be on the receiving end of her venom. Alice had been sitting, chatting away. Ruth only half-listened, enjoying the sun on her face, not bothered by Alice talking about things and people, books and plans, all blurring into one.

Helen, out of nowhere, had said, 'Oh, shut *up*, Alice! Nobody cares!'

Stunned into silence, tears welling in her eyes, Alice had stood up and just walked away.

Ruth had said, 'I don't think that was really called for, Helen.' It was just a matter of fact. She was not wanting to spoil the day but wanting to stick up for her friend too.

'Oh, blow you!' Helen marched off too.

Oh, well. The day had been spoiled, and she had piled the blanket under her arm and walked home. Alice was there, quiet, just at the kitchen table with a pot of tea.

'Tea?' she asked Ruth.

Ruth sat down. 'Sorry, Alice. Helen—'

Alice had cut her off. 'Don't make excuses for her, Ruth. You don't have to be sorry.'

Ruth really liked Alice. She loved the way the conversation never ended, though she could see how grating it might be for the likes of Helen.

She realised it was a joy to have her back, and she secretly thought – but would never say – that Helen was pleased too.

In true Helen fashion, she came back with a detailed account of Alice and Isabella's timeline, presumably badgered out of Alice by many probing and relentless questions. *Poor Alice.* She was already in a living hell without having to relive the hell she had gone through without them. Ruth was always amazed at how Helen could be a complete and utter wreck, wretched and emotional one moment, and act as if it never happened the next. Ruth had thought that was it for her, that she would have to look after Helen for the foreseeable future, but now she was sitting next to Ruth, recounting her news like she was sitting in the staff room at school, telling her about classroom antics.

'Sorry, Ruth.' She paused. 'Do you want to know what happened?' She had obviously seen Ruth's thoughts written on her face.

Ruth nodded, mute. Did she want to?

Chapter 12

It turned out that Isabella and Alice had been on deck, on the side the *Rangitane* was hit. Alice has debris lodged in her stomach and was actually truly lucky to be alive.

Helen recalled Alice's description. 'She said Isabella was just gone.'

There were tears again. She saw them on Helen's cheeks and felt them, warm, on her own. In the absence of mirrors, she used Helen as a reflection of emotion and aesthetic. She felt just as pitiful as Helen looked, and she knew she looked the same. Other women were talking in low voices in the room, and the scratchy sacking was making her nose tickle. She went to get up.

Helen took her by the arm. 'There's one other thing.' Her voice was low and serious.

Ruth stood still, looking down at her.

'Ruth, Alice lost her foot.'

She just stared blankly.

'Hello?' Helen waved her hand in front of her eyes.

'It's surreal, Helen. Is this actually happening to us? When will we wake up?' She was more present this time. 'Poor Alice. Poor, poor Alice.' She couldn't think of the words to express just exactly how poor Alice was.

The days had no real time to them, and there was definitely nothing productive to do. Ruth was worried that she felt nothing.

'Ms Helen!'

An urgent voice from behind made them both jump. They were silently taking in the vast expanse of nothing – just water, water, water. They had been lucky, if *lucky* was the word. It was ironic that there had been no bad weather, just dreadful hunger and dirty, cramped living conditions. They turned and saw Filip running to them. He seemed to be in the know with everything and have special treatment for some reason or another. Ruth thought better of asking him. It was best to just let people like that get on with things, and they could feed the information back, risk their own necks – their choice.

'Ms Helen! Ms Ruth!' He was panting slightly. 'I've been looking for you. Did you hear the commotion last night?'

The men's living quarters were well below the water line, so he must have been elsewhere in the ship to hear anything, but they both shook their heads.

'They sank another ship. There's new prisoners on board. That's why we have been told to stay down here. They're sorting them out.'

'They', like faceless, nameless beings, not human – Ruth felt sorry for the people. She and the other prisoners knew that terror so well. She wanted to go and tell them, 'It will be OK. Hang on. Then us seasoned prisoners will look after you.' She thought about Alice. *She will be getting new roommates in the infirmary. Those poor people.* There was that word again. What was a better word? *Unlucky* sounded crass. Lady Luck was AWOL; she was not only not on their side but also just simply cruel and unforgiving.

The evening was closing in, and they were told by the officers on their deck to go down to their quarters and stay there. One lady got a slap across the face for daring to ask about supper. Ruth winced at the memory. She thought about the lumpy, stinking concoction that was served to them in tin cups every night. *Would rather starve. Wouldn't risk a slap for that.* They slowly made their way down. The officers were barking at them, but there didn't seem to be much urgency about it. Some of the men had cigarettes hanging out of their mouths, waggling around when they spoke. They were teasing some of the younger women with what they thought were funny flirting remarks, but the circumstances and the odd translations of chat-up lines made it all feel more sinister. Ruth felt like she was in a suspense movie where you don't want to watch but you just can't turn away. She felt ill. Helen was behind her and tripped, pushing her into the lady in front of her.

They were told to stay there until further notice. She pondered the last time they were told that and how the new prisoners would be feeling now. At least some of the other women had cajoled the younger officers into letting them have the small space at the side of the stairs for a toilet. She didn't know how they'd managed it, but there was a big bucket and sacking blanket privacy curtains rigged up around it. She wasn't complaining – it was very good to not be sloshing around in human muck – but it stank, and if you did any more than urinate, you had to risk taking it up the stairs to empty over the side. There was also a line marked up the edge; if you were the one to go above that, it was your job too.

Inevitably, Ruth had never made it up the stairs without sloshing.

The first few times were utterly disgusting, but she worked out a way of holding it that meant it only splashed her legs. She made sure to tuck her skirt up into the waistband and tie the ends around her waist. She would never have been able to do that before being starved, not fat but not what you would call slender either. Her grandmother said 'pleasingly plump'. Ruth said 'frumpy'.

Ruth lay looking up at the roof, flat on her back, with Helen the same at her side. On the other side, two women were quietly talking face to face. She didn't really know the woman who had been sleeping next to her all these weeks. She felt bad for not making the effort. Obviously, there was the polite smile and nod, friendly enough; they were just not friends. They'd all been through so much; they were pleased to know who they knew and just leave it at that. Now with the possibility of having more people squeezed in here, the effort needed to socialise left Ruth feeling quite faint. She was drifting off to sleep, and a sudden, clear thought came into her head: Geoffrey. His face, round and kind, was close enough and real enough that she thought she felt his stubble on her cheek. She lay down again, on her side, crying into the sacking pressed against her face. *Will he only ever be a memory now?*

Ruth opened her eyes; she was stiff, and her right shoulder ached. It was the same every morning; she preferred to sleep facing Helen than a stranger. Helen could face the wall or Ruth; she was a lucky POW. She felt a pang of envy – or was it hunger? They just didn't have the energy lately to do anything. They had become shuffling, shrunken haunted house props, especially in their ragged clothes. Helen was still breathing softly next to her, and the two women on the other side had gone.

She thought about the time, but it needed not matter. How had time not come to matter when all she used to think about was time? Time for class, time for lunch, home time, no time . . . Her thoughts tailed off. She was thinking about her classroom and her children, thanking whatever or whomever it was that this happened on the way home and not with a fleet load of children, hoping against hope that they were still safe and sound in their new country. The sinking had been soon after their departure, and Ruth wondered if New Zealand could defend itself if they'd been invaded. Sleepy little Auckland wouldn't have known what hit it. She shuddered at the thought – and right on Christmas as well. *Christmas!* They'd missed Christmas! She shook Helen awake.

'Mm, why? What's happening?' Helen sat bolt upright and screamed, 'What's going on?'

'Shhh, shhh. It's OK. Oh goodness. Sorry, sorry.' Ruth felt dreadful. She looked at Helen sheepishly.

'What?'

Helen was grumpy, but Ruth had to think of something proper to say and not just 'We missed Christmas Day. I miss my mum and dad and food.' A tear rolled down her cheek; she had no control over it. 'Sorry. I thought something was going on. I think I was dreaming.'

Helen lay back down.

Clearly, Ruth couldn't be alone with her thoughts. She decided to go and talk her way past the guards in the infirmary and see Alice. 'I'm going up for some air.'

Helen nodded, grabbed Ruth's hand, and squeezed it. She wondered if her grandma Hetty had such good allies in her wartime escapades – or was she a lone spy? *Double-crossing, triple-crossing*. She tried to summon some of Grandma Hetty's spirit as she climbed the stairs and walked to the infirmary. She wouldn't make a good spy on an empty stomach; that was one thing she was certain of.

When she got down into the narrow corridor, she was surprised to see a line of other prisoners, waiting. She stood behind a woman with the rattiest bird nest hair she had ever seen. She immediately scolded herself for thinking so poorly of people. The circumstances were dire; she knew she looked exactly the same and smelled worse, probably. She wished she had her suitcase with a change of clothes. Thinking about all her lovely things, she was shocked at herself, how materialistic she was, but also so angry at herself for lugging it the whole way and then just losing it. She was filthier than she'd ever been before; it was like an outer layer had grown over her and her clothes. Maybe it was the tough exterior she had always wished she had.

She tapped the woman on the shoulder and asked, 'Is this the line for visitors?'

The lady turned, similar in age to Ruth, and even through the grime, Ruth could see she was very pretty. The girl nodded and smiled, a slight lift in the corner of her mouth. She turned back. Ruth understood that there was no need for chitchat. She had hated small talk at the best of times, but now, any more than a few words was all too much. She leant her shoulder on the wall and wondered how long she would have to wait. Again, she was thinking about time when time didn't matter. It wasn't relaxing; the unknown was stressful. Even when you're on holiday, you have access to time even if you want to forget it exists.

Alice was sitting up and looking a lot better than she had done. She was pleased to see Ruth and patted the bed eagerly for her to sit down. Ruth could close one eye and block out some of the hospital equipment to pretend they were sitting back at home. Even though she had only ever set foot in Alice's room that one time, she wanted to pretend they'd always been close enough to sit and giggle on each other's beds. Ruth needed Helen's hip flask right about now.

'The doctor said I can leave today,' Alice said gleefully.

Ruth mustered a wide grin, getting it stuck in her clenched-back teeth. She wanted to say, 'Stay here. You're better off – marginally, but you're better off.' Instead, she said, 'I'm so pleased. We will get you all sorted, next to us, with a bed.'

Alice's face fell. 'I haven't tried walking,' she said in a quiet voice, wavering.

Ruth swallowed hard and gave another wide grin. 'Shall we try now?'

'Ruth, you don't have to be jolly for me. This is shit.'

Taken aback by Alice's blue language, Ruth dropped the blanket on the ground and stared at her.

'Shit,' Alice said again, louder. 'Shit!' she repeated with more malice. 'Shit, shit, shit, shit, shit!' She was pounding the bed with her fists.

Ruth needed to be jolly for her own sake, or she would join Alice or, worse, end up with a panic attack on the floor, useless to everyone as usual.

'Stay here,' Ruth said.

'Oh, the irony,' Alice replied darkly.

'It's OK. I have an idea, but don't let them turf you out until I get back.'

'How can I do that?' There was indignation in her voice that Ruth ignored.

'You'll think of something, but you might not have to. Just wait there. Sorry . . .'

She smiled a bit and nodded.

Ruth needed to find Filip. She needed his authority on the ship and his canny no-questions-asked ability to find things. Where would he be? She tripped going up the steps in her hurry, bit her tongue when she banged her chin on the edge of the metal steps. She didn't stop; it was typical of her, and her grandmother's words rang in her ears – 'Ruth, slow down. Your mind works faster than that ungainly body of yours.' She really didn't have time to think at the moment. *Just find Filip.*

She rushed towards the end of the top deck and looked over the edge. Her hunch was right; he was playing cards on the deck below. Other men crowded round him, laughing and chatting. It felt odd to hear it, like they weren't POWs. They might have been on a cruise ship, the way he carried on. It took a couple of big breaths and a good clear shout with her hands cupped around her mouth, but eventually, Filip looked up. His face dropped when he realised the graveness in Ruth's. He rushed up the small ladder steps and jumped over the railings in front of her.

'You're hurt!' he exclaimed, gently putting his hand under her ear and lifting her chin to the side. 'Who did this?'

He was so calm but so furious, ready to jump into action for her. She was still and silent, his hand poised just at her neck and ear. His dark eyes were questioning, his face close to hers. She blinked, moved, broke the spell.

He let go but still with concern in his eyes. 'What happened?'

'It's not me. Don't worry about me, Filip.' She smiled, but he remained serious. 'I need your help, please.'

'Anything, anything at all. First, I deal with who did this to you.'

She smiled again. 'Dear Filip, it was me being clumsy. Alice – you know about her foot?'

Filip nodded, dropped his eyes, sad for Alice.

'The doctors are discharging everyone from the infirmary because there are so many more people injured in the last raid.' She stopped, caught her breath. 'It doesn't matter. What I need is a pair of crutches . . . please.'

He pursed his lips in consideration, scratched his head. 'Give me some time. I'll see what I can do.' He smiled. 'Anything for you, Ruth. He's a lucky man.' He winked and jumped back down again before she could say thank you.

Geoffrey was a million miles away, and she was a million miles in the other direction. Was there a point where you just start coming back again, a point where all lovers separated by miles could meet and live happily ever after? Her moment with Filip felt heavy in her heart. She hadn't done anything, nothing Helen wouldn't have done, and she was married. *Poor Helen – her heart must hurt.* Ruth made a note to talk to her alone at some point soon.

In the meantime, Alice was proving more uncoordinated than Ruth, and the pair of them struggled up the steps of the infirmary.

Alice kind of giggled and sat down – *plop*. 'OK, let's rethink.' She was puffing.

Ruth could feel her chest was tight with the effort. It was kind of comical.

'Don't laugh at me,' Alice said, playfully hitting Ruth's arm with the back of her hand.

'I can't help it. This is a fine pickle we got ourselves into.'

'Perhaps it might be easier if we swapped sides and you kind of hoisted me from behind on my missing side.'

Ruth couldn't help it; she burst out laughing. She was so weak with no food and emotionally drained that she just sat and laughed. It hurt so much, but she couldn't stop.

'You are dreadful.' Alice laughed. 'OK. Heave ho!'

At this point, Ruth just started howling and crying with laughter. Alice was laughing, but Ruth could tell she needed to pull herself together.

'Alice . . .' She was breathless and still overcome with giggles. 'Just don't talk, OK?'

Alice turned around and went up the stairs on all fours, and Ruth helped her at the top to stand and hop, holding under Alice's arm for support. She was a hopeless physical support and had been an even worse emotional support.

'Sorry, Alice.' She meant it.

Alice knew, patted her hand.

'Helen?'

They had got Alice settled and were heading up to look for an extra something to prop under her leg. She wasn't complaining, but they could tell it hurt her.

'You OK, Ruth?' Helen questioned, understanding the tone.

'Not really.' She paused. How could she explain what happened when she didn't quite know herself? 'I love Geoffrey . . .'

'I know you do, hun. I sense a "but".'

'But I did didn't do something.'

'"Did didn't"?'

Helen was confused. So was Ruth. They stopped, standing between the cabin wall and the railings, semi out of sight and with nobody else around, but Ruth still lowered her voice.

'Filip,' she whispered, ashamed.

Helen leant in and hush-hissed, 'What did you do?'

'Nothing. I did nothing. I could have. I wanted to . . . Nothing!'

Helen's eyes searched her face. Ruth felt judged, but she supposed Helen was right to judge her. How did she go about getting advice from her without offending?

'I need—'

She was interrupted by a loud hoot from above them. They looked up to see Filip himself waving something above his head at them.

'I'll come down!' he shouted.

'This isn't over,' Helen said and squeezed Ruth's elbow. Helen took the lead, standing between Ruth and Filip, making a point to Ruth, and she knew it.

'It didn't take me long, did it?' He winked at Ruth.

She smiled and went to say something, but Helen cleared her throat and said in her best teacher voice to the best pupil, 'Marvellous, Filip. We knew you could do it. You're such a wonder.'

Filip looked pleased and grinned again, still looking at Ruth. He slightly bypassed Helen and stood at her inside elbow to hand the crutches over to Ruth.

She kept his gaze until Helen said again, 'Thank you, Filip. Really, thank you. What can we do for you in return?'

He tapped the side of his nose – secret for now. Her grandma Hetty used to do the same thing when Ruth asked her anything about her wartime experiences, which only added to the mystery that was, and she was probably never going to find out. She had another pang for home; she hoped her parents were well and not fretting about her, but she knew they would be.

'I don't want anything, my fine friends. You show me a smile on her face, and I will be happy.'

Ruth still felt indebted and awkwardly pleased at the same time. He was wiry, with tanned skin, the opposite of Geoffrey – no uniform though, not his lovely, soft eyes, just the ragged feeling of flirtations too close to the edge. Her stomach was knotted.

'Helen, it was just harmless flirting to get what Alice needed.' Ruth was indignant now, ashamed she had even brought it up.

Helen wasn't angry, but her scorn was almost worse. 'The phrase "The lady doth protest too much" comes to mind,' Helen said with a flick of her matted hair over her shoulder.

They were sitting on the deck in the sun, and if it wasn't for the fact that they were on crates and not sun lounges, you could mistake them for gossiping ladies on a cruise liner. Alice had what remained of her cardigan over her eyes and was leaning back with her legs stretched out. Ruth couldn't help but look at the missing foot. Filip had also got her a big woolly sock to cover it. Alice had been in agony and complaining that it was freezing cold. Helen and Ruth thought she was feverous and delusional in the night, but Filip had said it was common with amputees that the sensation of a limb still being there was worse than the pain of losing it.

Poor Alice. Poor mismatched, uneven Alice. She had a lovely silk and merino sky-blue cardigan in tatters over her eyes – less sky, more murky pond now – a big grey grandfather-type sock on one leg and a boot with no sock on the other, a pair of black wool stockings with so many ladder runs, and a big green pinafore about two sizes too big for her with a cotton blouse under it. Where had they actually got their clothes from? Ruth looked down at her own dreadful clothes and sighed. She looked back out over the empty sea.

Chapter 13

Their sleeping arrangements had got even more cramped after they had emptied out the infirmary and taken on more prisoners. The poor women who joined them were mostly met with territorial stares and anguished blanket snatching. Ruth and Helen had set Alice up next to them by scrounging what they could and turning their bedding sideways to make a three-person bed. Ruth drew the short straw of being in the middle and so inevitably ended up with no blankets as both girls turned away from her. She was lying, staring up at the very close ceiling.

She hadn't exactly got used to the hunger pains in her stomach, but she was practiced at ignoring them – except tonight. Flashes of beautiful roast dinners with all the trimming kept appearing when she closed her eyes. Rather than dream of food, she lay with her eyes wide open. She couldn't see an end to this. Where were they headed? Was anyone looking for them? Tears came very easily, and she felt them pooling in her ears. Would they survive? If she did, she swore to herself she would tell her grandchildren everything, even if they didn't ask. *Of course, to have grandchildren, you need children.* As sleep took over, Ruth pondered if she could skip that stage and go straight to being a doting grandmother.

Alice rolled over and slapped her in the face. Even in her sleep, Alice managed to be awkward. Ruth had been on the cusp of proper sleep. She could tell by the way her heart was racing from the surprise. She sat up. What time would it be? She seemed constantly obsessed with time. In her mind, she scolded herself. *Honestly, you can never get your silly head around anything, and you're always in a muddle. How do you even function in the world? Really, girl – the time? Take note of the circumstances and find some gumption.* She pumped her fist across her chest in a decisive manner – *action stations* – but to do what? What could she achieve as a POW in the dark, under the waterline of a German raider ship in the middle of the night, the middle of the ocean, and in the middle of a war? She sank back down from her runner's stance. *Think.*

Intel. It seemed to come to her out of the darkness, as if from the ripple effect of the slap. *Knowledge is power.* She didn't remember much from her own primary school days other than being very badly bullied, but she did remember the school motto. Why? She screwed her face up in confused contempt at herself. *Knowledge is power.* What should she find out? She had nothing to lose. Alice snuffled in her sleep, and Ruth flinched. *Maybe work on being a bit braver*, she thought. The stifling smell of bodies packed into a confined, airless space made her gag. Sleep was illusive, and her brain whirred. She needed air, but during the night, the guards sat at the top of the stairs. They weren't allowed to go out. That was something she knew at least. She knew that all the sinkings and dastardly war actions happened at night.

Her immediate thought was Filip when she woke up. She felt guilty and made her brain think about Geoffrey and put an image of him in her mind's eye for the day. Really, it was because she had gone to sleep thinking about getting intel and naturally thought of Filip to help. Of course, it helped that he was very good-looking, but she again replaced her thoughts with something about Geoffrey and poked Helen awake. Helen seemed to be able to sleep on a clothesline if she had to, and Ruth was rather envious. However, she had a newfound fire in her belly and was ready to put it to good use.

'I'm going on a mission.' She was pulling her boots on like a child in a fairy story going on an adventure.

'A what?' Helen asked, half asleep.

'A mission. It's just something I need to do.' She paused, gauging Helen's reaction. She was rather hoping for a bit more hype than the shrug she got but took it to mean at least she wasn't going to be stopped. 'Look after Alice for today, please?'

Helen nodded. What else had she got to do anyway?

It was too early to find Filip playing cards. The sky was still that light peach colour that artists called Eos – the optimal, most beautiful time to capture. Somewhere, her befuddled brain remembered loose facts about ancient Greek mythology. Feeling pensive, she stopped to take in the view out over the sea like a Turner painting, though she thanked her lucky stars that it was just the colouring of the moment and not the turbulent oceans of his subject matter.

'Sunrise.' His voice was behind her. 'I wish I had beautiful things to say, but alas, my English is thus that I might spoil this beautiful scene.'

She turned. He was grinning.

'And yet you say "alas" and "thus" like a Shakespearian sonnet,' Ruth said, smiling back.

He winked at her and stood over the railings at her side. She turned back, purposefully turning towards him so her arm was pressed against his. He didn't move.

'I was looking for you,' Ruth said after a while. Their silence had been comfortable, but she wanted what she had come for.

'Oh yes?' His voice was pitched higher like a teenage boy's. He cleared his throat. 'Oh yes?" he tried again.

They were still facing out to sea, but Ruth could hear the delight in his voice that she was looking for him.

'I need to know all you know about Captain Earwig.'

In her eagerness for action, she let the nickname slip. She was mortified. At the first question, she had blown any chance of being stealthy and aloof and cool, calm, and collected. She had exposed herself as the bumbling, stumbling mess she really was.

He smiled, turned to her with a questioning smirk. 'Do you mean Kapitän Ewig?' he said in a mocking German accent and puffed out his chest.

Ruth laughed and relaxed again. She nodded, eyes slanted.

'What makes you think I know anything more than you?' He gestured with one hand on his chest and one hand out, palm up, still with the mocking smirk.

She noticed the definition in his arm and resisted the urge to squeeze it; instead, she narrowed her eyes more and pursed her lips. *You know.*

Filip nodded slowly, considering. 'Not out here,' he said and ushered her along the deck by her elbow.

Other prisoners were up and about now, shuffling around, mulling around, no purpose for anything – hunger, thirst, dirt, and the vast emptiness of the unknown. Ruth actually felt quite desperate. What was she really going to be able to find out that would be of any use? She just wanted to know, she supposed, hold some kind of power, some thread of something. *A loose end is better than no end – or the end?*

Filip had guided her along the deck they were on and headed her down towards the infirmary, but before they reached the double metal doors, they went down another, smaller set of stairs. There was no room for two people at the bottom, and she had to squeeze past him to get into the narrow gap that doubled back. He held her a moment too long, breathed down her neck closer than he needed to be. Her body hummed with excitement and guilt. He had to stoop his head as he led the way down the narrow corridor.

There was a door at the end, barely wide enough to warrant being called a door. Filip opened the door for her, and she stepped inside without a second thought.

She couldn't believe it; there was an actual bed in the room, albeit a very small bed, but she was so overcome at the sight, she forgot herself and flopped down on her back. It was just a hard base, which knocked the wind out of her. She gasped without taking a breath, both arms up like a stranded beetle. She began to panic. She managed to wheeze a puff of air out and started to breathe normally again, still flat on her back.

Filip lay down next to her. Ruth took air in through her nose now but not daring to look at him, her heart beating fast. She was excited, thrilled, dreamlike, head spinning, nothing in her thoughts except reminding herself to breathe. His hand came up to her cheek. Then his face came into vision, hovering above her. She hadn't moved.

'Are you OK?'

She nodded. He kissed her. She kissed him, her heart beating nearly out of her chest, excitement and guilt making her feel sick, but she didn't stop. It was what it was: desperate need.

The wooden base of the bed was now scratching her bare skin, and Filip's snoring was grating on her. It had been glorious, but now she was uncomfortable; there was no two ways about it. She crawled about, collecting and putting on her clothes, feeling very shameful and silly. What had possessed her? *Intel*. She was none the wiser and had only gained splinters in her bottom.

Ruth winced but shook off her shame and woke Filip up. He groaned, rolled over, smiled, and pulled her into a deep embrace again. Before she melted too much more and lost her senses again, she wiggled out from under him. It took all her resistance; that body, just near her at any time, made her weak.

'You have your own room?' she asked, meaning, *Who are you? What makes you the king of all prisoners?*

He grinned and kissed her collarbone. 'Are you impressed?' He was genuinely wanting to know.

She gave in and kissed him back but pulled away again. 'Very,' she said slyly.

This was going to take some extra effort, but what else did she have to do?

Chapter 14

Helen looked fed up and was sitting with her back half-turned to Alice. As Ruth walked towards them, she could see Alice chatting away to Helen, oblivious to the fact that she had probably stopped listening half an hour ago. When Ruth got closer, she realised Helen was crying. She quickened her step, sat down next to her, and mouthed, 'Are you OK?' *Obviously not, but what else do you say?* Alice was talking about home. Ruth put her arm around Helen. She didn't want to cry, but there were those tears again, always unstoppable.

'Alice?' she said, in a tone of *Are you hearing yourself?*

'Hi, Ruth. What?' As she was turning to face both of them, her face dropped when she saw them both crying. 'What's happened?' There was fear in her voice.

'Alice, stop talking about home, for Christ's sake,' Helen choked.

'Oh dear. Oh no. Gosh, I am sorry, Helen.' She was remorseful, shocked her words had made someone so upset without her meaning to.

Helen pushed herself up and stood, wiping the tears on her grimy blouse sleeve and making a smudge through the grime on her cheek. 'I could have stopped you sooner, but it was nice to listen to for a while. Sorry I snapped.'

Ruth decided now wasn't the right time to tell them what she had gleaned from Filip so far. She was also glad the flush in her cheeks could be mistaken for crying.

The ship was packed, but not a lot of socialising went on among the women. There were pockets of friends like them, and they largely stayed to themselves. The men were more easily distracted and seemed to be able to entertain themselves well with cards and made-up physical games. How they had the energy, Ruth didn't know, but it was sometimes fun to be a spectator.

They picked Alice up and moved over towards the crowd to find a good vantage spot. This time, it seemed to be a type of football game with makeshift goals at either end of the deck between two building stacks. She couldn't quite work out what they were using for a ball, but of course, Filip was in the mix. She wasn't surprised to see him, even though it had been less than an hour since she left his little room. He spotted her in the crowd, winked. Helen didn't notice, and Ruth was pleased. She smiled back and half-wave-motioned him to play on. Ruth needed time to come up with a plan to inform Helen and Alice without giving herself away.

The game wasn't all that thrilling, but it was a good excuse to just sit and be mildly entertained. Sporting events at home had never interested her, and she wasn't about to start now. Ruth was still giddy with what had just happened, and it hadn't mattered in the heat of the moment, except now she was extremely conscious of how she looked. She remembered what it felt like to care about her appearance. Why was it suddenly an issue? She felt like a silly teenager with a crush. *Will he notice me? What can I do to get his attention? Now that things have happened, will he even care? Why would he want someone like me in the first place?*

She recognised the signs before hyperventilation could fully kick in, and she tried to relax and enjoy the game; it was entertaining enough, and she could pretend to be excited. They also knew some of the other players from the *Rangitane* crew, and she cheered them on, choosing the opposing team on purpose to make Filip notice. It was all quite jovial, and they could try and forget the squalor and fear they lived in. It was a distraction from the hunger pains, but only if you could block out the miles of sea, the miles and miles of open water.

She decided to drip-feed the information, to casually drop it into conversations. The fact was she really didn't know all that much, and it was frustrating as well as very debatable information. She wanted proper insider information, which she was sure Filip had, but he was holding back. It was so-called midday mealtime, where they lined up to get a tin cup full of watery paste. Some days, they held their noses and tipped it down their throats, but most of the time, there weren't many takers.

The three of them were choosing to be brave today, so to distract them from a necessary evil, she said, 'Kapitän Ewig has a stuffed toy he hugs in bed.'

Helen snorted the mouthful she had just taken and laughed out loud. 'No! What? What on earth made you say that, and how do you know?'

Alice was in giggles next to her. 'Well, it's distracted us, hasn't it?'

Gulp – down the hatch. It was useless information but successful enough to provide comic relief and make him seem less of a threat.

It seemed like Helen and Alice were glued to her side over the next few days, like a bizarre barn dance where she was the leader and they followed her every move. She tried not to show her impatience, tried to act normally, but she couldn't remember how she had been acting before her encounter with Filip. Would she have asked for time on her own? She decided against that and played a little spy game with herself to try and lose them. It didn't really work – not for long enough anyway. Alice was getting better at using the crutches, and Helen and Ruth were encouraging her to race along the walkway, trying to beat her time each way. It was also a fun distraction, and it was also good to see smiles on both their faces.

'Was that faster?' Alice beamed at her.

Ruth shook her head.

'You're off in la-la land today. How did you count that one if it wasn't faster then?' She was still laughing, but Ruth could tell she was a bit upset at her lack of enthusiasm.

'OK, I'll do the elephant count on your way back. That seemed to be the most effective.' Ruth raised her voice and shouted down to Helen, 'The time to beat is ten elephants!'

Helen gave the thumbs-up, and Alice swivelled round and charged back down the other way. Ruth smiled; this was OK for now.

The darkness hadn't lifted in the room when Ruth opened her eyes, wide awake. Everyone else was in the low hum of various states of sleep. She could tell she was in for a long wait. It was hard to keep the lid on her excitement, but she was daring herself to be brave and conquer whatever it was that she was after. The days had long ago blended into a mass, pocketed only by brief moments breaking the monotony. Even the people dying and their burials at sea were happenstance enough to be forgotten.

She felt sick at the state of mind she was in – a person's life just tossed overboard, a throwaway thought. Isabella's must have been one of the very first bodies. They had not known at the time but had been in attendance when the German sailors and crew had stood to attention and saluted as the bound bodies were hefted into the sea. She remembered being offended by the swastikas at half-mast but now just felt nothing. She got up, stepped over sleepers, and went up the stairs. Was she forcing herself for a real cause or doing it just to feel something, anything?

It wasn't very light outside either, but she must have timed it just right to either miss the changing of the guard or be right on time. She didn't stick around to find out. She hurried along the deck and down the now familiar set of stairs to his door. She stopped, took a deep breath, in through the nose, calming the pulse she felt in every body part. He was bleary eyed but seemed pleased to see her, pulled her in by the wrist, and shut the door behind her. He pressed her against it and kissed her. She felt. It was a small feeling, but it was there.

'Hello,' he said in her ear.

She was melting.

'Are you a spy?'

She tried to be casual as they lay tangled together. 'Yes' – she was laughing – 'and now I have to kill you.'

She was cross that he didn't share anything and hadn't really said anything about the earwig either. He had whisked her away like there were secrets to tell, but nothing had come of it. She was beginning to feel a fool, but she supposed at least it was a feeling.

'No joking, OK?' she asked, propping herself up on his chest.

'OK, no joking.' He put on a mock serious face.

'You know things, and I want to know them too.'

His mock seriousness turned to real seriousness, and a greyness took over. For the first time, she saw just how much the circumstances were affecting him too – the deep furrow lines in his forehead, caked in dirt except where they creased and un-creased as he thought.

'I have secrets, it is true, but I have to be wary of who I'm with, who I'm meant to be.'

'I'm nobody. It's true. Ask anyone.' She was too eager. She knew she'd blown it this time. *Be more aloof, Ruth. Subtlety is not your specialist subject.*

Filip laughed, a hearty laugh which moved her up and down with it. 'Oh, my darling.' He was patronising, patted her head.

She went to stand up, to get up and get away, but he grabbed her, pecking at her – kiss, kiss, kiss, kiss, with every kiss 'sorry'. She relented and fell back down – fell.

Somehow the danger and excitement of what she was doing outweighed the guilt. Even though the guilt was extreme, Ruth couldn't help but be drawn to Filip. The morning ritual of walking along the outside deck, admiring the sunrises and descending the little stairs to his room, gave her thrills beyond anything else. This was lust – lust for him, lust for what he would tell her, and lust for what he wasn't telling her. The information he was holding close kept her going back. She was careful not to go every morning and careful not to make a pattern of it either.

Ruth was proud of herself and was just thinking that perhaps Grandma Hetty the spy would be too when Helen popped out in front of her.

'Where have you been? Don't lie. I've been following you.'

Ruth's stomach lurched, and she knew guilt was written all over her face. She was silly to assume she was any good at espionage and was glad that none of her intel was of any particular value. It was merely an excuse, but now the guilt had caught up with her. They sat down at the back of the top deck so they wouldn't be disturbed from behind, and they could see people approaching.

'I know,' Helen said reproachfully.

What could Ruth say? She just had to face it and tell the truth.

'He's out there fighting, defending his country and your freedom.'

Helen was almost crying. She wasn't just talking about Geoffrey. She went on. Ruth took it all; she deserved it.

'I honestly can't believe you. What a thing to be doing.'

Helen wasn't shouting, but she was almost snarling the words. Tears ran down Ruth's face.

'Don't cry. You knew what you were doing. You're only crying because you got caught.'

At this, Ruth opened her mouth to defend herself. 'I'm—'

Helen screamed, 'Don't!'

Other people were further along the deck. They looked over in surprise.

'Don't even think about making excuses.' Helen brushed her dirt-caked, wrinkled skirt and tried to smooth it out in disgust. Helen went on and on. She was crying, and through the sobs, she said, 'I just thought better of you, Ruth. You sit there, all judging of everyone else, and then you betray.'

Ruth couldn't take it. *Betrayal* was the worst word in the worst of circumstances, and before she could stop, she said, 'You can talk! You're a hussy, Helen Masters! A flirting, shameless hussy.'

She regretted the words as soon as she'd said them, blank, unforgiving eyes staring back at her.

'Helen, I'm sorry.'

Helen got up, walked away. Ruth had never felt so angry or so sad all at the same time. It boiled over, and she punched the wall behind her – hard.

At least the throbbing pain in her hand was distracting from the mess in her head. She had berated herself over and over and over since she watched her friend walking away. Helen was rightly not having anything to do with her, and poor Alice was the go-between, trying to mend fences while Helen and Ruth smashed stuff around her.

Alice was leaning on the railings, looking down at the water next to her. 'I think that hand is broken.' Alice wanted her to go to the infirmary.

Ruth was bitter and angry and couldn't help but bite. 'What would you know? Are you a doctor?'

Alice was silent for a moment, breathed in deep, took the hit, and lightly said, 'Come on, Ruth. Be nice. I know you're hurting in more ways than one, but we all are. I could pull the "selfish only child" card on you right about now.'

Ruth scowled. She hated that. She prided herself on being generous, friendly, helpful – everything the opposite of the only-child stereotype. It was exhausting. Who was she trying to prove what point to? She flexed her fingers and winced in pain. Alice was right, but she didn't want to go to the infirmary. She wanted to stay out of sight of everyone.

The rift between them had caused chaos for the hard-fought-for sleeping arrangements. Ruth had begged a younger woman to swap with her, but to swap, her friend wanted to swap with her, and so began a chain reaction until most of the cabin was furious at her. In the end, an older woman came to her rescue – a direct swap with her. Ruth was now positioned with her head in the corner by the metal bars that sectioned off the steps and a big metal door that was welded shut. She had no blanket, and the metal plate and screws dug into her. She couldn't sit up for fear of losing more space, so she chose to sacrifice her left hip to the bolts and the left side of the crown of her head to the metal edge. This was what she deserved.

Her right hand was beginning to cease up. She had to face fears and go to the infirmary tomorrow. Would anyone go with her? The type of hardship her grandma Hetty had to endure was probably never self-inflicted. Ruth was very sorry for herself, and deep sleep never came.

She dreamed – a fitful, agonising dreamscape of familiar places mixed with dread and foreboding. She awoke in a cold sweat. The pain in her hand was immense. It was still very dark, so she thought it must be about three o'clock in the morning. Sleep was impossible, and she lay with her eyes open. The woman next to her was too close for comfort. *It's amazing how comfortable you can get with your surroundings, even when they're dreadful.*

She missed Helen next to her. Her body could sort of relax on that side and know it wasn't imposing on a stranger. When Alice asked to switch places with her, Ruth had got used to the breathing patterns and movements of the other girl, not familial but a sort of comfort in the circumstances.

This woman seemed much too close for comfort, and because she didn't have a blanket, there was no sense of a barrier.

Ruth felt exposed and very, very sad. She hadn't meant to hurt Helen. She hadn't even been thinking about her, but she supposed that was the point. *Selfish old Ruth, always out for herself and her comforts.* Was she really that bad? Would Helen forgive her? Throbbing pain in her hand made her snap out of her thoughts.

When the cabin started stirring and the women snuffled and began to talk in low tones, Ruth stood up and stretched. She wanted to get out straight away, just out and away, but she did have to get her hand seen to. Her middle finger was now drooping down to her palm. The look of it made her feel sick. She stretched again and groaned at her stiff left side. How had that poor woman slept there this whole time? Was she from the newest group of sunken civilians? *Poor woman.*

She stepped over her still-sleeping neighbour and braced herself. *Be brave, Ruth.* Her internal monologue used to run wild and accusing; it now just chanted steady beats. *Be brave. Step one, two, three. Go, go, go. Be brave. Walk.* Her feet knew what they were doing. Did she have to get a story straight for the doctor? *'I slipped and pushed my hand into the ground'? 'I got it caught between a crate and the wall'? Maybe that one.* Ruth's head was spinning, and she could feel the panic attack coming. *Be brave. Be brave. Breathe, breathe, breathe. Brave, brave . . .* She sat where she was and put her head as far past her heart as she could. There used to be a time when her head met her knees easy. Now there was a strange pulling in her back and neck and no stretch whatsoever. Was she stuck? *Don't panic about that too.* She breathed in, out through her nose. *Deep in. All isn't lost. You're alive.*

There was a tap on her shoulder, and someone sat down next to her. *Oh joy!* Her stomach made a little leap, and she looked up to see Filip, his grinning face.

'My Filip.' Had she said that out loud?

'My little English lady,' he said quickly and smirked at her.

He was mocking her affection, and it hurt. She didn't let on. She held her hand up with the droopy finger and started crying, sobbing like a child.

'Yeeeee.' He breathed out. 'What happened? You punch someone? That's a good boxer's injury. You set up secret betting syndicates?'

He laughed but took her hand gently, turned it over as she flinched and stopped herself from crying out.

'How do you say this?' He said something in Polish like she was expected to understand. He shook his head.

She realised how matted his hair was, but she still wanted to run her hands through it. They were sitting close, and he had her hand in his. Ruth wished she wasn't in so much pain, yearned to tell him she was fighting with Helen because of him, but he would mock and make her feel worse.

'Ah! Dislocation!' said the doctor after one little look in her direction.

'Dislocation, yes, Herr Däkter,' Filip said.

Ruth looked at him, screwed up her face in vexation and questioning. He winked. Only a few moments ago, he didn't have the English word, and now he was spouting German nonsense too. The doctor ignored him. He was a tall man, with a classic white coat and clipboard, peering over his glasses and pursed lips. What frightened Ruth the most was his eyes. They were hooded and deep, almost no life behind them. She shuddered. She had an impeding sense of doom and wouldn't be at all surprised if he pulled out a big syringe and stuck her with poison, tossed her overboard. Filip would surely do something, though he was much larger than Filip. The doctor gave Ruth a rolled-up rag. She took it, confused. He motioned for her to put it in her mouth. It was quick – she gave him that much – but it wasn't painless, and he sure didn't care when he slammed his hand down on her knuckles hanging over the edge of the desk. She screamed. She really, really screamed – and then blackness.

She woke up spluttering and coughing. The doctor had thrown water in her face, and she was lying on the floor.

'You fainted,' he said shortly.

Ruth sat up, spinning, unable to tell where the worst pain was. She just felt like her whole body was buzzing with pain.

'I have nothing else for you.'

Ruth thought better of saying he'd not given her anything in the first place, except more pain. Filip got her under the arms and semi-hauled her through the door. The doctor slammed it shut behind them, and they were left in the hall. She leant on the desk – palms flat, head bent, just breathing – not quite head-in-hands defeated but pretty near, mentally checking her body from the toes up, scanning for the pain, isolating it, and trying to forget it. Filip was silent and stepped back against the wall. He'd read it right; she didn't want him to touch her.

She thought about when she was in the upper primary, about 10 or 11 years old, thinking that she might like to play hockey. She had enjoyed it for a couple of years, but the other girls had got a lot bigger than her, and what wasn't above their knees was well above hers. The stick marked bruises on her thighs, and she thought of the pain she thought she was in then.

She gave the desk a little shove and stood up. *Onward we go.*

Chapter 15

Helen walked right by her. Ruth had smiled and beckoned her over, but Helen glared and turned her head towards the girl she was with, as if chatting, but Ruth knew Helen. She wasn't even friends with that poor girl; she was making Ruth jealous, and it was working. Ruth had been trying. She thought she was making progress by just being as relentless as she could, but Alice had said that was making Helen furious. Alice had been stuck in the middle for well over two weeks now. *Poor Alice.*

Filip had managed to find her a pencil and some paper. There was German writing on one side, and it was only the size of a writing pad, but it was something. She had never been good at drawing people; landscapes were her thing – and not realistic ones either. Ruth preferred to say she was inspired by the expressionists, trying to sound as if she knew what she was doing and what she was talking about. In actual fact, she was trying to cover up her mediocre skills. She loved art. People had said she was talented – but mostly family. This, however, was laborious. She wanted it just right for Helen, just to show her how sorry she was – perhaps a picture of the three of them, heads only, smiling.

'I can't do it, Ruth.' Alice was pleading with her. 'It's just gone on too long.' She sat on the crate next to Ruth and let out a big harrumph like a child sulking. 'I just don't think she will ever forgive you.'

Forgive – that was an intense word. Ruth hadn't thought about it like that. She was under the assumption that Helen just wasn't accepting her apologies until she got it right or had paid her dues. Forgiveness was another matter entirely.

'Do you think I should be forgiven?' Ruth asked, emphasising the *you* rather than the *forgiven*, gauging Alice's response.

Alice shook her head but said, 'Yes, of course,' in a bright, cheery voice.

Ruth's heart sank. They sat in silence, always looking out to sea, with all the time in the world to think, to overthink. Ruth had been searching in the wrong direction. Helen was not going to forgive her, but did she really have anything to forgive? Ruth hadn't done anything to her personally. If anyone, it was poor sweet Geoffrey. She wondered if her drawings had ever found him. She wondered if he was writing to her. She was wretched; her hope was running low.

Ruth had successfully managed to persuade Alice to give Helen the picture, but listening to Alice retell Helen's reactions and words was cutting deep. Alice had a way of breathlessly recounting every minute detail.

'Ruth, she screwed it up. She just more or less pulverised it and threw it over the railings. The look in her eyes was terrifying.'

It was dramatic but, Ruth assumed, accurate. She was going to have to face Helen herself, physically make her sit and listen. What would she even say? *I've given up hope of ever seeing anyone ever again. I'm afraid we won't be getting off this boat alive. I'm frightened of everyone and everything. Most of all, I've given up hope.*

'Thank you for trying, Alice. Thank you for sticking by me.'

Alice nodded, her head low. 'It was a lovely drawing, Ruth. I'm sorry.'

Ruth was touched, but the only reply she could muster came out all squeaky. 'Mm-mm.'

She stood up, and Alice followed, but Ruth put her hand up to stop her following. Ruth walked away but thought better of it and turned back to Alice's pained face. She gave her a big hug, Alice tensed for a millisecond and then hugged her back hard; she might never let go.

There was nowhere to go other than the decks. Ruth had chosen a spot to sit in between two big pillars. She had no idea what they were or what part of the ship she was on, but Ruth didn't care. Her heart was so low; her mind was scattered except for vivid images of home and her parents. She had been coming to sit here for the best part of the day since everything had happened. Helen was still not showing any signs of relenting. Between the pillars on one side, the railings were solid except for a letterbox-sized slit through the middle. If she sat with her back on one pillar and her legs bent, she could pretend she was sitting in a window seat of a beachfront mansion.

She was pleased with her spot, and for the most part, nobody really bothered her. It was a slight relief from the squalid conditions, the hunger, and the increasing overcrowding in the quarters. Her spot on the bolts had shrunk even more. They had devised a way of lying like toppled dominos, stacked on the long edge. It seemed like the ship was taking on more prisoners every night. She couldn't decide if all emotion had left her or if she was feeling too much at once to process anything. She was overwhelmingly lonely.

The morning was cooler than it had been. Ruth could see her breath as she emerged from the depths. The blouse she had on seemed even more threadbare, and she shuddered. Anything was better than down there, and she walked on, heading for her spot with her head low. It was busy on deck for the time of morning, and she stopped to take in the happenings. The crew, who usually sat about, were scurrying about like ants, stopping to pass information or papers or equipment, some with big boxes and even suitcases. What was going on? A few other prisoners were leaning over the sides like her and watching, with ponderous faces and low chattering.

Something was definitely happening, and if anyone was to know, it would be Filip. Would it be worth it? She didn't want to ask a crew member; they were harsh at the best of times, and at this moment, Ruth thought it best not to even make eye contact for fear of retribution. The other prisoners would only speculate, and she couldn't be bothered with that. Fact finding had become her mission. It was keeping her going, but it had also got her into a lot of trouble. She realised she hadn't really found out all that much either, but what did it matter? Filip would know.

Ruth knew she couldn't sit down all day if she was going to find out what was happening but didn't really know where to start. In the end, she decided on doing laps. She supposed the exercise would do her good either way. The card spot had got busy with all the new arrivals, and it took a while to search all the men's faces. All of them looked the same, with beards and long hair, sunburnt arms, and dirt-caked clothes. Where was the dirt coming from on a ship?

She thought about home comforts and the people at home. She had lost all sense of what month it was; she figured it was 1944 by now, January, perhaps February, but the stretch of time blurred into the blank horizon, and the weather was nothing to go by as it was hot and sticky one day and freezing the next. On and on, they sailed. Did they have a destination? For all she knew, they were just going around and around. Before setting out for New Zealand, Ruth had been on ferry boats and in a small dinghy on someone's farm when she was very small. That was the extent of her watercraft experience and knowledge. Now she was going to die on a godforsaken German raider with no friends or allies. She was crying.

Ruth circled back towards her spot. She hadn't found Filip, and she was even more disheartened than before. By the haze on the horizon and the pink tinge in the sky, she could tell it was almost time to line up for the slop in a cup they called food. Her stomach twanged at the thought, as if to tell her not to do it. She wasn't going to. She wished she'd eaten the food on the ship over. *What a priss I was. Who did I think I was? Lady Mac? More like Lady Muck now.*

She froze. He was waiting for her in her spot. Was he waiting for her, or had he just chosen to stand there? How did he know about her spot? She had every intention of sitting there until the bitter end tonight until she heard the guards yelling their nightly chorus of 'All POWs below deck! Schnell!' Even then, she thought she might risk a night in the open, away from other people's breath. What was that look on his face?

'I heard you were looking for me.'

She hadn't asked anyone, so she must have been a tad too obvious, a tad too desperate looking. She nodded sheepishly.

He grinned his knee-wobble-inducing grin and had his palms up. 'Why?' he asked.

'I know you know what's going on, and you're going to tell me, Filip.'

Still with his palms up but a downturned mouth, raised eyebrows in mock misunderstanding, he shook his head. 'I don't know what you are talking about.'

Once again, he had convinced her that talking in the open was not a good idea. They were sitting on the bench bed in his room.

'What do you want to know?'

She thought hard about how to phrase a question to get the best possible answer and the most information. Her head hurt with the effort, and in the end, she asked, 'How is it that you have personal quarters?'

He looked up to the corner of the room. Somewhere in her memories, she had heard her grandmother talking about body language. Was it up and to the right for lying or eyes down? Either way, Filip was thinking of how to answer, so she knew she was either going to hear a lie or an edited version of the truth.

'I won't tell a soul,' she offered. 'Not even Helen.' She hadn't told him they weren't speaking. *He wouldn't have cared anyway – not his problem.*

He looked at her again. 'You know I was crew on the *Rangitane*, but I used to be . . . I don't know the word. The second from the captain on a, you know, a working boat? How do you say it in English?'

She shrugged, a bit confused. He was frustrated with his English. The furrows in his forehead deepened, and his dark eyes squinted at her in the dim of the room. She managed to work out that he was some sort of ship's command back in Poland and had managed to wrangle the very proud and patriotic Earwig to give him quarters, something to do with gentlemen's etiquette at sea, regardless of wartime, peace, or country of origin. Ruth found it hard to follow and hard to believe. Filip reckoned he didn't know what was going on this morning, but she wasn't convinced.

'Are they going to attack another boat?' she pressed. When he didn't really respond, she changed tack and said, 'What's your hometown like?' as sweetly and airily as she could.

'You're full of questions today.' He laughed.

He play-tackled her backwards, and she let him, even though she was cross at being dismissed all the time.

'Do you know what I think?'

His face was close to hers and a cheeky one, a surprisingly trim eyebrow cocked at her.

She went on. 'I think you got lucky. I think you're nothing special and you got lucky!' She regretted her outburst a little bit when his face fell, but she was still cross.

'You're right. I'm lucky, lucky that I am who I am.' He sat up, serious in his movements; his long arms and legs seemed even longer in the small space. Sitting to face her, he pulled her closer, wrapped his legs around her in a bear grip. 'I truly don't know much. I am largely ignored by the crew, which means I can slip in and out of places and hear things and see things, but they don't directly tell me. You think I'm in their planning rooms and their confidant. I'm not.'

She listened. He was staring directly at her. She felt slightly uncomfortable at his seriousness, but she had asked.

He went on. 'I can tell you we are still in the Pacific Ocean. Other German supply ships come at night to refuel and restock.' He paused then. 'Surely, even from below deck, you hear the noise of sinking ships?'

She did. They did. She always thought about the survivors, that at least they'd be on board soon, and willed them to not be scared, sending silent prayers into the unknown. She had never been religious. Her family went to church briefly, and she remembered having a good time at Sunday school. She wondered why they had stopped; she hadn't even thought to question it. Grandma Hetty always used the Lord's name in vain, so Ruth was pretty sure she wasn't religious.

'Yes,' she said quietly.

They had chatted a long time, and Ruth was getting a little bit anxious as to how she was going to get back to the quarters undetected. She didn't voice her concern. Filip was chatting now, and she didn't want to stop the seeming normality of it. He'd found his voice, and they had talked about all sorts of different things. *How can he remain so cheeky and cheerful and have seen and done what he's done?* She wanted to know how he had avoided frontline duties or, in fact, any wartime duties. He was a totally able-bodied man, but she didn't know how to ask or to break his enigma, which was part of the pull for her.

'I have told you a lot, no?' He smiled, ducked his face into hers, questioning, 'No?'

She grinned back. 'Yes, a lot. Thank you.' *Thank you? For just talking?* Why did she always submit? It was a constant battle between her brain and what her mouth chose to say. Inside, she rebelled, but outwardly, where it counted, she would just roll over and say, 'Yes, please. I'll do anything for you if you scratch my belly.'

Her thoughts were broken by Filip launching himself at her.

She pushed his shoulders up enough to be able to gasp out, 'What are you doing?'

He pushed back, and her elbows buckled. He kissed her and pecked her all over her neck and cheeks. She squirmed.

'Why are you fighting me? What's the matter?' He was cross.

She pushed at him again to move off her left side. It was hurting from the bolts, and she was panicking about being trapped. He was heavy and bullish, and it wasn't the same feelings as before. He was uncaring and distant. It had come out of nowhere, and now her heart raced in a different way. She wriggled again and got her leg out from under him.

'Why are you fighting me? This is our deal, yeah?'

He kissed her again, rough, squeezing her chin. She kicked like a bucking donkey, and he bit her lip with the jerk. She screamed.

'Shhh,' he hissed. 'This is our deal? I tell you things, and you give me you?'

The shock of this statement rang through her whole body. Was this waking up to reality? Gone were the rose-tinted glasses, her beautiful love replaced with a beast. Wasn't it meant to be the other way around?

She could taste the blood down the back of her throat. She thrashed again, and he released her. He was really cross – wild eyes and breathing hard. She sat up gasping and crying. She stood up and tripped on the blanket twisted round her ankles. This time, the blood dripped down her cheek from the split on her temple. Filip barred the door, getting there before she could. Ruth grabbed and pulled at his arm, but it wasn't any use. She went to scream again, and he clapped his hand over her mouth.

'I'll tell you this for free,' he said, his accent making the anger into a snarl, right in her face. 'You women POWs are doomed.'

She narrowed her eyes at him, his hand still on her mouth. She shook her head free.

'I know this much from listening and watching.'

Ruth didn't reply; she wanted to ask questions. She just stared him down.

'They're searching the maps for an island to dump you all on. There's not enough food for everyone. Even the crew.' He was calmer now, still blocking the door but stating things as if it were a normal thing to be sent to your death on a deserted island. Filip relented and let her out without a fuss.

Ruth was too exhausted to run and shaking too much to even walk. She wasn't even worried if a guard caught her, but she wasn't going back to the quarters. She found herself in her spot. She looked out through the gap to the deep black of nothing. Was he telling the truth or trying to scare her? She curled up into a tight ball, managing to squeeze herself facing in, her knees tucked almost to her chin. Adrenaline was still pumping through her, and she was wide awake.

How could she be so stupid? She paid the price but had also got off lightly, she suspected – rattled but not broken. Alice had more or less given up being the go-between and had chosen to stick closer to Helen. Ruth didn't blame her, but she now felt more alone than ever. Thoughts turned to home, and the beats of her heart were softer in her ears, but they were broken beats.

Chapter 16

Ruth woke up. It wasn't the type of peaceful wake-up you get from sleeping in a bed, but she felt all right. Then she moved. Stuck between the two pillars, she had somehow wedged her foot in behind one and twisted in her sleep. If it wasn't for last night's events and how sore she felt, she might have even giggled at her predicament. Turning halfway back and bracing her other foot against the side, she pulled her trapped foot out. She could see it was going to bruise; it was already swollen. Was she going to end up an amputee like Alice next?

Her thoughts were always more malicious than her words or actions. She counted herself as a 'nice' person, and other people always said so too, but internally, she was thinking some horrid things. Was she a nasty person, or was it like a release valve in her head, stopping her actually saying nasty things out loud? Whatever it was, she sure was paying the price now. She didn't intend to leave her spot.

The whole day had passed. She had stood up once or twice to stretch and look over the edge at voices or sounds, but she had not moved. She now needed to go to the toilet very badly. She wasn't about to pee where she slept. There were more pillars further down, a little more exposed but not too bad if she was going to squat. Holding her breath and praying to whatever it was that was going to prevent anyone from seeing her, she darted over, lifted her skirts, and squatted, eyes darting everywhere, ears pricked to every noise. Was this the longest pee in history?

She breathed out and scampered back to her spot. If one thing was good about no food, it meant that bowel motions were few and far between. She settled back down to look out through what she now thought of as her bedroom window. She was slightly worried that Filip would know where she was, but what could she do? *Another night in the open.* Were they missing her at all? At least at roll call, they would genuinely be able to say they didn't know where she was. *Nobody cares.*

The anguish of the night before had worn off, and the desperate need to be anywhere other than Filip's room had faded. Now her spot was cramped and cold. Ruth awkwardly lay on her back and looked up. *Weren't you meant to see the stars at sea? Something to do with navigation?* Even the stars didn't want to be out on this night. She thought about Filip's last words – threatening. Was it true? She ran through the facts in her head. He was extremely good at sourcing things out of nowhere; he seemed to have a strange rapport and connection with the crew. However, he possibly did make up most of the things he had told her about Captain Earwig. The fact that he was here, there, and everywhere meant that he could have picked up a few pieces of information along the way, but was his German that good?

She wanted to hate him for what he did. She wanted him to pay, but mostly, she just wanted it to have never happened and be happily back in his arms. That way, Helen would still be wrong, and she would still have someone. *I've failed you, Grandma Hetty*, she thought. *It's adventure I craved, but I'm useless and stupid.*

Sleep out in the open was good for the lungs and nostrils – no bodies crammed in, no rotten-smelling breath fug – though it was damp and cold. Ruth was just opening her eyes, and she saw a strange face peering down at her. She scrambled backwards in fright. It was a seagull. He took flight and swooped back along the length of the ship before climbing higher and carrying on into the distance. She stood up over the railings, and with one hand shielding her eyes from the glare off the water, she strained to see where the bird had gone. She didn't know much, but she knew they should be too far out at sea for birds. Did seagulls migrate? Had he lost his flock on the way? What was the collective noun for seagulls?

Ruth remembered one summer they had spent as a family with her father's parents. They lived too far away and were too old to travel. She hadn't really known them all that well, but she remembered her grandad loved to do crosswords. They were sitting at the little round table in the kitchen, always with a pot of tea among them.

Ruth might have been drawing – she couldn't quite remember – but her grandad had asked her, quite genuinely, involving her in his puzzle, 'What's the collective noun for owls?'

The look on her face must have given her away as her grandad had chuckled and explained what the term meant, using some funny examples. She remembered them clearly, thinking through them as she gazed after the seagull – a family of sardines, an army of caterpillars. She had found 'a glaring of cats' the best. All the cats she had ever known could easily kill with one glare. Of course, 'a parliament of owls' really stuck in her memory. Ruth thought she was right with *flock* though; she thought that might be while they were in flight. Would a 'colony' be better?

She had nothing else to think about and, quite frankly, didn't want to think about anything else. What was there? Were Helen and Alice at all worried they hadn't seen her for close to a week? She thought again about the bird. Was it an omen? Had she actually dreamed it into existence? They hadn't been in sight of land since they had first been captured. She wished she had kept a record of days. How long had they been out here? She was going to have to go and line up for food today; she was becoming delirious, seeing birds. She was weaker than she had ever been as well, so she mustered up the courage and went to be one of the first, hopefully missing Helen and especially to avoid Filip. How could she be so stupid? She stopped herself from running through the events in her head for the umpteenth time.

It was too early, and she was one of the first few to be there – empty, expressionless faces, skinny and sunken looking, no smiles among them, the faces all familiar but with no names or history to put to the bodies. It was like they were extras in the background – the silent chorus, the villagers filling up the scene. She took her place in the queue, silent and expressionless herself, but she did acknowledge the woman she sat next to with a straight-lipped smile. The smile was returned in the same way before both sets of eyes dropped back to the ground. Silence was broken by a familiar sound, one that broke her thoughts and her dream – a great squawking cry of seagulls overhead.

The lady jumped to her feet. 'Land. There must be land.' It would have been a yell if she was not half starved.

Ruth's heart stopped. *Land.* Of course, that was what it meant to see a seagull. She searched the horizon. *Nothing – yet.*

The hunger had gone, replaced by an extreme urgency to find Alice and Helen, to tell them what she knew. She hurried as fast as she could, desperate to rouse them and get as much so-called food and water in their bodies before they were left on a deserted island to fend for themselves. She couldn't help thinking. If she'd given Filip what he wanted, would he have saved her from this fate? She shuddered. What was worse? She decided being alone without her friends and not knowing what had happened to them would be much, much worse, and she hurried on.

Flip-tripping down, she barrelled into a woman too close to the foot of the stairs. She yelped as Ruth's full weight pinched down on her side. Ruth apologised, but it would have come across as meaningless as she kept on barging through to the back corner of the room. She shook Alice first and realised she was awake but still kept on shaking her.

'What . . . are . . . you . . . doing?' Alice said between jolts.

Helen sat up, silent and staring at the mad woman shaking her friend.

Ruth took a big breath. 'Land. Seagulls. There will be land.' She was gasping. 'It's too full. We have run out of food. There's land.'

Realising the blank faces staring back at her were confused and everything was coming out mixed, she started again. She was quieter now, but most of the people close by had heard what she said and came closer to hear.

'Trust me. I saw.' Her voice was lower still. 'They're planning to put us all out on a deserted island. There's no more rations, and the crew are hungry too. They're desperate, and they never have cared about us, just about saving face and seeming like they're treating us right.'

She got madder as she talked, more and more aware of what was actually happening, piecing together the events and fragments of information, the things said directly to them by Earwig, all coming together to form a grand finale of a Greek tragedy. She turned to Helen, who was stone-faced and disbelieving.

'I find it hard to take anything you say seriously, Ruth,' she said, a cutting tone at the end, her name used as an insult.

Dear Alice – if it wasn't for her, they wouldn't be back in the queue, waiting for slop in a cup. Ruth remembered when anything that Alice did got on Helen's nerves. Now neither of them could function without her, the way she could just muddle on through things and make it possible to see both sides of every story – not exactly *impartial*; that wasn't the word. She was able to get people to do things by being a little bit lost herself, as if everyone had to look after her and show her what to do, and in doing so, everyone ended up doing what Alice wanted to in the first place. Was it an act?

Ruth had always had a lot of time for Alice and always enjoyed her little tangents and stories about people Ruth had no idea about. However, this morning, like everything and everyone at the moment, Ruth saw Alice in a different light. The 'Oh, Alice' days – 'What have you gone and done now?' – were over. She really saved the day today, and Ruth felt much calmer and braver with her at her side again, even glowering Helen. If they had to turn to cannibalism, would Helen taste like sour grapes? Ruth snorted and held back a giggle, masking the noise by having a fake coughing fit. Alice patted her back. Helen turned towards the fuzzy haze of the horizon, fate before them.

They had not heard from Kapitän Ewig for many days. He had been in the habit of lecturing them on the latest conquests of Germans on the front line and even past conquests of his own. Most mornings, as they were waiting in the breakfast line or while they were milling about deck, he talked from the top deck, but sometimes he would stroll about in an almost friendly manner, always with great tales of Nazis winning out over the Allied forces, British planes crashing into the sea, troops retreating over hills or being captured. To give him his due, he had great English and great storytelling capacity.

Ruth couldn't help but listen. That was the point, she supposed – a literal captive audience. His stocky figure, immaculate in dress and stance, appeared at the top deck railings, his ragged subjects peering up at him, waiting for the news – how their future was in his puffy hands. He sucked in air, sharp, and clicked his heels together, stuck his chin out, and greeted them in his thick accent and air of grandeur. Ruth suspected he wished he was talking at a big rally with cheering supporters and flags waving. In his mind, he was destined for bigger things, but somehow – with some turn of the key, a decision made in the past – they had all ended up together on this ship.

'To be precise,' he said as he stood over the top of his prisoners, official and booming, 'it is no longer sustainable for all of us to be together. It is with great sadness that we will soon part ways.'

The food line hadn't moved, and Ruth realised it wasn't going to. What else was there to do but just stand there, waiting? It wouldn't be food they got, but they might get off the boat first. The other prisoners in the line were no doubt thinking the same way.

Ruth muttered, 'It is with great happiness that we part ways with the earwig.'

Alice patted her shoulder. Helen shuffled but didn't say anything or look in Ruth's direction. It was heart-breaking, standing in a line to the unknown and feeling more alone than ever – heart pain, physical heart pain for anyone and anything she ever loved, including Geoffrey and Filip. It was possible to love in different ways. Ruth supposed Helen would argue it was lust that led to betrayal. She tuned back into what the captain was saying in time for his customary gloat session. She tuned back out again, and tears trickled down her face.

It ended up being quite a warm day as they waited on deck, still in quite an orderly line, though most of them had sat down. Ruth was picking at lint on her cardigan sleeve. Alice was asleep on Helen's lap, and Helen was leaning against a crate, still staring out to sea. The haze on the horizon had got darker; their deserted island was coming slowly into view. It reminded Ruth of a suspense thriller her grandmother had taken her to. Ruth had held her breath the whole time. She didn't remember much, just a dreadful terror feeling. Was that where and when she had lost her brave? *Ha!* She thought.

'I'm sorry, Helen.'

It just slipped out. It broke the silence with a jolt, but Helen didn't move or motion that she had even heard. Ruth was sick of it. She just started talking.

'I don't know what I was thinking. I was wrapped up in my own selfish world. I didn't believe I was doing any harm. I'd lost hope and felt as if we would only ever be on this boat for the rest of time. I am sorry it hurt you. I can see how bad an idea it was now. I hurt everyone and ruined everything, and it's unforgivable. If it's any consolation, I got what was coming to me . . .'

She tailed off. She was crying, and Helen had turned to her inquisitively at the last comment.

'He tried . . . He tried . . . He thought . . . I got away . . .'

Silence fell between them. Helen looked down.

'Everything will be OK,' she said quietly and to nobody in particular, but it was good to hear her friend talk again.

They waited, long past dark and long past curfew. Nobody came to tell them to move to their cabin, so they remained. Not a single prisoner had moved, and more had joined – less in a line, more in a congregation now. Ruth missed church; she didn't regularly go, but she made a silent vow to attend as much as she could, if they ever did get home. Home was always on her mind, but she tried to suppress the memories. They were painful and full of regret. *If you're close to the edge, are you always filled with regret, or do some people see a fruitful, philanthropic life?* Ruth pondered. She didn't regret anything she had done, just regretted she'd had no time to do anything more. Was that selfish? She supposed it was.

'It's hard work being a POW,' said Alice, yawning, standing up to stretch. Supported by one crutch and the wall, she had actually got quite nimble.

'Does it still hurt?' Ruth asked.

'You can't ask that!' Helen shushed.

'Why not?' Alice replied. 'It's just a missing foot.'

Helen was muted.

'Sorry, Helen. I know it's not "proper"' – Alice quoted with her fingers by her temples – 'but what is proper these days?'

'Does it feel dreadful to stand on it like it was still there?' Ruth wasn't stopping now.

'Well, let's just throw away all common decency while we're at it, shall we?' Helen was at fever pitch.

'Scream at me, Helen!' Ruth knew she wanted to.

Ruth baited Helen. Looking back on it, Ruth knew it was mean, but she needed Helen to get it out, get past the action, and move onto being friends again. They needed each other more than ever.

'I was only thinking of myself when I fell in his arms—'

Helen stood up. 'You're a selfish slag!' She went on. 'You're a vicious, worthless cow!'

Her nose was flaring, eyes wide but full of tears, and Ruth noticed the vein in her forehead protruding. She had wild fury for Ruth, fuelled by the dread of the unknown, her own heartache, everything they'd been through to this point, and it had boiled over.

'Wretched and useless – I hate you! You're a slag!' Helen paused, breathing heavily. She looked Ruth dead in the eye – 'I hate you, you whore!' – and launched at her before Ruth had a chance to even register.

Helen was on top of Ruth, pummelling at her – head, face, stomach. Ruth had her hands up to protect her face but moved one to yank Helen's hair. It was more to try and get leverage to get up, but it made Helen worse. She was screaming and clawing and crying. Ruth was too.

Somebody came over the top of Helen and pulled her off, and someone came behind Ruth and dragged her under the arms before she had a chance to stand up. Helen was still screaming insults as she was pulled off Ruth.

There was a stunned silence around them, the other prisoners unaware of the background that led to what seemed like two lovely young ladies having a bar brawl. Helen hadn't realised who had pulled her away. Ruth was staring hard at Filip, but he wasn't acknowledging her. He held Helen by the elbow, and she wheezed in and out, puffing and gasping with every sob.

Ruth felt her heart breaking. The word *heartache* is true. It physically aches in your chest when a lover rejects you and a friend hates you. Ruth dropped to her knees, head in her hands, willing the earth to open up and swallow her. Like all the Greek and Roman stories she loved so much, would a god of one kind or another take pity on her now and transform her pain-stricken heart into a creature, one to be named in tragic honour of her pathetic loss?

'Get your hands off me!' Helen was screaming, seeing who was holding her back.

The fists came out again – she had seen red – but Filip was able to just grab and hold Helen's wrists. She struggled and twisted; he gripped harder and pushed her violently backwards.

'No, no, little lady,' he said, half-grinning.

Helen didn't move, shocked into freeze mode.

Filip pulled her arms into her chest, lifted her off her feet, and shook her again. 'Calm down. You are making a big scene.'

Ruth and Alice charged at Filip at the same time. The sight of their friend being attacked had flipped a switch in both of them – Ruth for all the good times taken away, for her friend, for every woman taken advantage of, Alice for the sheer audacity of someone laying a finger on her friend, let alone someone who had caused so much trouble. Alice had her crutches, and like a scene from a movie, she threw one at Ruth, and they both started laying into Filip. He dropped Helen, who immediately pulled at his legs. With the shock and timing of everything, Filip was powerless under three attacking women. Hell hath no fury. In a foetal position on the ground, he lay motionless as he took hit after hit, kick after kick.

'*Enough!*' Boomed a voice, right in Ruth's ear, and at the exact moment, a jet of water hit her hard in the chest. She was knocked backwards into the railings.

Helen and Alice were hauled over by two guards. Filip got up, brushed his top with the flat of his hand, brushed his pants, looked up, caught Ruth's eye, grinned, and walked away. Something lurched in the pit of her stomach, an ear-piercing scream wretched out of her throat. She wanted it to form daggers and stab him in the back, in the heart.

Chapter 17

It was almost pitch dark in the cabin they had been locked in. Ruth and Helen marched, pushed along with their hands held tightly from behind, Alice carried like a sack of potatoes over the shoulder of one guard. They had been here for a long time; Ruth couldn't tell, but it had been hours. With her not being able to see much, her ears pricked at sounds, but there had been nothing of note. They knew what they'd done. They didn't know what was to become of them.

'It didn't hurt. It just felt strange to put weight on. I didn't think, and I just used my leg like I still had a foot.'

The long silence was broken by Alice's sudden blurt. It shocked Helen, and it took Ruth a moment to realise she was answering her question about standing on her leg. Both of them watched as Alice hauled herself up the wall to a standing position.

She grounded herself on the good side and then gingerly put even weight on both legs. She stood. 'Shall I try and walk?'

'Yes, dear friend. Let's take a turn about the room,' Helen said with a posh voice, making Alice giggle.

Ruth stood up in the middle of the room, and like a horse being led on a dressage ring, Alice held Ruth's hand, and Helen had her under the arms while she slowly walked around.

'I'm walking,' she said, just matter-of-factly. 'Thank you.'

Helen was sitting close to Ruth, and in the gloomy room, with no idea of their fate, Helen hugged Ruth hard. 'I'm sorry for everything.'

Ruth was taken aback. 'No, Helen. You do not need to be sorry or say thank you.' She put her hands on her friend's shoulders. 'I broke everything. I destroyed trust and friendship.'

'We got the sucker pretty damn good though, didn't we?' Alice picked up her crutches and waved them above her head in victory.

Helen and Ruth laughed and nodded in agreement, though Ruth couldn't get Filip's last look out of her head. She had been very, very stupid and had paid the bitter price. She knew it would take more than her verbal apology for Helen to forget, but she vowed to make it up to her in any way she could.

Keys jangled in the door, and they clutched together. The guard who had carried Alice came in. His large figure blocked the door menacingly. He was ragged looking; they had seen the deterioration of the crew over their time on the boat, and circumstances took a toll on their demeanours as well.

'Follow me.'

They followed in silence, Alice first on her crutches. The ship was eerily quiet. It was early evening, and they were led to where the gang plank would be if they were in port. However, instead of the red carpet treatment, they got a red rope ladder down to a lifeboat.

'Down!' the guard barked at them.

Another crew member was in the boat already, staring up but not helping.

Helen bravely struck out first, calling back up, 'How do you propose to get a person with one foot down here then?' anger and desperation in her voice.

Ruth called down, 'They're hitching ropes around her now!' with worried and fearful tones.

Helen wasn't halfway down, and she looked far away and little already. Alice's face was ashen. She gulped, tears welling in her eyes.

'It's OK. You'll be ok' Ruth's heart was beating out of her chest.

The guard tied the other end of the rope to a metal ring. 'Get over the edge. Sit.'

His English wasn't as good as others, but his accent also wasn't as thick. Ruth wondered where he might be from, shaking her head back to the reality of the situation when he put the rope in her hands.

'Pull. Feet here.' He demonstrated bracing himself and then walked off.

'Ruth?' Alice gasped.

'This is not going to be how it ends, girl!' Ruth was sitting beside Alice, still holding the rope.

Helen was screaming from the boat below, but it was too hard to hear her, the words blown away over the water.

'This is exactly how it will end.' Alice was crying.

Ruth was panicking. She could feel it welling inside her. Instead of letting it out, she harnessed the strength. 'You're going to have to trust me,' she said through gritted teeth. 'Get yourself on the edge as far as you can.'

Ruth put both feet on the railings, pulled the rope tight by coiling it around one arm, and, with her free arm, pushed Alice as hard as she could.

Alice screamed, the rope pulled back, and she hit the side of the boat with a sickening thud – silence, out cold, dead weight. Ruth inched the rope, letting it slide over her arm on one side through both hands, holding tight. Every part of her body was exploding with pain and every part of her straining to keep her friend safe. She shut her eyes and let the sensation of the tugging rope take over. The pain in her arms was like hot needles, and then the rope went slack. She didn't wait for anything or take a second look back; scrambling, she put one arm through each of Alice's crutches and almost slid down the rope ladder after her friends. She took the drop into the boat from the bottom of the ladder like a rag doll, crumpled. She promptly threw up. From the angry screaming, she must have got the guard. She didn't care.

Alice was sitting up and awake but looking so pale and gaunt. Helen was staring in the same direction as Ruth, at land. Ruth turned her head back towards the ship – still looming and huge set against the grey water and sky. It looked like some kind of prehistoric insect with sharp features and lots of antennae. She shuddered. Was it 'out of the pot, into the fire'?

The evening could probably be described as pleasant; there were stars in the sky, and the lapping of oars was methodically peaceful. Were they the only ones heading for land? At least three fewer mouths to feed was a start for the starving crew. Land was visible, but in the distance and in the dark, no details could be seen. How did the man rowing know where to head to? Were they getting rid of him too?

'Where are we going?' She felt brave. What did she have to lose?

The man just kept rowing, staring straight ahead.

'What's your name?' Ruth was feeling brash.

'Shhh,' Helen hissed.

Ruth took heed and stopped talking. The darkness was soupy and enveloping; land had disappeared.

'There's rocks!' Helen screamed. 'Stop! Stop!'

They had been semi-drifting for a while; the guard rowing was obviously tired but didn't want to show it. He grabbed up the oars and furiously hauled to one side. Fortunately, the night was still calm, and the water was flat.

Helen peered over the edge and strained her eyes. 'If there's rocks, there's land?'

They seemed to be staring into a black hole. Anything outside the edge of the boat was pitch dark. It was very lucky Helen had been looking down when she was. Ruth didn't fancy shipwreck number two being added to their already long list of woes.

The man stopped rowing again, sighed, and then let it all out in a loud, angry vent of air. Ruth could tell he was lost and angry. She worried they'd drift far away. Then there really would be no hope of being found. At least on a deserted island, you were in one spot. There was a small anchor at their feet. She felt brave again.

'What if we threw the anchor at the rocks and just waited the night out?'

Alice gasped, did a little whine, and slid further down into the boat. Ruth could see Helen thinking about it, weighing up the risks. The guard looked grim and kept his eyes down, though he had stopped rowing again.

'We'd have to keep a watch, awake at all times, in case we were dashed in the rocks if the wind gets up.'

Alice whimpered again.

'*No!*' The guard leapt to life. 'I am commander!'

'What do we do then, Commander?' Helen asked. 'We are lost, and it is better than drifting away, never to be seen again.'

Helen was using the tone she applied to naughty teenage boys. It was hard for Ruth not to smile.

Helen continued. 'Do you want that on your official transcript your family gets?' She put her fingers in quotation marks. '"Lost at sea with no glory. No hero actions. Just lost because he ran out of ideas and ran out of puff."' She said the last word very close to his face and emphasised the 'ff' with a tough girl spit.

Ruth sat with her mouth open in amazed pride. The guard readjusted himself and stood tall over Helen. She didn't budge, but she tipped backward, and he grabbed her by the shoulders.

'OK, little lady. Lady commander.' He said it almost jovially. 'You are our commander. You must throw the anchor. Go on. You know best.'

Helen bent down and tried to pick up the anchor. Her wrists were thin before; now they just looked like dry twigs that would snap with the weight of a feather. Ruth tried to help. They got it up, but there was no way they would be able to throw it anywhere. The guard smiled, smug and amused at his own game.

'I'll drop it on your foot!' Helen screeched. She made a move to swing it.

Ruth pulled back on the other side. 'You'll make a hole in the boat. Gentle. Easy. Put it down.'

They both released it slowly, and then from the dark depths of the boat, Alice started to scream, 'Do something, you lily-livered bastard!' She sat up. 'Do something! Do something! Do something!' Alice had reached crescendo; she had her fists clenched and was waving them in useless fashion about her face.

'Do something!' Ruth joined her in yelling.

The guard picked up the anchor. They stopped screaming and held their breath. Then he stared at something beyond their heads and suddenly put the anchor down, picked up the oars, and started rowing furiously. Ruth turned to where he had been looking and saw a little pinprick of light. It was moving, winking in and out of sight, but it was definitely a light. *Maybe from a lamp?*

They had to get closer, risk the rocks to get within shouting distance. Even though they were screaming, they were too far for their voices to carry to shore. Any screaming, no matter how loud, would always be picked up by the sea fog and taken in the wrong direction. You have to be proper men of the sea for the deities who dwell in the depths to do you any favours. Even then, you have to catch them on a good day. Frustratingly, the light did not seem to be getting closer, but fortunately, the rocks where they had drifted seemed to be craggier, more obvious, and, she hoped against hope, not under the surface, ready to pounce.

Ruth remembered a holiday when she was little. She had gone with a friend and her family to a farm and a lake. Her friend had an old dinghy, hardly seaworthy, and was allowed to go out in it on her own. Ruth remembered feeling very nervous and worried but not wanting to look silly in front of her friend; she had got in anyway. She can't have been more than 10. She quite clearly remembered the grass slope from the back door to the lake's edge. The water lilies were flowering. Her friend had leant over the side of the dinghy and picked one. Ruth was horrified, not only because she was scared out of her mind to even move but also given the fact that she had picked the flower in the first place. Ruth had been brought up to look and not touch, to ask first, and to respect other people's things, and this was clearly destruction of somebody's property, surely? She had looked around to see if anyone saw and if they were going to get into trouble. Why couldn't she remember the girl's name? *Jenny? Jane? Jenny perhaps.* She had just laughed and giggled the whole time. It was why Ruth had become friends with her in the first place; she was fun. Ruth was always the fearful one, the one having fun by proxy and worrying all the while. The fear she felt now was ten times worse.

As they were bobbing about in the pitch dark, following an apparition was now almost comical. The guard was heaving big, puffed breaths with every stroke, and he was making similar whimpering sounds to Alice.

'Can you hear me?' Helen cupped her hands and yelled loudly towards the light.

Was she imagining it? Did the light stop? 'Keep yelling,' Ruth urged.

'We are here!' Helen took another big breath. 'We are here!' She paused to listen back. 'In a boat!'

Silence was the worst sound in the world; Ruth really thought so at this point in time.

'Help!' she yelled. 'Help! Help! Help!'

Where were they? What language did they speak here? The light was still in the same place, unwavering now. As Ruth looked at it, she noticed it was flashing in a semi-rhythmic pattern. She grabbed Helen by the sleeve.

'Morse code?' she hissed.

Helen shook her head. 'Maybe, but I don't know how to spell in Morse code.'

Alice spoke from the bottom of the boat again. 'Dot, dot, dot. Dash, dash, dash. Dot, dot, dot.'

'What's that?' the guard asked in a hoarse voice.

'SOS,' Alice said quietly. 'That's all I know.'

The three of them more or less pushed the guard into rowing again, mostly by yelling at him and Helen by pulling at his arms. He was so pathetic and pitiful that he simply obliged, slow and laborious. Painfully slow, they inched their way towards the light. Ruth thought it was like rowing in unset cement. She rubbed her eyes, blinked, and looked at the light again. She rubbed her eyes again and nudged Helen, who was slumped next to her. Helen looked up, looked towards where Ruth was pointing.

'Two lights?'

They had to be close enough to yell again by now. Ruth stood up.

'Sit down!' the guard roared.

She plopped back down but cupped her hands around her mouth and yelled, 'We are coming!'

There was silence and then . . . Was that a call back? Faint? One light flashed again.

'Were we ever taught Morse code in school?' Helen said, frustrated.

Ruth knew she wasn't; she couldn't remember being taught anything of all that much use. She pondered why she herself had become a teacher. *Just something to be.* She did enjoy the children but mostly their company and doing anything creative with them. She wondered what had happened to the lovely painting they'd done on the ship to New Zealand, a thousand years ago now.

'You are very lost!' the voice by the lantern lights said, hoarse and old sounding.

Ruth imagined a pirate or a rugged lighthouse keeper from a storybook, perhaps. The other light was silent. They were still beyond the waves but now on a more steady pitch straight for land. The guard seemed to have a renewed energy and was rowing with all his might.

Helen shouted, 'Where are we?' but her voice was spat back to her on the sea spray, too light to carry.

'Keep going!' the pirate voice said again.

The wind must be blowing off the land. Ruth supposed that would make it hard going to row into it but was thankful that it made the water flat. What on earth were they heading for? *Friend or foe?*

Alice said, 'Well, we now know it's not a deserted island, I suppose.'

It was more factual than funny, but the three of them laughed quietly.

'Why are you laughing?' the guard said crossly between pants. 'Are you laughing at me?' He sounded really quite indignant, like an offended child.

How can you explain laughing at a situation when you're in the situation? Ruth thought. *You can't explain all the feelings that built up to that moment.* It was inexplicable to add all the nuisances of past experiences, thoughts, emotion, and personality into a single sentence or two. So Ruth replied, 'Yes.'

The guard roared, 'I will tip you out!' He stood up, waved an oar above his head, and started to rock the boat with his legs, up and down, side to side.

Alice was screaming, 'We weren't laughing at you! We weren't! We weren't!'

Ruth clung to the side and wrapped her legs under the seat. Helen was doing the same on the other side with her head under her arm, hanging on for dear life. What had she done? With one word, she had put their lives in jeopardy again, ruined any hope without thinking, *again*. What was wrong with her?

Ruth shouted, 'I'm sorry! I'm sorry! It was a misunderstanding!' She was screaming, crying.

All of them were being jolted about, so weak from hunger and exhausted from everything; it wouldn't take much to break them now. Ruth let go. With one big dip, she fell into the water. She wanted to let it take her. She didn't struggle, didn't try to swim. She wanted everything to just dissolve into the water.

The boat had stopped rocking, and Helen was screaming her name. Ruth wanted the water to take her, to mass a great swirling whirlpool and take her to the depths. Instead, she floated. She just bobbed next to the boat with no effort and no drama at all. She just floated. The water was cold; it would get her with hypothermia first, and even then, she would probably just bob along merrily to shore.

'Hand! Give me your hand, you stupid girl!' The guard was leaning over the boat. 'Stupid girl,' he repeated.

'Don't forget selfish,' Helen added darkly.

'Don't forget thoughtless,' Alice added.

'Stupid, selfish, thoughtless girl.' The guard was getting her back for her mean words.

He hauled her up by one arm, and she twisted and flipped into the bottom of the boat. She slapped at Alice trying to take her clothes off.

'You'll die of cold. I'll keep adding adjectives, but it will always start with *stupid*.'

When Alice is angry at you, you know you've done very wrong. Ruth behaved.

Ruth's jaw was uncontrollably chattering when they reached the shore. Helen and Alice were hugging her, but Ruth could feel the cold seeping into her bones. Her whole body was shaking. Two men, pretty much how Ruth had imagined them, waded out waist deep and took her.

'Take her first. She has one foot,' Helen said, ever the organiser.

'Dear me.' It was another gruff voice.

Poor Alice was slung over his back again; she must be getting used to this treatment. Ruth and Alice hugged, sitting on the cold sand. Alice tried to get Ruth inside her cardigan as best she could. Helen came in by piggyback, and the guard waded in; the other pirate pulled the boat up onto the sand.

The bigger pirate scooped Ruth up in his coat, signalled the other man to pick up Alice, and said, 'Can you walk, miss?' to Helen.

She replied, 'Yes,' but was only just audible.

It was a slow procession, an odd collection of people who had no business being together or ever meeting in their normal lives. What was normal anymore? Two big, burly pirates rescuing three, mostly whole, young women and their captor from near dashing on rocks – yes, perfectly normal for now. Helen stumbled and slipped on the loose rocks. The guard stopped to pick her up, but she hit him away. Ruth was mildly amused that they didn't actually know his name. He must be as scared and worried as them, perhaps more so, considering these pirates might be more inclined to rescue the three women and POW roles would be reversed. If that did happen, Ruth vowed she would try to make sure he was fed better, also find out his name.

They marched on through the dark. They were going along the water's edge, a rock scramble Ruth would have loved as a child. Ruth couldn't see much more ahead of them; the lanterns only cast light at their feet and about two to three steps ahead. How they had followed them in was a near miracle. Her eyes were so heavy, she was freezing cold, and the wind seemed to be rushing right through her ears.

Everyone was silently walking along – nothing to say except everything to say. Ruth had so many questions, but she just let the men carry them to wherever it was they were going. What could she do anyway? It was certainly better than being in peril on the boat, and she would rather try her luck on dry land than ever have to go on a ship again. She also thought that any amount of distance between her and Filip was a good thing. Geoffrey came to mind; she wished him well and safe. Home came flooding in too. Was anyone at home still holding out any hope for them? Ruth thought if she was in their position after this long, she probably would have given up hope. She thought of her parents having Sundays without her. Were they even home now? If only she had gone with them instead of Helen all those months ago.

They had reached a small headland of larger rocks. The palm trees that had been marching along next to them ran out – water on one side, craggy rocks on the other. The men stopped to consider.

'Go around the edge.'

Ruth was on his back and, up until now, had every faith in him, but now she wasn't so sure. Alice's pirate went first, and they all trailed in single file around the headland, Helen next, and then the guard and then Ruth and her pirate. Around the rocks, Helen let out a little scream.

'You OK, miss?' asked the pirate carrying Alice.

'Yes. Yes, thank you. Are we going over there?' Her tone was almost excited.

Strange little buildings were scattered on the flat. Ruth could see their outlines in the clearing from the beach to the trees. *Very strange.*

'Yes. The other people from the big ship are there. You got caught in the currents that swirl around the headland. You are extremely lucky. There was someone watching you all tonight, that's for sure.'

Ruth wasn't a firm believer – no way – but tonight she could make an exception and quietly thanked her grandmother too. A miracle, they were walking along, a miracle.

Ruth couldn't work out the man's accent. Was it English? It sounded vaguely American, but there were certainly no familiar enough cues to pick, no clues as to where they might be in the world. *Not that you'd know anyway*, she told herself. The knowledge that everyone from the boats was there excited her and frightened her at the same time. They had all easily rowed here, but the four of them were gallivanting around, dodging rocks. She tried not to think about the possibility of Filip being there, grinning. She shut her eyes tight and tried not to chatter her whole jaw off.

The buildings got closer, and there were more lights in lanterns, and the low hum of many voices greeted them on the warm wind. Ruth could feel that the wind was warm on her face, but it was not enough to be warming her up at all.

'I'll take you as far as here,' said her pirate kindly, 'but I'll leave it to the women folk to help you get warm. I'll come back for my coat.'

He smiled, and Ruth saw he wasn't as old as the sea after all. He obviously wasn't a pirate either, but she couldn't help thinking he was.

'Thank you . . .' She paused. 'I'm Ruth.' She smiled up at him. 'Thank you for rescuing us. We owe you our lives.'

He smiled back. 'I'm John. You are most welcome, brave girls.' He looked like a proud father when he said that or uncle, like they'd known him all their lives. He turned to the other man who had plopped Alice down and made her giggle. 'This is Scott.'

The man nodded.

'Thank you too, Scott. We owe you everything.'

He nodded again and half-smiled. He wasn't as old as the sea either; their big beards and gruff-sounding voices were deceptive.

'We had best be getting back around the shoreline again in case there are more.'

There was no mistaking that accent; it was Scottish. It sounded nice, so out of place on a tropical island.

A woman came out of the hut behind them and bustled them all inside. She reminded Ruth of Cook, and when she said so to Helen, there were tears in her eyes. They all missed home; it was so nice to be on dry land, to see a sense of normal living, albeit so foreign and unknown. The unknown was hardest of all.

The little hut was dim inside, but it was made up beautifully with two neat rows of what looked like the most comfortable mattress in the world. The lady brushed in past Helen and Ruth, with Alice between them.

'I see you met my husband in a most dramatic manner.' She was smiling a big smile, had a Scottish accent. 'I'm Mirren. Now we don't have much, and we haven't gone through all the items that came off the ship, but we do have a lot.' She stopped and put one hand on Ruth's shoulder and one on Helen's firmly and smiled. 'I'm so glad you're here. You're safe now, girls. We will look after you.' The relief was palpable. 'You're the first ones in here, so pick beds, and I'll be back with the clothes.'

Helen looked at Ruth. 'All three together, please.'

She was saying it as reassurance to all of them but also to say that bridges were mended. Ruth was so relieved.

They chose three beds in a row. Between laughter and tears, they came to the conclusion to be comfortably in the middle. Ruth was shivering uncontrollably now. Mirren reappeared with another woman, carrying a suitcase in each of their hands.

'There's bound to be something in these,' she said chirpily. 'Then you can settle down for sleep and worry about a wash in the morning. Too late for all that now.'

Ruth looked up as the other lady put her cases down. 'That's my case!' She leaped for actual joy and ran to the shocked-looking woman. 'It's mine! Oh, thank you! Thank you!' She flung it open on the bed, and everything familiar spilled all over the place. She wanted to swim in it, bury herself in it. *Everything*.

Alice gasped, and Helen said, 'I'm surprised Kapitän Ewig didn't keep all this.'

Mirren coughed. 'Well, they're all still here, love.' She looked worried, uncertain of what it really meant to have a German ship captain, his crew, and his guards on the island with them. 'Never mind,' she said, brighter. 'We need to get you dressed and warm. I'll go and make a pot of tea.'

Ruth jolted, shivering – plus the shock of how normal that sounded. *A cup of tea.*

'Oh, Ruth!' Alice exclaimed. She was sitting on the mattress, pawing through Ruth's suitcase. 'Oh, Ruth, don't you just want to put these on and dance?' Then she started to cry, big plopping tears with no sound, just a pained and sad face.

Helen sat up and hugged her. Ruth put down the dress she was holding, the one from the department shop in Auckland. She knelt next to Alice and just held her hand, put her other hand on Alice's arm.

'I will never be able to dance again. I do so love dancing.'

The three of them sat, just sat in the comfort of one another and the comfort of real sheets and blankets, the comfort that they were safe now. They were safe. It was an odd feeling. They had obviously been in grave danger in the rowboat; that was an experience of danger. They'd also been through the bombing of the *Rangitane*, but she just hadn't really fathomed the real peril they were in from day to day on board the ship. She hadn't considered it until now, until she felt the safety of *now*.

They were sitting like that when Mirren brought back a tray of tea and biscuits. *Biscuits!*

'We are making up some food for everyone, but it is taking quite a while to organise. I brought you these in the meantime, and I will go and find some bread. Don't go to sleep on an empty stomach, girls.'

They all thanked her profusely, and she left grinning, happy to be of service.

'What we already know of going to bed on an empty stomach,' Helen said with a laugh.

True to her word, Mirren came back with a plate full of bread. It looked homemade and smelled so fresh that Ruth's mouth began to water as soon as Mirren walked in. They held back from pouncing on the poor lady while she explained what it was; none of them heard or cared. The butter was smothered from end to end, and the crusts were so crispy looking. She set it down on the end of Ruth's bed in the middle.

'Now eat this and sleep,' she said – commands of a caring nurse maid to three mischievous little girls. 'We will sort everything out in the morning. Never you worry.'

They waited until her footsteps on the gravel outside had faded, and then they pounced, chewing and grinning and not savouring one single bite, just devouring. The tea was even better with real cream and sugar lumps. *Sugar lumps!* There was enough for three each. Ruth never took sugar in her tea, but she put them all in now. It was the best meal she had had in her life, sitting in a strange little hut, on a strange – was it little? – island, with strangers outside the door, but they were safe, and they were happy, together, alive, and that was all that mattered.

With a wonderfully satisfied stomach and wrapped in her green coat like a cocoon, Ruth fell into a deep sleep. Thoughts of home briefly went through her mind, but the exhaustion quickly took her to the Land of Nod.

Chapter 18

They all slept well into the next day. Ruth opened her eyes, and Alice was still peacefully sleeping. She rolled over, and Helen was sitting up, watching the happenings. There were other women in the room, all familiar faces. Ruth couldn't tell if all the beds had been slept in, but there were a lot of women all chattering away. It really was a wonderful sound to hear.

Ruth and Helen sat next to each other in comfortable silence, watching the women tip out and sort suitcases. Some of the clothes looked expensive, and Ruth was a tiny bit envious. Of all the suitcases Mirren could bring in, what a fluke that it was her own – but imagine if she'd got a luxury one. She had used her case as a bed head last night instead of putting it at the end of her bed like Alice and Helen had done, partly because she thought she may trip on it if she got up in the night but mostly because she didn't want to let it out of her sight again. She tipped the entire contents out in the bed again.

'You really should have made the bed before you did that,' Helen said shortly.

Ruth gave her a sideways look. 'Back on dry land, and suddenly, bed-making etiquette takes priority? Blow that. I want to wear something nice today,' Ruth bit back, but Helen smiled, quickly pulled the covers up, and tipped out the case that Mirren had given her the night before.

'What fun! We should find the owners?' Helen said, concerned suddenly.

'What if they're dead?'

Ruth didn't mean it to sound as harsh as it did. It burst their fun bubble, and they sat back down quietly. They had upset themselves, and talk had turned to Isabella.

'We didn't even have a memorial,' Helen said sadly. 'I hate to think of her at the bottom of the sea, in the middle of nowhere . . .' She trailed off.

'I can't even bear thinking about her alive. It makes me too sad,' Ruth added. She was fiddling with the edge of a thick woollen cardigan, too hot for this weather and too drab to wear too. What should they do with all of it that they didn't wear?

'I wonder if we will find her suitcase,' Helen said, half hopeful of any memorabilia of their beautiful friend.

'Find whose suitcase?' Alice mumbled and flopped over towards them. She had that crumpled and wrinkled look of someone who had slept, half dead, in one position all night.

'We were talking about Isabella.' Helen said it carefully, not wanting to upset Alice but not wanting to lie either. The blast that had killed their friend and maimed Alice was always something that went unsaid – not exactly off-limits, but there was no need to drag it up either.

'I think we should look for it,' Alice suggested. 'If yours is there, then others are bound to be. Shall we go now and find Mirren?' She was getting quite excited.

'Do you want to look in your suitcase first? We were going to get dressed up,' Ruth said with overzealous glee that she regretted instantly, but the others didn't remark.

There had been nothing much in Helen's suitcase. The shoes were strangely mannish and much too big. Ruth pictured a goblin-type creature, hunched and little but with huge feet. The clothes were all brown and lumpy like she imagined a goblin's attire to be. They chose a thin brown blouse because it was silk and folded everything else back in to take to Mirren. Perhaps they could swap it.

Ruth put on her blue floral dress and light cardigan. She thought about the lovely floral dress that Isabella had. She wanted to cry all the time. Ruth took in a deep breath to calm herself and put on her matching plimsolls with the blue trim and felt like royalty. There was one problem. She felt disgusting; she was absolutely caked in filth and, in her excitement, had forgotten all about getting clean. Hurriedly, she changed back into her mismatched and grimy clothes.

They decided to choose outfits first and then go to find Mirren for a wash and hopefully some food too. The bread and tea had whetted their appetites, and now Ruth's stomach was being very vocal about being empty again. Alice giggled at the sound, and Ruth gave her a playful shove. They were already thawing out and starting to feel more their normal selves. It was hope, but dread of the unknown was still heavy in their hearts and minds.

There were other women walking down a little sandy path between some palm trees. It was well trodden and quite firm under foot. They had ditched the too-big boots and were going barefoot like children. Alice picked her way gingerly along as every step she took, her crutches dug into the sand and she tipped backwards. Helen walked like she was floating, and Ruth wanted to skip and prance and kick the sand up. It wasn't like the forest at home when she was a child – with the soft, springy grass under her feet – but it was the only other time in her life that she had been purposely barefooted.

The other women also had suitcases, so they followed them along. Three big buildings, long and wooden with pitched roofs, were circled, end to end, around a dirt courtyard. Makeshift signs had been pitched in the ground on what looked like banisters from a grand staircase in a London homestead. Ruth stopped and stared. Ablutions, the sign read, with an arrow pointing to the right.

'Over here!' Helen shouted cheerfully.

Ruth turned and saw them with Mirren, waving to snap her to her senses.

'What were you doing?'

Helen half-giggled, embarrassed. Ruth shrugged, turned to Mirren, and smiled.

'Now did you have a lovely sleep, or did you have a lovely sleep?' Mirren asked.

'It was total bliss. Thank you. Thank you so much.' Alice was staring up at the top of the palm trees, looking all around, searching. Then she said, 'Where on earth are we, Mirren?'

'Ah yes . . .' Mirren was proud to say, 'You are on Emirau Island in the South Pacific.'

It meant nothing to any of them, but it meant so much to be standing on dry land in front of a beautiful Scottish woman, safe and about to be clean. They told Mirren about their clothes situation, and she was very understanding. She took them to the back, at the opposite end of the bigger building, where there was a stack of suitcases taller than them and about as wide as a small pond.

'Well, I just grabbed three off the top that looked vaguely like they would have women's clothes in them. I figured, since mostly women turned up and only a few old men, that my luck would be striking cases with dresses rather than trousers.'

A few old men? Did that mean that Filip was still on board? Didn't make it? She suddenly feared for his life. She hated the guy but didn't wish him dead. She thought about the other young men, crew from various sunken ships from all around the world. *Why just women and old men?*

Mirren snapped Ruth out of her panicked thoughts and said, 'The Germans are still here, up at the estate. That captain is a piece of work. He commandeered our vehicles and just demanded we feed him and his crew. We had no warning.'

Ruth was concerned. 'Will they leave again?'

She suspected they might start just living it up, eat everything on the island before heading off, leaving all inhabitants and prisoners stranded and starving. Mirren shook her head and shrugged. She suddenly seemed like she had the weight of the world on her shoulders. It wasn't a good feeling that Earwig and his crew were on the island too. It brought a cloud down over their feeling of relief. They would never be truly free until the island was empty of anything resembling the war.

'Does this island belong to a fighting nation?' Ruth asked quietly. She felt sorry that they had brought it here and frightened Mirren and the other people of the island.

'Emirau is part of New Guinea. The fighting is not ours.'

There was silence for a moment, and they scuffed their feet in the dirt.

Ruth looked up and smiled. 'Thank you for everything, Mirren.'

Mirren smiled, and as she turned to leave, she spun back and added, 'The showers are signposted. They're at the side of the main hall. It says Male and Female, but nobody has been minding since there aren't that many male shower takers.' She grinned. 'Also, you will have to drip-dry or use your bed sheets . . . Sorry. We have tried.'

It was an odd feeling to be suddenly back on dry land and some kind of normal where people took showers.

Ruth couldn't wait. 'I'm going to have a shower and come back to this.'

Alice hurried along next to her, and after a moment's pause, so did Helen, all opting to retrieve their bed sheets first.

Back at the pile of cases, they started opening and sorting, creating a system. They were even more thrilled than before now that they were clean. Ruth felt lighter and freer – her thoughts as well.

'Do you think we should order them? Line them up?' Alice asked, ever the neat one.

Helen looked up from an open suitcase she was rummaging through and said, 'What, like colour coordinated? Alphabetical? Size?'

It was a tad too mean, and Alice went white, her face dropping.

'Sorry. I'm sorry. That was not called for. Alice, I'm sorry. Forgive me.' She was pawing at Alice's sleeve.

'OK, OK. It's OK.' Alice patted Ruth's hand, nodded into her face.

Helen was just about to say sorry again when two other women were brought to the pile. They had suitcases to swap as well. Polite smiles were exchanged. Ruth recognised them both from the ship.

Ruth felt slightly territorial but was snapped out of it by Mirren as she left saying, 'I'll be up at the main estate for tonight, helping my husband with the kitchen duties for the Germans. If you need anything at all, there is a new tent set up which will be manned all the time. You only need ask, and we will try.'

She sounded worn out; she looked stooped as she walked away. Ruth wondered what the estate was before Earwig took over. *Maybe some kind of farmstead like in American stories, with slaves.* Were they going to be the slaves?

'I have an idea.' Alice had obviously been thinking while they were looking through the clothes. 'Helen, you've had retail experience from home. Let's set up a clothes shop!' She was excited.

One of the other women said, 'That's a lovely idea. For everyone to come and get what they need.'

'Only we won't charge, obviously. Just have to limit the numbers at a time.' Helen putting on her organising hat. 'Ruth, you're in charge of display.'

Ruth was quite chuffed and excited about the role. It gave her something to think about, something different to occupy her thoughts other than Geoffrey and Filip. They were a constant; they had crept in and never left. Ruth's efforts to forget only made their faces more prominent in her mind, their words louder in her ears. She longed to hear Geoffrey chattering away again. It seemed impossible. Her daydreams always involved Geoffrey being with her at home. Her fretful dreams at night were Filip, always. Now she could focus on a cause – she hoped.

'Can we help too?' asked the lady who had spoken before.

'Yes, please. The more, the better. I'm Helen. This is Ruth and Alice,' Helen said, briefly flicking her hand towards them in an official way.

'I'm Iris, and this is Gita.'

Gita waved, and Iris said something to her. *Polish?*

'Gita doesn't speak much English. I only know a little Polish from my grandmother, but we have got by these past' – she paused, gulped – 'hellish months.'

She had a posh English accent, the kind from old England, and before she could think, Ruth said, 'Do you go fox hunting?'

Iris looked at her the way you look at an invalided child, with sympathy and concern. She was thinking Ruth might be a bit touched. Ruth was certainly acting like it.

'Forgive me. My mind has no filter these days. I was thinking your accent is lovely, wondered where you were from, and then imagined you with royalty, in the country on a fox hunt, and I just said it.'

Helen and Alice were hiding giggles behind their hands. Gita was awkwardly smiling, not knowing what was being said. Iris still had the pained look on her face; it was so out of context. Ruth just shrugged, palms up, and started to laugh, shaking her head, baffled at herself. They all laughed.

'Well, that certainly broke the ice,' said Iris, still laughing a bit.

Poor Gita was not in the loop even when Iris tried to explain, but her Polish was definitely not up to describing the nuances of the English class system or the strange goings-on in Ruth's head.

She smiled politely and said, 'I can help?' picking up a suitcase and offering it to Ruth.

'Yes, please.' Ruth smiled back.

Helen had already marched off to find Mirren. Alice was sitting on the dirt ground, surrounded by the contents of a suitcase. She was holding up garments and putting them into odd piles. As she held them up, the warm breeze took them, and Ruth watched the fabrics dancing. Feeling the freshness on her face and the warmth from the sun, she turned her face upwards. It was a brief pause for her mind, a reset for her body, just that spare moment, until the chattering started again. She must try and find a place to go to soon that was hers to be alone in.

'Which ship were you on before . . . before the . . .'

The words were getting stuck in Iris's throat. She was a slight woman, made to look gaunt and even more drawn than she probably would have been if they'd been properly nourished. She still had an air of glamour about her, and Ruth wished she hadn't acted so strangely. Iris had directed her question to Alice and was semi-avoiding direct interaction with Ruth. Maybe it was for the best.

Helen came breezing back and announced like a public meeting that they were allowed to set up in one of the empty cottages. 'Let's carry as many cases as we can. Follow me.'

Iris and Gita collected three each, and Helen put two small ones under her arms and a large one in each hand. She staggered off like a pack horse.

Alice giggled as Ruth helped her up. 'Find one with a long strap you can hang round my neck. I don't want Helen to think I'm slacking off,' Alice said, mostly jokingly.

'She won't expect you to carry anything.' Ruth was laughing too, but they both were a little sceptical.

In the end, Ruth found three little handbags she hung around Alice's neck before quickly grabbing two large cases herself. The other three had rounded the corner of the building, out of sight. Helen would be cross at them if they didn't hurry. Ruth looked back at Alice.

She laughed. 'It's OK. You go on. This lame pony can manage. I'll sit down at the other end like the stubborn ass that I am.'

Ruth giggled too. It was nice to have Alice's humour back. They had lost sight of themselves on that ship – the mundanity of grave danger, hunger, dirt, violence, death, the fears of never returning home, that they would be floating in the sea for the rest of what might be a very short life. She shuddered. She was safe now, able to think of other things, including clothes – her favourite.

When Ruth got to the little cottage at the side of the kitchen block, Helen was already up and running. Tables were out, chairs being arranged as makeshift shelving. Ruth marvelled at Helen. Ruth had been about ten minutes behind them, and already, Helen had managed to enlist several men to climb and lift. The little round cottage had a compacted dirt floor. The entrance came straight into an open room. A wall with two doors went right from one end to the other but didn't meet the ceiling, which was pitched and trussed. Ruth had obviously never seen anything like it in her life and stood staring for a moment.

Helen snapped her fingers at her. 'Why are you staring at the roof like a dummy?'

Ruth shrugged; a lot of shrugging was all she could muster about anything. She put the cases down.

'Iris?' Helen called briskly.

Iris walked over primly, with Gita behind, happy to take orders from a person who was younger than her but obviously 'in charge'. Anything was better than what they had got used to on the ship, she supposed.

'Can you and Gita please keep making the trips with the suitcases? If you get tired, just stop or ask one of the men to help you. They're very obliging.'

Iris nodded, and Gita smiled a neat-row-of-teeth smile, and Ruth noted that her eyes were sparkling too. Did it really mean that they were going to be OK? Ruth didn't feel OK, but she was beginning to relax into island life and supposed that if this was them for the rest of the war, that would be OK too.

Alice came through the door huffing and puffing, and two of the men rushed to help her. They scooped her in a fireman's lift, which made her giggle and blush. Ruth realised that just because of their bulk and height, she had assumed they were older men, but looking now, she saw that they were about the same age as them, skin a beautiful dark caramel. She caught herself staring and, for an awkward instant, didn't know where to put herself. She dithered and knocked over a pile Helen had been working on and sat down in the middle of it.

Helen was so wild. She stood over Ruth with her hands on her hips. 'You are an honest-to-god liability,' she scolded. Then she started to giggle.

Ruth started to giggle too, and then it was free for all to laugh at her expense, sitting in a pile of clothes, staring at the roof like a stranded beetle. Helen put her hand out, and Ruth scrambled up, still giggling.

'Well, that's your pile then.' Helen gave it a smug kick and grinned.

Ruth got to work. She was in her element. She set Alice up behind a table and gave her the bits and bobs to display – hair pins, some makeup, brushes, small things that seemed so frivolous now which made them all the more inviting. Helen was talking to Mirren, who had come in to check on progress.

'Well, I'm pleased someone had the initiative, you know. Those cases would have stuck out there for the rest of time, I'm sure. Thank you, ladies.'

Helen beamed at Mirren's approval. 'I'm going to arrange the small amount of men's clothing we have to one side. I don't think we will have too many customers, so we can have a separate line for them to have better access,' Helen continued.

She was still organising, and Ruth was very happy to leave her to it while she got to go through and display some beautiful garments. She tried not to think of their owners. Her chest was tight as she was thinking about the many times they had stood on deck and watched silently as the crew saluted wrapped bodies into the water. The process was never something they got used to; they just got numbed to paying respects and were deaf to the drivel that Captain Earwig would spout at each ceremony. Was *ceremony* the right word?

She clutched a purple silk scarf in her hands; the edges were beautifully hand stitched. She imagined the woman who owned it standing on the balcony of some country estate, summer breeze blowing, the war having never happened. Then she supposed that it was probably more likely the scarf of a poor teacher, nurse, or nanny who had saved it for best and would never wear it again.

There were tears. It was too hard not to think of all those women. She was so glad to be alive. She hadn't once thought she would be better off dead, but those women died needlessly. She wanted to go screaming up to the captain, scratch at him, beat him, yell at him. It would be no use, but it might satisfy her anger and sadness.

She shook her head and continued sorting. Iris and Gita were bringing in the last of the cases, and the room was looking good.

Chapter 19

It would soon be time to start spreading the word. There was a small gathering of women outside already, chattering as if they had met up on the high street.

Alice suggested, 'We have all these empty suitcases. Why don't we give them each one to put their clothes in?'

Helen nodded, put her finger to her mouth, thinking logistics. Then she turned to the two who had been helping and lifting all morning. 'Can you please line up the empty cases outside the door?' She smiled her best smile, and they obligingly stood up from their rest. 'Good,' Helen said, clapping her hands. 'Almost there.'

She had even set up a couple of makeshift dressing rooms with sheets and big sticks. It was their very own island department store – haberdashery, intimates, cosmetics, formal, casual, men's, accessories, the lot, all set up as appealing as Ruth could make it. Alice was still sitting down behind her bits-and-bobs table. Ruth was eyeing a pink lipstick that Alice had displayed appealingly, with one half poking out, leaning up against the gold lid. Ruth didn't even like pink all that much, but she wanted that lipstick.

She turned to Helen. 'Can we all choose just one thing?' She sounded like a little child asking their mother's permission.

'One. We deserve one item. Yes.'

They let Iris and Gita go first. Gita was so excited, she skipped straight to the dresses and chose a flowing off-white cotton dress, which she immediately put on. She didn't even bother with the changing room. Iris surprised them all by choosing a little lace hat. It was very crumpled and sorry looking, but when she put it on her head, it made her look like a fairy, a jaunty fairy godmother from a storybook. She grinned at Ruth, and Ruth grinned back. This was fun.

Alice went next and chose a blue skirt which might have had a matching blazer at one point, but the gold buttons at the front were still very smart. Helen went straight over to a deep red dress that Ruth had displayed on two crossed-over sticks like a scarecrow. When she got it out, Ruth had the thought that Helen would love it. She smiled. Helen deserved it. It might have been, before all that they had been through together, that Ruth would have got jealous and angry, but now she was happy picking up the little pink lipstick. She popped the lid on and felt the weightiness in her hand. *Quality.* She looked in the little compact Alice was holding up for her. The pink slid over her dry, cracked lips like silk. *Bliss.*

Some of Ruth's best memories were of her and grandma Hetty poring over purchases from the high street. If they'd gone together, it was reliving the finds. If they'd gone alone, it was showing off their finds to each other. Ruth's mother had never understood the frivolity, choosing practical. This day, in the dirt floor hut, with all the women chatting and excitedly showing one another things, was somehow just as thrilling as those days with her grandmother – the genuine joy and carefree feeling, the happiness the clothes were bringing.

Ruth was relaxing into it and starting to let go angst and worry when a hush settled over the room. She looked up to see the captain in the doorway with his half smirk and menacing, creeping stance. Even the few men who were in their corner of the room stood still. Earwig stepped in, ducking a little bit to get through the door.

'My men have wives and girlfriends who are missing them terribly,' he said in his thick tone, trying to garner sympathy from a room full of people he had tortured for months on end; it made Ruth feel physically ill.

Ruth turned away. Most people's eyes were on the floor. Mirren was staring at him dead in the eyes from halfway across the room. Ruth could feel her seething.

Her nostrils flared. 'What's that to us?'

Nobody had dared stand up to him before. There was a quiet, collective gasp at her brazenness. Mirren stood up taller and puffed her chest out, elongated her neck. *Don't mess with Scottish lasses.*

Earwig laughed, a sullen, indignant noise that was more scoffing and mocking than anger. 'Well . . .' he said, sliding towards her. 'It means that you will have to wait while my men choose what they think their women folk would like.' He smiled, with teeth, lips peeled back, and added, 'Also maybe some things they would like too. You have arranged everything so nicely for us. Thank you.' It was sugar, fake sweet, sarcasm bristling off him.

Mirren stepped forward again. 'No!' she said. 'I won't let you!' she added, not shouting but strong.

Ruth gulped; she couldn't look away, but she was rooted to the spot in fear.

'You? You won't let *me*?' He emphasised the *me* with feigned surprise and a raise of the voice.

Mirren stepped forward again.

'Don't,' Ruth managed to squeeze out. 'Don't.' She was breathless and hardly audible.

She shut her eyes when Mirren stepped closer again. She heard Mirren hitting the floor hard. She opened her eyes and lurched forward. Mirren was already getting up, holding her face. Ruth remembered how much that hurt, winced at her own face, touched the lump that hadn't gone away after the initial swelling.

'Yes, me!' Mirren shouted and lunged forward again.

This time, the captain put his arm out, charged towards her with his fist, and hit Mirren square in the chest. This action, this horrific scene as Mirren flew backwards and landed on the floor again, winded, made everyone snap out of their trance. As if by some magical click of fingers, all the people in the room ran towards the captain. Three women blocked the door as he turned to leave, and the whole mob engulfed him.

There was a heaving pile of people just overtaken by the animalistic need to fight. Ruth got a good couple of punches in, in the guts. Then she herself received a kick to the back of the head, which made her pull back from the pile. Crawling backwards, untangling herself from the writhing pit, she realised how silent and motionless the Earwig was. She scurried backwards towards Alice's table. Mirren was clutching her, and Alice was patting her back like she was a frightened child. Ruth wanted to do the same.

'Are you OK?' Ruth asked Mirren, helpless to do anything if she wasn't.

Mirren nodded, still looking at the punching mob. 'I didn't mean for this,' she said, her voice sounding stronger and more together than she looked.

The women started pulling back after what seemed like a very long time. Helen had come over to them shortly after Ruth and stood in silence, watching. It was brutal. The women staggering away were disoriented and bedraggled. One woman had a bloody nose, and another with a torn blouse rushed to her aid. Ruth had flashbacks to the days after their ship was bombed. It was scary how easy it was to compare the scene in front of her now.

She hadn't dared look down. Was he alive? She didn't have to in the end. She heard someone say, 'He's breathing,' as if that was all that mattered. *Would he still keep breathing?*

Two German officers appeared in the doorway. Ruth held her breath. This was it; they were all going to be taken out the back to the firing squad. Mirren stood up.

Alice yanked her back down, hissed, 'No.'

Ruth and Helen moved closer to Mirren, instinctively knowing that they needed to stop her doing or saying anything. *Just let the officers do what they will.*

The two of them were in silhouette in the doorway and darkened the room. In the gloom, the dresses and other clothes that Ruth had strung up looked like shadows of a ghost army – all the men and women they'd killed along the way. The men walked over to their captain, picked him up under his arms, and slapped his face, reviving him enough to claim back supposed dignity. Swinging between his two officers, his clothes ripped and his face swollen and bleeding, the Earwig left their lives. It was a dishevelled, pathetic end, like something out of a dramatic production. They had all been holding their breath, and it wasn't just for the duration of that scene. Ruth knew that it was release from months on end.

The woman with the bloody nose came over to Mirren and hugged her hard, grabbed her and hugged so that Mirren's arms were stuck out sideways like a squashed insect. She laughed, gasped. 'Thank you!' the lady said.

Then the room erupted into clapping and cheering, and more people came up to hug Mirren and thank her. She was quite overwhelmed.

The clapping was so loud, and someone starting singing, 'For she's a jolly good fellow, for she's a jolly good fellow, for she's a jolly good feeellow . . .'

Then the whole room sang, *'And so say all of us!'*

Mirren was staunch and proud but not smug; she knew what she had done. 'Not on my watch! Not in our village!' she yelled.

There was cheering and clapping. Ruth wouldn't have been surprised if confetti started falling from the ceiling. Ruth was smiling and clapping and cheering too. Elation after suppression and fear was a rush she had never felt before – swept up in the madness and then the celebration. Her heart was pounding, her head light and spinning but not with panic – with joy. The difference was her heart was singing and her feet were floating. The heavy, sinking feeling gone. Would she feel this wonderful forever?

It was hard to get back to task after the excitement. Alice suggested they shut the shop for the rest of the day and start fresh in the morning. Nobody minded. Mirren walked back up to the homestead. Ruth watched as far as the bend up the hill into the trees where she couldn't see her anymore. She had refused company, but Ruth was scared she would face repercussions.

'Never mind me,' Mirren said. 'I have my men up there too.'

Ruth still wasn't sure, but she turned back to head in the same direction as the others. It was hot; she was sweating. Her dress and shoes were not really suited to tropical conditions, not for sweltering, more for swanning. Her grandmother used to say, 'Stop swanning about. Find something productive to do.' She supposed she hadn't really had a 'hard' day's work ever. If they were to be stuck on the island forever, would she and Helen have to set up a school? It seemed the sort of place one would have to start from scratch, like missionaries. Ruth didn't fancy that. She wanted her family legend to be one of mystery and intrigue. She'd have to get home first; she'd have to have children too. The family name stopped with her.

The others had gathered in the clearing where some odds and ends of furniture had been set up. It was quite ridiculous to see a comfy armchair and a full dining table just set up in the open. What would happen when it rained? The chatter was inevitably about the Earwig. Ruth sat down next to Helen, and she spontaneously put her arm around Ruth's shoulders, comfort and camaraderie.

'I was too far away, and it all happened so suddenly, but wouldn't it have been good if I'd got him with my crutches?' Alice poked at the imaginary man on the ground with her tongue stuck out to the side; everyone giggled.

One lady showed them the back of her hand, scraped knuckles like a bare-fist boxer. Had it been worth it? Ruth looked at her own hands, still sore from – she was ashamed to think about it – when she punched the wall.

One lady giggled. 'His belly was surprisingly jelly-like! That's where all the food on the ship went!'

They stayed talking for a long time. Conversation turned to homelands and family, and there were quite a lot of tears. The three of them stayed quiet, mostly choosing to ask questions and commiserate. Ruth probably wouldn't have been able to stop if she started, and she knew she'd cry too.

Chapter 20

'Noooo! No, no, no!'

She heard screaming, crying, begging. Ruth was walking to their shop, but when she heard Helen screaming like that, she broke into a jog. She had been taking her time, enjoying the morning by having a wash and carefully getting ready for a day of glamour as an albeit makeshift shop assistant. She thought the Earwig was back, and her heart was pounding in her ears. It was just Helen and her this time, no angry mob of women possessed by collective hatred.

She could still hear Helen sobbing. She burst into the hut expecting to see Earwig and his men destroying the place. Instead, she saw a woman and Helen fighting over a dress. They were pulling like tug of war, but Helen was being so very dramatic. Ruth's eyes took a moment to adjust to the light. She walked closer and realised the fuss. Calmly, she laid her hands over the top of Helen's, turned her back towards the other woman who was still holding on, and looked directly at Helen. Kindly, so as not to set her off again, she loosened her grip while talking, almost a whisper.

'It's OK, Helen. She can have it. We love Isabella. This dress means an awful lot to us, I know.' Her voice was shaking.

Helen was crying but had stopped tugging.

'Remember how beautiful Isabella was. We just think of her like that. She wouldn't have minded. She is a lovely girl who would have gladly shared. It's OK. It's OK. It's OK.'

Helen let go. The other woman stood with the dress in a limp-fisted grip – a sorely won prize. She looked upset, and Ruth felt bad.

She patted Helen on the arm and turned to her, saying in her best high street voice, 'You will look lovely in that. Please take it with joy.'

The woman smiled and bowed her head in thanks. 'Sorry,' she whispered.

'It's OK. Sorry too,' Helen said. Then she added, 'You will look lovely.'

The woman left, and Ruth turned back to Helen. 'Are you OK?' She wasn't used to bailing Helen out of irrational binds.

'I don't know what came over me. I was absolutely fine, but when it came to that particular dress, I don't know. I just lost it.'

Ruth nodded. She must admit, she felt the same – but what to do? She made a mental note to ask Mirren where in the world they actually were and if they had such a thing as a postal service to alert home that things were ... were what? Fine? They weren't fine, but they were alive – not all of them. *Who alerts those about the ones who didn't make it?*

They had a lovely day in the shop. They congratulated themselves on how smoothly everything had gone and how polite and calm things had been in the end. After finding Helen playing tug of war with a dress that morning, Ruth was very glad it hadn't happened again. There were lots of people jammed in the small hut at one time and a large line out the door, but it was like Oxford Street, and if you just looked at the ladies shopping, you could imagine yourself there – nearly.

Ruth felt guilty that she was one of the only ones who had found their own case. She had given some of her clothes for the shop – just some – as she thought it would be a good swap if something caught her eye. She wasn't so greedy as to look before everyone else, but she did have her eye on a few things. The last few ladies were leaving, thanking them over their shoulders as they left, beaming. Ruth's heart felt lighter than it had in such a long time. She realised she didn't really know what time of year it was. Was it 1940? No, they'd had Christmas when they were sunk.

'What year is it?' Ruth asked.

Helen looked up from folding and shrugged. She didn't seem to care, and Ruth found she didn't either. Time had become a foreign concept.

Mirren came in the door just as they'd packed the last of the things back in the cases. She had managed to find a pretty green smock-type dress with a rounded collar.

Ruth smiled at her and said, 'Do a twirl for us,' and Mirren twirled like a little girl showing off.

'It has been a long time since I had anything of the like. Thank you for such a good idea.' She was still beaming; she jumped on the spot and gave a little squeal.

The three of them looked back at her, surprised at the sound.

'I have some even better news.' She took in a deep breath and blurted, 'We are going to have a party! A celebration! Tomorrow evening.' She looked at them, mock serious. 'Why, you ask?'

They nodded silently.

'Well, the Germans are leaving in the morning!'

A rush of excitement, anguish, and relief came over Ruth, all the emotions at once. Helen and Mirren were doing a semi-dance and hug for joy, and Alice was clapping her hands. She walked over to Alice and gave her a big hug. She should feel better for the fact that they were going, but Filip was on the ship. He'd hurt her beyond measure, but while they'd been in view off the island, there was room for redemption. She never wanted to see him again but wished him no harm either. It was hard to keep all her emotions in check when she felt she couldn't talk to either of her friends.

Ruth hauled a few more cases to the doorway and then left without a word to the others. She went back, through the trees, along the path to the beach. She could see the raider out past the headland, like a floating black beetle. She sat on the warm sand and dug her toes in, looking out at the ship, willing Filip to come out and see her. There was no chance of that, really; the ship was too far away, and even if she could make out life on board, she wouldn't even recognise her own mother. She was deep in thought, thinking of home and the very start of their adventures, wishing and willing for people to be OK.

She didn't realise someone else had come down to the beach until they sat down next to her. She gave a start and gasped when the guard who had rowed them ashore sat in the sand next to her.

'I'll answer your question now,' he said in a quiet voice. It was unexpectedly low and soft.

Ruth remembered the gruff, angry man from that night but realised he was probably just as scared as them. Her heart was pounding. 'My question?' she said, echoing his quiet tone.

'Well, you had questions,' he said, emphasising the plural. 'My name is Karl. I am from Hamburg. I am 31.' He turned to her and smiled, a straight smile with straight teeth, but his eyes were sad looking.

She smiled politely back. 'Thank you. I'm Ruth. I'm from England, and I'm 27.'

They sat in silence, looking out to sea. Ruth was conscious of how loud and fast she was breathing. She tried to slow her breaths and act as if a German navy officer sitting next to an English woman on the sand, on an island in the middle of nowhere, in the middle of a war, was perfectly normal. She thought about her Geoffrey and then scolded herself for thinking he was hers. How badly she had treated him. If she ever did see anyone ever again, she willed it to be him, at home with her family.

Karl moved slightly in the sand and shifted his weight, lying back, propped up on one elbow. *Oh gosh*, she thought. *He's getting comfortable* now. *This is beyond belief.* Her grandmother used to say things like 'You wouldn't write about it' or 'Try making that up. I dare you'. Ruth had no recollection of what she may have been saying, but it was probably a story she had embellished or indeed made up. The more experiences she had during this confounded adventure, the more Ruth thought that it was probably more than likely that her grandmother had been caught up in espionage and happenings in the First World War. She sent a thought up to whoever was listening. *Please don't let my future die in the war.*

They hadn't said a word since their first exchange of names. Ruth had calmed down enough to sit there with her own thoughts but didn't know how she could leave. She jumped when he spoke.

'We are leaving in the morning.' It was matter-of-fact, but through his accent that didn't sound German, she detected a tinge of fear and sadness.

'I heard,' she said. Then she added, quietly and leaning forward, close, like they were old friends, 'Thank you for saving our lives.' It just came out; she meant it.

He looked at her, deep blue eyes in the hollowed-out sockets. 'You are most welcome, fräulein.' He meant it too.

They sat and stared at each other. Ruth didn't know what to do; she smiled sheepishly and probably a bit too coy. Karl put his hand up to her face. Was she ever going to learn her lesson not to fraternise with the enemy? Her heart actually felt like it stopped when his hand met her cheek.

'*Ruth!*'

A scream was heard from the trees behind them. She jumped up, slipping on the sand, scrambling and stepping on the hem of her dress. *Helen.* Must she always be her Jiminy Cricket? She felt ill. Karl hadn't moved; he was still leaning on his elbow like he was on holiday, except he was looking away from them with the stiff neck of someone very conscious that they had done wrong.

Ruth was crying. She was upset with the situation and herself; it was annoyance and embarrassment at having been caught, but she was also sad at a broken moment. It wouldn't have been anything – they both knew that – but it was a 'goodbye and good luck' of sorts, no hard feelings.

'I'm sorry,' she managed.

As she walked away with Helen pulling her by the elbow, she heard him say, 'Farewell, Fräulein Ruth,' and then something in German she completely missed.

She pulled free of Helen, throwing all caution to the wind, and ran back to Karl. She knelt down in front of him, kissed him quick but deep, stroked his cheek, and ran away. Tears streaming, she ran past Helen, who had a wide-open mouth in horror and disbelief.

Ruth ran. She didn't know where she was aiming, but she just ran. She didn't stop at the huts; she kept going – up the dirt track, off the track, and down into a sandy gully of banana trees. She sat in the shade, catching her breath. She stayed there in the cool silence. She didn't care if people were looking for her or not. She just wanted to be back home so badly, to remember how to be herself, to be away from her irrational mind, the constant unknown, and back in her attic room.

Instead of going to find Helen or Alice, Ruth went to search for Mirren. She found her talking to one of the men who had led them ashore. They were talking earnestly but stopped and smiled as she approached.

'I was wondering if I could please trouble you for a pen and some paper,' Ruth asked Mirren.

Mirren nodded and said, 'I think you already know my husband from the night you landed.' She gestured towards the man.

He grinned and put out his hand.

Ruth shook it and said, 'Thank you very much. We owe you our lives and some.'

He beamed. 'Not at all, not at all. All in a day's work.'

She nodded with gratitude and turned back to Mirren, who said, 'I'll drop some pens and paper to you soon.'

Ruth nodded.

Mirren kept talking. 'We are just discussing some orders we have had from the German captain.'

Ruth winced.

'It's OK. Don't worry. We will sort it out. They have told us we can't contact anyone about the German raiders in the Pacific. Do you know anyone who can draw?'

Ruth was confused but replied, 'I can draw,' without thinking.

'Enough to capture what the ship looked like?'

Ruth nodded slowly. This was a secret war mission, but it probably meant going back to the beach. She had been trusted to the inner confidence of Mirren and her husband.

'We can't go back down to the beach. I was just there, and it is crawling with Germans,' she said – a white lie to save her more embarrassment.

'That's good to know,' Mirren continued. 'We can go on up the headland instead. The cows sometimes graze up there, so it won't cause suspicion.' Her train of thought kept flowing.

Her husband looked at her intently, memorising the plan. 'I'll fetch you paper and some drawing equipment, and you can pretend you can't resist drawing the views. If you're asked, that is,' he said.

They trusted her immediately and wholeheartedly. *For God's sake, don't mess this up, Ruth*, she thought. She started to doubt her ability to even draw a stick figure. She thought about the drawings she had sent Geoffrey. *What a stupid thing to send someone in the middle of a war.* She remembered why she had wanted to find Mirren in the first place. 'Do you have a post office on the island? I want to send to home. Can we get a message home? What's going to happen to us?'

She was getting panicked, but Mirren put her hand gently on her arm.

'Let's get the Germans off the island first,' Mirren said gently. 'Wait here so as not to arouse suspicion, and we will be back shortly.'

They walked back up the road to the homestead. Ruth sat down in the shade on the bigger hall steps. The place was busy with people, seemingly oblivious to their island setting, sitting and chatting or walking through. Were they not worried that they might never leave this place? She started to feel sick again and put her head down on her knees, trying to conjure up any remnants of home, her parents, her life before this. She was scared she had forgotten what everyone looked like. She pictured her father at the kitchen table with a cup of tea and a book. He could sit for hours with a book, much to her mother's annoyance sometimes. She pictured her mother fussing with Sunday lunch as she talked to Ruth and her father. She would either talk serious politics, mostly, or talk about other people's goings-on or, in fact, both.

She missed her home. If she ever got back, she swore she would never take it for granted again, though she knew she'd probably get lazy and complacent. She smiled to herself. She had made a couple of very poor choices, but nobody could say she'd taken things lying down. Maybe Grandma Hetty could be proud of her after all, especially if she was successfully able to draw a great replica of the raider.

Mirren returned, and she gave Ruth a big metal easel, a roll of what looked like parcel paper, some pencils, and a pen. Ruth had the funny thought that there had been art involved in almost all the crucial points of their journey, but this was a real expedition, a real war effort. She looked at Mirren and laughed. She was wearing a pair of far-too-big overalls and huge Wellington boots and was carrying a shepherd's crook.

'You look like a scarecrow.' She laughed out loud again.

Mirren giggled. 'That's the idea. We haven't got much time. Stop laughing at me.' She was laughing too, and they set out to follow the path along the waterfront and up to the headlands.

It was easy going along the sandy path, but they could hear the Germans on the beach, and Ruth was pleased she'd known to avoid it. The path got rougher under foot, with small shells and gravel. Then as they made their way up, the trees thinned out, and the terrain became rocky.

'There is grass at the top, but we just have to do a rock scramble first,' Mirren explained.

Ruth was worried about losing her footing. Mirren turned to take the load while Ruth climbed and then turned to do the same. It didn't take long to get up.

They stood and gazed down at the water, catching their breath. Ruth was disappointed that it wasn't as high up as it had seemed, but it was jutting further out, and foreshortening meant that the ship was in full, side on view. She set up and got to work, a sense of urgency coming over her. Looking at the ship, she had to turn off emotion and concentrate on the shapes. She chose to do a strong outline and as much detail of the ship's construction as possible. Mirren stood at her elbow; it was slightly distracting, but Ruth carried on.

'I think that the ships had contacts out there too,' she explained to Mirren. 'On occasion, another raider would pull alongside, and fuel and provisions were passed over.'

Mirren took a scrap of the paper and a pencil. 'Do you mind if I write while you talk? I think this kind of information will be helpful.'

Ruth nodded and carried on. 'We weren't allowed out at night, and sometimes we were locked in. Those were mostly the nights they sank other ships . . .' She paused, swallowed hard.

'It's OK if you can't,' Mirren said anxiously, but Ruth knew it was important to recount the details she knew. Then at least her times with Filip were not a total disaster, not totally heart-breaking.

She drew furiously and talked furiously. Talking about things was bringing back the form of the ship; she could draw the outside by referencing the times on board.

'I remember one night quite clearly. It was before they sank the ship where all the Australian men came on.'

Ruth paused and waited for Mirren to catch up. She had filled two pages already and was starting a new piece.

'I wasn't supposed to be out, but I was. It was in the half light of morning, and the German crew were down the sides of the boats on pulley things. I thought at first, they were just doing some maintenance, but it looked like they were painting different markings.'

Ruth stopped talking then and looked at her drawing, held it up in front, closed one eye, and compared it. She wasn't happy with it at all. She wasn't a realist, and she was envious of those who were.

Mirren said, 'That's what we had heard about raiders. Not much, in all honesty, but the rumours are that they repaint to look like peacetime ships going about their cargo-carrying business.' She looked grave.

The wind had picked up; it was warm and not very refreshing for a late afternoon or early evening, as the case was.

'Are you finished, do you think?'

Ruth nodded slowly, held it up one more time, making it the last time to ever look.

The walk back down was much easier, and even though they had a sheep and cow viewing and tourist story planned, no German stopped them. They were obviously very preoccupied with leaving in the morning.

She wondered how Karl was doing, wanted to reassure him that everything would be OK, but how could she? She was surprised that someone fighting with the Germans was scared and unwilling. She hadn't really thought of them with lives outside war, with homes and families to go back to. She was leading her wartime experience and assuming everyone on the other side was against them and enjoying it. She could hear their chatter through the trees. German always sounded cross, but there were bursts of laughter. *The island will feel better when they're gone*, she thought. It was going to be OK, she told herself in Grandma Hetty's stern but caring voice. *Now is not the time to collapse in a heap. You've come this far. Try to think about other things.* Now Grandma Hetty's voice was becoming too contrived, and Ruth thought she'd never stand for such sap. *Pull your socks up, Ruth – things to be done.*

Helen and Alice were sitting outside.

Ruth plopped down next to them and said, 'Did you ever think that the German soldiers don't want to be part of all this?'

Helen looked at her sideways. 'Where's this coming from, Ruth?' Helen was obviously concerned about witnessing the stolen kiss.

'Don't worry, Helen. That meant nothing other than we weren't enemies for that brief moment.' Ruth looked at Alice too; her head was bowed, and her expression was knowing. 'Helen obviously told you then?'

Alice nodded.

'You were talking about me?' It was an accusing question that came out harsher than Ruth intended, but Alice nodded again.

'We are worried about you, Ruth.' Alice said her name like she was pleading.

'Ah, don't worry about me. We have to get off this island and home now, yes? The three of us.'

Helen patted Alice's knee and smiled at Ruth. 'The three of us,' she said.

Alice said, 'We will have to get on another ship, won't we?'

'I don't see any way around that. Unless we stay here for the best part of the rest of the unknown,' Helen said, despairing. 'Which would you rather?'

Ruth was feeling more energised, but the thought of being sunk again filled her with dread. 'Perhaps . . .' Ruth offered. 'The fact that we were too much to cope with on board may mean that they're not blowing up other ships anymore? That word has spread?'

'Or they just don't take survivors anymore,' Alice said darkly.

There was that. They sat in silence again.

Chapter 21

In the morning, they were awoken by great shouts and applause and singing, an eruption of sound that yanked Ruth, bleary eyed, out of a rare peaceful slumber. She had a decent mattress and pillow and enjoyed going to bed immensely. She had got used to sleeping in and waking up to a leisurely breakfast and time to swan about for most of the day. The singing was louder, and she realised it was 'God Save the Queen'.

The three of them rushed out and down to the beach with some other stragglers. They were in time to see the last of the German row boats leaving, solemn-faced men off to serve their country again. *For what purpose? Half-starved in squalid conditions.* What were they really achieving out there? Obviously, the Earwig thought he was adding to the German war effort and winning the battles single-handedly. *Good riddance to bad rubbish*, she thought, and she joined in the singing with heart. Alice and Helen were also singing with all their might. It was an odd ragtag of people, mostly women, and they were not holding back, not exactly wishing the Germans 'bon voyage' but truly happy to see the back of them.

The two women who had helped them set up the clothes shop came up and stood next to them. Gita was grinning from ear to ear and doing little excited jumps every now and then. Iris was more reserved but still smiling. It was wonderful to look around and see smiling faces. Ruth caught sight of Mirren, and she was smiling and laughing with another group of prisoners. Ruth thought she should stop referring to themselves as prisoners. *Ex-prisoners? Stranded castaways?* Mirren looked somehow younger, a huge weight lifted off her shoulders.

'This is a good feeling,' Alice said.

'I feel better than I have in a long time,' Iris said. 'It's hope.'

Alice nodded and looked back out to where the rowboat was now just a smudge of black and a smudge of grey heading to the bigger smudge of grey. Ruth was going to remember every little detail, perhaps write it down for her grandchildren one day, but today it was good to just think of those dreadful times as a smudge.

Helen clicked her heels. 'Right!' She grinned. 'I believe a celebration feast was promised. Where do we start?'

There was a murmur of agreement from the other people standing around, and off they went to find out. Ruth was pleased that they were back to being ruled by their stomachs and not by shouting Germans.

It turned out that not only did Mirren and her husband directly disobey Kapitän Ewig's orders, but also, they hadn't even waited until they were off the island to call Australian officials to relay what had happened. Mirren was the centre of attention as they all ate. This wonderful woman and her husband had saved them, and they were forever in their debt.

'The range is so limited on the radio phone.' Mirren was breathless with the excitement of reliving the danger. 'We had to make extra cord and extend it further and further from the house each day. We buried it and worked at night.'

One woman asked, 'How did you manage to stay out of sight?'

Mirren explained, 'Most of the young officers were preoccupied drinking our liquor night after night, and the others were actually in bed by eight o'clock.' She laughed heartily at this and added, 'Imagine if Hitler found out they lost the war because most of his army were old grandads who needed their nightcaps and slippers.' Everyone laughed, and then she said, 'In all seriousness, we made contact with Australian officials the day before yesterday, and they are sending ships immediately to come and collect you. You're all famous!'

Applause and cheering went up at the back, and suddenly, everyone was clapping and dancing up and down.

Ruth couldn't muster the strength to get back on a ship. She had packed the night before, said a proper goodbye to Mirren, and vowed to write. Now her body wouldn't move. She was conflicted with yearning to be home but never, ever wanting to see a ship ever again, let alone set foot on one in her lifetime. There were two big ships in the distance, and even from the beach, she could see they were nothing like the raider, but her feet were firmly on the sand, her hands clutching the handles of the suitcase in a white knuckle grip. Helen was staunch beside her, and suddenly, Alice let out a whimper. It was like a little dog whose tail had been trodden on. Then she sat down and whimpered again.

'We have to do it, girl,' Iris said from behind them. 'We have to do it!' It was not exactly comforting, but Ruth assumed she was more telling herself than Alice.

'The three of us,' Ruth managed, again telling herself more than Alice. They were grouped in lots of twenty to get them on the lifeboats quickly. The Australian soldiers were extremely nice to them, and one came over to them to check.

'Can we do anything for you, miss?' a young tanned-faced and blond man asked.

Alice whimpered again, but Ruth wasn't so sure it was stress more than swoon.

'She will be all right in a minute, thank you.' Again, Iris was being efficient.

'Thank you for your concern,' Helen said politely. Then when the soldier turned to leave, she called him back. 'Excuse me. Can you please tell us a little bit about what to expect? I think it would help us immensely' – she gestured to poor Alice still crumpled in the sand – 'especially for the sake of none of us ever wanting to get on a ship again.'

The soldier grinned, white teeth against the dark skin. 'Sure, miss, sure.' His accent made him sound like he was saying 'sewer', and Ruth thought that he wasn't half wrong with the raider in mind. 'It won't take very long in our zippy little boats to get you onto the main boat. As you can see, you will be properly fitted with a life jacket.' He pointed down the beach to the next lot of people getting into boats. He continued, 'We will probably have something to eat ready by the time we get down to this end of the beach, and we will set off in the evening. Best time.' He searched their faces to see if that was enough information.

Helen nodded, satisfied. 'Thank you. You have been a great help indeed.'

The soldier tipped his hat and bowed a little bit. 'My pleasure,' he said, and then he turned towards the next lot of twenty and so on down the beach.

There were two more lots before them, and they more or less waited in silence, each with their own thoughts. Ruth was happy enough to stay here. Island life suited Mirren, so maybe it might suit her too. No, perhaps not – not Ruth. Where would she get all her clothes?

Gita had curled up on her coat and suitcase and gone to sleep.

Iris was shaking her. 'It's our turn now. Wake up! Wake up!'

Gita scrambled up, and a soldier in a hurry immediately put a life jacket on her. The soldier who helped Ruth into hers was even more in a hurry. Ruth gasped as he pulled and tugged and adjusted.

'All set, miss. Follow them down to the side of the boat. Don't get in yet.'

She giggled to herself as she waddled to the water's edge like a penguin. Alice couldn't reach her crutches over the padding. Poor thing – she really did try. Two soldiers put their arms round her, and she dangled off their necks down the beach. They more or less tipped her head first in and instantly felt so bad, they both jumped in and started fussing over her and fetching things to make her short journey more comfortable. Alice was grinning from ear to ear by this stage.

'It's OK, lads. Nothing I wouldn't do myself. How do you think I lost the foot in the first place?' she joked, but that made them fuss even more. 'I'm OK.' She was holding up her hand and smiling. 'Help the others. I'm fine, thank you.'

They jumped out and went back to life jacket strapping. *What a difference to be handled with care, as people.*

It was a much quicker and obviously far less dangerous journey than their previous trip in a lifeboat. They also didn't even have to get out of the boats to scramble up the ladders. The boats were hooked to big winches and heaved up, inch by inch. It did take a long time, but Ruth thought she probably wasn't alone in thinking that this slow process was better than anything else they'd experienced on the raider. Looking back, she had a great view of the island. It somehow looked even more overgrown and deserted, small and lonely from this distance. She was glad to be going, sick to the stomach with dread and worry but glad to be going.

'Do you think the Australian ships have better warning than the English ones?' she said to Helen.

'You mean like they'd be able to pick up the raiders' chatter or see them first?' Helen asked.

Ruth nodded.

'I'm scared too,' Helen whispered, clutching Ruth's arm and pulling her closer.

'Us three together,' they both said at once.

'Let's just hope – all we can do,' said Helen.

Ruth nodded and put her head on Helen's shoulder.

The first soldier had been right. By the time they made it onto the boat, a meal was ready in the dining area. It wasn't lavish, but at least it wasn't rotting mystery in a cup. There was lots of bread and a vegetable soup. It actually smelled delicious. The room was crowded but hushed, everyone still in the shocked, silent stage. Ruth supposed that once they relaxed into their journey, they'd be a lot more chatty.

'Are we going to England or Australia on this ship?' Alice asked quietly.

They didn't know, but the Australian soldiers had been so wonderful with anything they needed. Helen said she would find out later. Ruth was more concerned with the sleeping arrangements. She hoped to go straight home but also wished to see Australia as well. It was a shorter distance too; maybe if they covered short distances along the way and land-hopped, they would be less likely to be overrun by raiders. She had a good mind to go and tell the *kapitän*. She thought again, *He wouldn't be called that, would he?* He'd be Australian, so she assumed a captain like the British Navy. She wondered why she was giving it this much thought; it didn't matter.

Tea and coffee were put out on a table near the door, and they could help themselves. There was quite a crowd, so they waited, chatting quietly. A radio crackled suddenly and made them all jump, and a few shrieked. Being on a ship again made everyone on edge. It was the intercom, and the captain cleared his throat.

'I am Captain O'Brian, and Chief Officer Baldwin is my second in command.' He cleared his throat again – nerves? 'It is my responsibility and pleasure to return you, my precious cargo, back to England safely.' He said this with such gusto and heart that everyone cheered and clapped. 'It is my duty, but I consider it a great honour, and you are most welcome on our humble vessel. Godspeed.'

The microphone chirped again, but it was drowned out by the excited talking and clapping. They were headed home. Excitement was stuck in Ruth's throat; it was joy and anxiety. She was happy; she really was. Home had started to feel like a dream place that didn't actually exist. Ruth had almost resigned herself to never going back. Helen looked at her; the disbelief and uncertainty on her face said it all.

The dining room had been slowly emptying out. The crew had been calling table by table to register their names and home addresses, next of kin, and assign them a record number. Then they were being taken to the cabins. The three of them were sipping what Ruth was considering to be the best cup of tea she had ever had in her life. She was truly marking it up as a great moment.

'It seems funny to say the word "home", doesn't it?' Alice said. She was excited, and her smile nearly reached her ears. 'What is the first thing you are going to do? I mean, after we see everyone, of course.'

Helen scrunched up her chin and pursed her lips, thinking harder than

Ruth was about it. 'I think . . .' Helen paused. 'I think it would be nice to just sit alone, surrounded by my things, in my own space.' She was crying. 'Alone.' She said the word again, quieter.

Alice put her hand over Helen's. Ruth knew what she meant. Alone was the best, but completely alone was another thing entirely. Ruth didn't know what to say. There was really nothing. She shuffled closer to Helen and put her head on her shoulder.

'What are you going to do, Alice?' Ruth asked light-heartedly.

Alice beamed like she had a cunning plan.

It was very late by the time their table was processed and they were led to their cabins. The sailor showed them the wash facilities, and one of the women jumped for joy.

'If you're that excited about a loo, miss, then wait to see the beds,' the sailor said.

The word *beds* came out like *beads*, and Ruth was confused.

Alice giggled. 'What does that mean?' she hissed.

Ruth shrugged. Even after the relative comfort of island living, she was tired and just wanted it all to be over; the excitement was wearing her down now. The big metal doors seemed to be a feature of any ship, regardless of country of origin – also the confusing passages and stairwells. Their corridor had lots of doors off it and was obviously crew cabins they had given up for them.

'You're down this one, ladies. There are eight to a room.' He swung the door inwards. 'I am sorry to say that the lights are on timers, so I will shine my torch in here as best I can while you arrange yourselves.' Even in the dim light of the corridor, Ruth could see he blushed. 'I meant sort out where you will sleep before I leave,' he stammered.

Ruth lay in the bottom bunk, the one behind the inwards-swinging door. She thought she had probably willed it into happening, but as soon as she saw the door flung open by the crewman and hitting the side of the bed, she knew she was destined for one of those bunks. Alice was above her, having claimed claustrophobia, and Ruth was too tired to care or argue about how she'd get up and down with one foot. Helen was feet to feet with her on the next bunk. They hadn't known how to arrange themselves, as the crewman put it; they had just chosen bunks and let him move on. There had still been two more tables to process, and he needed to get back. Helen decided she didn't want a kick in the head and so chose to go feet end together.

It was taking Ruth a long time to wind down. She lay and listened to the others breathing and lightly snoring. She remembered the excitement of their first day at sea all those many months ago. She was desperately trying to muster the courage for another long time at sea. It was the thought of her mum and dad and even bad-tempered Trudi that kept her going. *Won't it be great to see them? Even Cook and Helen's family.* She was mercifully drifting off.

The lights flickered on in their cabin, and almost at the exact moment, the door swung inwards and – *bang!* – hit the bunk. Ruth was startled and almost fell out of bed. She heard Alice moan at the top.

'We set sail during the night!' a woman yelled into their cabin. 'No more island! We are on the way home!'

A sleepy, subtle cheer went round the room. Most people wanted to have found that out on their own after a sleep in – no chance with the lights coming on, anyway. Ruth slid off the bed and crumpled on the floor. She rubbed her eyes and tried to get motivated to be motivated. Others were doing the same. Alice had procured a fancy eye mask from one of the suitcases and had actually gone fast back to sleep. Ruth didn't have the heart to wake her but did worry about how Alice was to get out if nobody was here.

Helen stood up, hugged Ruth, and kissed her on the cheek. 'Morning, sunshine,' she said so cheerfully that Ruth almost laughed in her face. 'We are on the way home.' She grinned. 'Let's see what there is to eat!' She was like a child on holiday for the first time.

Ruth did want food, so she quickly got dressed and looked in the shiny metal that was supposed to be a mirror. *That will do for now.*

It was absolutely glorious to come out onto the deck, feel the breeze on their faces, and see the open water. It seemed freer; they seemed freer, just to be with the Australians, not in squalor and, for the most part, dressed appropriately. POW life was behind them, and even though they would probably never relax until they were safely on British soil, it was a wonderful feeling.

Helen squealed a little noise, like pinched air out of a balloon. 'Oh, Ruth . . .' She tailed off.

'I know,' Ruth said. 'Hard to explain, but we are feeling good.'

A crewman came up behind them. 'Morning, ladies.'

They turned, and he tipped his hat.

'Is there anything I can do for you?' he asked, the Australian accent making everything sound like 'e' was the only vowel. He smiled.

Their grins were ear to ear. *These boys*. Ruth grinned back; she couldn't help it. It was all so jolly.

'Could you please tell us if we are allowed breakfast and where to get it?' Helen asked.

'You are our VIP guests who are allowed anything your heart desires as long as we can get it, and if not, we will try hard for an alternative. It is our job to make you as comfortable as possible. Captain's orders!' He grinned again. 'Follow me.'

They went back along the deck and down into the corridor before entering the dining room they had been in the night before.

'Ladies.' He tipped his hat again, and they thanked him.

Buffet tables were to their left with platters of fruit, bread, and butter and what looked like delicious porridge with raisins and honey drizzle but smelled like dirty socks. They laughed; it was good to laugh. Bread and butter was still a luxury item to them, anyway, and the fruit was obviously from the island.

Chapter 22

Time seemed to go a lot faster on this ship. Ruth supposed it was knowledge of a real destination and also many more things to do. In the past few days, she and Helen had taken up playing poker in a big way. Alice wasn't so keen, which Ruth thought was a good thing as she could never seem to get the hands straight in her head – always betting high on absolutely nothing, not bluffing, just thinking she had things. Ruth saw her fold on two aces in her hand, with a third already dealt on the table. *Hopeless.*

She and Helen, however, had got quite good. They had a few decent wins under their belts, though they had both drawn the line at taking people's personal jewellery and trinkets. They played for odd coins and tokens and sometimes the odd pin badge, but it was more a thrill and a way to pass the time. It was a way to quell the fear of raider ships stalking them on their way over the open seas. The lady sitting opposite them was *um*-ing and *ah*-ing over her turn.

'You're first after the small blind, so you could check instead of fold? See what others do?' the lady next to her offered.

They were both older than them – forties, Ruth guessed – but the lady whose turn it was looked a lot older, especially when she rapped the table with her knuckles and shouted, 'Checkmate!' Everyone at the table laughed out loud. Ruth felt bad when the woman stormed off.

This time, they came away with two pounds, two tin tokens from a Sydney sightseeing attraction, and a tiny shamrock pin, and what Ruth was most pleased with was a small silk handkerchief with violets on it. Helen said she could have that and one token if she could have the rest. Ruth agreed. She felt like a child again. She had done similar trading for treasures in the playground that meant absolutely nothing outside the gates, but during school hours, the person with the most loot was king or queen. The Australian crew really were trying their best to treat them like royalty too, always asking if they needed anything. 'Anytime' and 'no worries' were their favourite things to say, and they meant it.

One sailor had said to them in passing, 'You know you're famous, don't you?'

They were baffled.

'The Emirau Island prisoners? You're all famous. Every newspaper wants your story, I can bet.'

They felt chuffed and a bit worried. Would they be mobbed? Helen quite fancied the idea and had got Ruth to help her pick out the outfit she would wear. She topped it with the shamrock pin, and when Ruth asked her why it meant so much to her, Helen began to cry.

'I'm sorry. It's a very sweet little pin. I was just wondering.' Ruth was confused.

'It's OK. It's just that Elliott's mum . . .' Helen stopped and sobbed even harder.

Ruth sat next to her on the ground as she couldn't crouch on the edge of the bunk without burying her chin in her chest.

'His mum put a pin just like this into his jacket lining . . .' she said, again unable to carry on.

Ruth was crying now too. Things were not OK. Every day Ruth had to stop herself from crying over what had happened to them. Helen had stood up remarkably; Ruth knew she would never have been as strong. Now she held her dear friend while she sobbed and sobbed.

Alice came in, and Helen cried even harder and, through the sobs, said, 'For . . . good . . . luck . . .'

Alice collapsed down next to them and hugged Helen too. What else was there to do?

It was late afternoon, and the day had been getting hotter and hotter. They were out on the deck, enjoying the sun lounges, when a loud voice boomed from above them.

'Land! Land ho!'

For some reason, this made Ruth and everyone else scramble off the chairs and rush to the side of the boat. They couldn't see anything, but it was exciting nonetheless. It hadn't been that long since they left the island. Ruth supposed it seemed that way as anything would feel shorter than the time they sailed the unknown.

'What land will it be?' Alice asked.

Ruth squinted out to sea but couldn't make anything out, not even a haze.

Helen said, 'Does it matter?'

Alice was indignant. 'Yes, it matters! I'm hoping it's closer to home than that godforsaken island at the end of the world.'

'Mirren wouldn't like to hear you call it godforsaken,' Ruth said slyly.

'Blow Mirren!'

Alice huffed away on her new steel-and-wooden crutches. They were slightly too tall, so she swung both legs as she went. Mirren had found them for her in the endless pile of paraphernalia she seemed to have in the homestead. Ruth knew Alice didn't mean anything; she was just anxious – and rightly so. Ruth was anxious too.

The crew had called them to the middle deck, where they could see and hear the captain from the top deck. It had an eerie resemblance to the Earwig's daily addresses, and it was making everyone uncomfortable. Fortunately, the news was good and not boasting of latest conquests, though later on in their time with the Earwig, he had resorted to past victories as there hadn't been a sinking for a good few days.

The Australian captain explained that they would be heading into Sydney Harbour. 'We will only be here two days as we stock and reset for our longer journey to London. You are welcome to get off the ship each day and look around. You are expected and very welcome.'

The three of them hurried down to their room to get dressed. There was going to be quite the celebration on board tonight as they entered the harbour, and everyone was extremely excited. They put on the outfits they had chosen before, and Ruth's stomach did a flip. She was genuinely excited.

Nobody wanted to be below deck; they wanted to get that first glimpse of land and then watch it get closer and closer. It was hot in the late afternoon sun, but the sea breeze was refreshing. Everything was more refreshing when they knew their fate. It was their luck that they were on the wrong side when land could be seen.

'Rotten luck. Trust us,' grumbled Alice, but she soon perked up when she saw just how close it was.

They only had a few hours left, and their feet would touch dry land again. Ruth didn't want to think about the much longer journey home. *Weeks, not just days.* Music had started playing, and they realised it was coming from the parade speakers. It was old jazz, but it was very upbeat and made their toes twitch. Soon, they were linking arms and twirling with everyone in sight. People were laughing and singing and clapping. It was wonderful, just what they needed. The crew joined them, and some of the sailors were quite good dancers. A ring formed around a couple who were performing a wonderful routine. The sailor would do a little routine and twirl, and the lady would copy. Then they'd join hands and do flips and all sorts like they had been dancing together for years.

The audience, including Ruth shouted, 'More, more!'

Everyone was cheering; it was amazing.

They danced for a long time, long into the evening. Ruth sat down to catch her breath and suddenly realised she was famished. They had danced and chatted and laughed past dinner and supper. There were still just as many people on the deck as there had been in the afternoon. She sat and looked for Helen or Alice. She spotted Alice sitting with a couple of other women and some members of the crew. She was proud of Alice and glad to see her having a good time. One foot and crutches made for some very funny dance moves, but she was up and happy, and that was all that mattered to Ruth. Helen was also sitting down; she looked more solemn and was talking close with an older woman whom Ruth recognised but didn't know. She wondered what they were talking about, but she could have a wild guess and say their experiences, swapping stories.

Ruth didn't want to think about things. Australia was in sight, and they were alive, but she couldn't help it – her parents, home, Geoffrey. Not knowing about Geoffrey was hard. She had been suppressing the thoughts of him on the front line. She would never know what happened to him; she wasn't his next of kin like Helen to Elliot. Ruth would keep that thought to herself – no point in being outwardly horrid. She couldn't help what passed through her mind, but she was grateful for being able to filter her thoughts.

Ruth looked back over at Alice. She was secretly hoping some kind of connection would form with one of the dashing crew members. *Only a few hours left on board.* Then the music stopped with an ear-splitting crackle.

A voice came over the speakers. 'Ahem. Sorry about that. Just thought I would give you a brief update on our status. We will anchor here for the night and row in tomorrow morning. Supper is now served in the captain's dining room. We hope you enjoy. Keep dancing.'

The music screeched back on. Everyone clapped and cheered. Ruth went to eat; she was starving and curious to see the captain's dining room. She asked a passing crew member and had to hide her giggle when he called her 'meese' and she imagined herself as a scurrying mouse.

The dining room was unnervingly like the dining room on board the raider. When she walked in, Ruth shuddered. However, the carpet was plush under foot, and pictures were framed in gold, including a large picture of the Queen at the head of the room. She was pleased to note that pictures of Hitler were nowhere and relaxed after her initial shock. The tables had been spread right across the room, so only half were accessible. On the other side was rather a grand wooden table with big chairs. When did a ship's captain have time to dine?

She picked up a plate and filled it with biscuits. *Shortbread. Like Cook makes.* She didn't feel bad taking as many as she did because there were at least twenty plates full of them and some sort of raisin loaf, but she left that. Then she poured herself a cup of tea. She had been the only one in there, but a few more people came as she left. She suddenly had the urge to be on her own. She wanted to enjoy her tea and biscuits and be alone with her thoughts. She figured it would have to be on the other side of the ship from where everyone was looking at the twinkling lights of land. She was careful not to choose a spot like her 'room' on the raider. Her thoughts were confused, and she tried to just concentrate on the biscuits and tea.

Chapter 23

The lights clicked on, and everyone groaned. Ruth rolled over and faced the room. She had actually come to bed after everyone else, which had surprised her. She hadn't realised the time at all, lost in thought. The only reason she had come in was that it got too chilly to be on deck.

One of the women asked the room, 'Are we to pack and take our suitcases, do you think?'

Nobody knew for sure, so when the morning knock came at their door, the poor young sailor was met with eight women in their nightclothes all chattering at him, his stunned face opening and closing like a drowning fish.

'Ladies, excuse me. Ladies. Ladies, if I may?'

They finally stopped and let him speak.

'We will be here for the next two nights. Please bring your suitcases. We have booked hotel rooms for you all.'

Everyone squealed and set about packing as fast as they could, and the poor sailor shut the door as fast as he could as well. Ruth grinned at Helen. She grinned with her cheeky shoulder lift and chin out, mischief in her eyes. It was pure excitement.

Ruth reached the edge to be helped into the long boat. It wasn't a big step, but she froze. Her legs decided they'd rather stay on the ship. The memory of the last time they had got off a big ship and into a small boat came flooding back. She began to shake all over.

'Meese, are you OK?'

She couldn't even laugh when she heard 'meese'. Her legs began to move again but took her backwards. She stepped on the women behind her and stumbled back onto the deck.

'Meese, what's wrong?'

She looked at the young sailor, but no words would come out. He helped her to lean against the wall and catch her breath.

After a while, she managed to say, 'I can't do it.' She gulped in air but couldn't breathe it out again. She kept gulping.

There was another voice, a woman. 'She's hyperventilating. Please get a cool wet cloth.' Then to Ruth, she said, 'Put your head on your knees. You're OK.'

The feeling of the cloth pressed firmly on the back of her neck made all the difference. Her breathing came back, and the calm voice of the woman talked her down.

'What did your mind say to you there?' she asked with kind, understanding eyes.

Ruth managed to talk again. 'I got a shock, a memory of the lifeboats.'

The woman nodded. 'Let's do it together. You're safe. We promise.'

Helen and Alice had saved her a seat. They couldn't get off to help but had seen everything.

Ruth thanked the woman, and she said, 'All in a day's work. You're welcome. Take care.' That was that.

Ruth cursed herself and her stupid mind. It kept failing her. She tried to concentrate on land and chat to Alice, who was almost leaping over the edge with excitement. Ruth realised she was talking about a man – 'Frank' this, 'Frank' that, 'Frank said', 'Frank did'. She tuned in a bit more, and Alice was saying something about Frank taking them somewhere.

'Frank told me that you can walk up the Harbour Bridge. You can get all strapped in and walk up one of the side supports. Oh, I'm going to do it. Will you come? Frank said he can take us all.'

Helen replied, 'I'll come. Something to say we did, isn't it?' She nudged Ruth. 'Isn't it?'

Ruth nodded and smiled at Alice.

Alice clapped her hands with glee. 'Frank said there are stairs, but the last part is a ladder, but he can lift me.'

Ruth nodded and smiled again, pleased for Alice but sick of Frank, whom she hadn't even laid eyes on yet. It was lovely to see and hear Alice so genuinely happy. They had all stopped being upbeat and just let things happen to them, given up expecting, even rescue. Now it was going to be different. Ruth nodded firmly to herself, set on the course for home.

They were received at the wharf with great fanfare and music and cheering, confetti everywhere. Ruth pondered on what the sailor had said about the Emirau Island POWs being famous. They were ushered to waiting rows of seats and sat while the next boats rolled in to the same pomp and circumstance. The women in the boats were waving and cheering, everyone was clapping, and the music got louder. Ruth just wanted to go to the hotel they were promised. She wasn't being ungrateful but surely wondered if all this hype was really necessary. Helen and Alice were clapping along and waving, and Alice was bumping off her seat to the beat of the music. Ruth sighed, relented, and joined in. It was hard not to.

They were facing a big raised stage with a podium and banners. Ruth was admiring the lovely dark blue drapes along the back when she realised it was the Australian flag, a shrunken version of the Union Jack. A soldier came on stage, tapped the microphone, and cleared his throat. The crowd hushed after a while, and he cleared his throat again. He introduced another man; Ruth wasn't listening, but the crowds behind them started to cheer and clap again. The man walked on stage; he looked official in a crisp suit. Ruth was too far back to see properly, and she felt she really didn't care. The man did drone on and on about the war and Australia's part in it, but he also said they were pleased and honoured to be host to 'the Emirau Island returnees', as if they'd just been misplaced for a moment. Australia had played a huge part in their rescue, and he said he was personally honoured to have them stay in Sydney. The crowd erupted again – more confetti.

It was very nice of everyone, and a lot of effort had been put into their arrival, but Ruth just kept thinking about the hotel bed. They were escorted as a big group down a wide red carpet and onto buses. The barriers were lined with people jostling to see them and to talk to them. Ruth was pleased she was in the middle of their group. Other women were pleased to talk, and she could hear them recounting everything, from the sinking to their experiences on the raider and the island and, one lady said, 'the brave and handsome rescue by the Australian navy', and there was giggling and cheering. Alice was finding it hard to stand up in the pressing crowd, and Ruth could tell she was getting over it.

'Let me take one crutch, and you lean on me, OK?' Ruth had got used to helping Alice when she needed and felt a slight pang.

'Why are you crying, Ruth?' Alice said in amazement. 'This is perhaps the best day of our lives! Well, I suppose a lot is left to come, but this day is a start! We are here to carry on and have the best days of our lives, yes?' She squeezed Ruth's arm.

Ruth nodded and laugh-cried. 'I just want to go to bed.'

Alice laughed and put her head on Ruth's shoulder. 'Me too, actually. Me too. Let's sleep for a week?'

There were more crowds of frantic press with flashing cameras at the hotel, men with the cameras right in some women's faces, yelling at them, 'Give us a twirl, ladies!' Some women were jostling to get pictures of themselves, but some were being quite roughly pulled aside to get an exclusive chat. Helen and Alice were both just slightly in front of her now, and Ruth felt panic rise up. She swallowed hard. *Come on, girl. You've been through worse than this.* She elbowed her way through, pretending she was being thrown about by the mass madness, and caught up to Helen.

'Hold my hand. Stick together so we can be bunked in one room, yeah?' Helen grinned and squeezed her hand.

Helen and her missions. Ruth was secretly pleased.

The hotel doors looked like the large picture windows on Oxford Street. Ruth got a flashback of all those years ago in the crowds there and her green jacket. She regretted not wearing it. It was too hot for the jacket anyway, much too hot, but it would have been comforting. Her grandmother was not one for too much emotion, too much sentiment, and she'd fake-gag at anyone. She would have loved the attention of the press – but then again, if she was a spy, perhaps not. Ruth was so tired, memories and people's faces swimming in her mind. As usual, she let Helen do the organising.

Alice said, a little frosty, 'She's using my foot as an excuse to get a room upgrade on the ground floor.' Then she added sadly, 'Or lack thereof. Ruth, I'm so tired.' She slumped where they were sitting, on low red velvet couches under a big floor lamp that was giving off too much heat; Ruth could feel her cheeks glowing red.

The crowds were not allowed inside the lobby, which was a small mercy, and they were left with the hotel staff, who quickly organised the few men in the party to their rooms and left the porters to organise the unruly women who were sick of standing in lines and being organised into groups. Some of them were being particularly difficult, and one even bopped an exasperated porter on the head, pushing his hat over his eyes. It was a rather comical sight, and there were a few quiet sniggers. Helen came over and plopped down next to them. She didn't even say, 'Excuse me,' to the other person sitting at the end of the couch.

Alice leaned forward and said, 'Pardon us,' but the lady harrumphed and turned her head.

Oh dear. We aren't being very polite as a whole, Ruth thought. She was very much sick and tired of everything too, and the waiting wasn't helping when the beds were so close yet so far away. 'What are they doing about rooms then?' she asked Helen hopefully.

'We just have to wait. The man at the desk said that there's two more hotels on this street that the group has been placed with, and if he can't find anything here, we might be moved.'

Alice groaned. 'Not on my account, please,' she begged. 'I could just stay here. Look, it's comfortable.' She leant her head on the armrest and shut her eyes.

Ruth sighed inwardly and tried to sound as upbeat as she could. 'It's going to be OK, Alice. Thank you, Helen, for organising us.'

Alice grunted.

In the end, they didn't have to move. They followed the porter down the long corridor behind the main desk. The lights were low, and the carpet was plush and squishy underfoot.

The porter said, 'These rooms are larger, but being on the ground floor, you have shared facilities. I hope that won't be a problem. They're very close to your room.'

He stopped and pointed at a door with a silhouette of a lady's head on it. Then he opened the door opposite and held it open as they piled in. He gave the key to Helen, and before she had even said 'thank' and 'you', he was briskly walking off, calling behind him, 'No worries.'

Ruth thought that 'no worries' must be a key phrase in Australia as all the sailors said it to them as well. 'No worries.' She grinned at Alice and Helen.

'No worries.' They both grinned back.

Their room was bright and airy and even had room for a little table and chairs by the big window. It looked onto a large leafy courtyard that opened out to a main area linked to the rest of the ground-floor rooms. The trees were lush. Ruth felt like they were in a rainforest. She turned back from looking out the window, and both Alice and Helen were, face first, plonked on their beds. Ruth took off her dress and followed suit. *Bliss.*

Chapter 24

Everyone was very eager to help in any way they could. The hotel staff were immaculate in their dress and manners. Ruth admired their smart dresses with small floral print that was barely distinguishable and made the material look textured and expensive. Some of the women were taking full advantage of having their every whim catered for. It was slightly embarrassing for everyone involved.

The three of them were out in the foyer, waiting for the infamous Frank. Alice was a complete jittery mess, though she was trying to hide it. The foyer was busy, but Alice suddenly gripped Helen's arm.

'He's here!' It was a squeakier voice than she had intended, and she cleared her throat before Frank got to them.

He wasn't as young and boyish as some of the other sailors, and his kind eyes had the beginnings of crow's feet when he smiled. He was in uniform and had his hat tucked under his left arm. He heartily shook their hands when Alice introduced them.

'Nice to meet you ladies. Are you ready for an adventure?'

Adventure is what got us here in the first place, Ruth thought, swallowing hard, but she grinned back, linked arms with Helen, and nodded as enthusiastically as she could. Frank held out his arm for Alice to take and then blushed when she moved her crutches round to take it.

'It's OK,' she said kindly and grinned with a cheeky smile. 'You can take my purse.'

They got to the ticket office at the bottom of the bridge quite quickly. The walk had been downhill, and the views of the harbour had been wonderful. Ruth looked around the kiosk and thought a postcard might be a nice idea to send home. The officials on the Australian boat had organised notifying their families, but she obviously hadn't written herself since Auckland. That was too long ago and too many memories ago to think about.

As she turned the postcard stand, she remembered. 'Helen, do you have any money?'

By the shocked and worried look on her face, she could tell that she had forgotten about money too. It had been too long ago that they might have forgotten how to even use it, let alone have any for Australia.

Helen poked Alice in the back and hissed, 'Do you have money in that purse of yours?'

Alice shook her head. 'No, it's just for show. It's completely empty.'

Helen winked at Ruth and patted Frank on the arm. 'Dear Frank...' she began, but Alice elbowed her out of the way.

'Frank, kind Frank, we have just realised we have no money between us...' She tailed off. That was the truth of it – no money.

After a lot of back-and-forth on Frank's part because he wanted to pay for them all, it was decided that Frank would pay for Alice and himself to go up only. However, he insisted on buying four postcards for them and walking them to the nearest café. They couldn't get around it and had to get over their embarrassment, especially when he walked into the busy café and announced they were Emirau Island survivors.

The head waiter came bustling up to them. 'Do sit, do sit. You're welcome here, and of course, everything you desire is on the house. So brave, so brave. Coffee? Cake?'

All they could do was nod and smile in gratitude.

Frank winked down at them. 'Enjoy your morning, ladies. Stay here as long as you want. We might be some time.' He smiled again – gentle eyes, not a dominating presence but a commanding energy about him.

They thanked him, and he went off to join Alice. Just how they were going to manage the stairs was beyond Ruth. *But not my problem*, she thought as she relaxed back into the wicker lounger.

'He's delicious,' Helen said with a mouthful of chocolate cake, not ladylike at all.

Ruth giggled. 'The cake?'

'He's smitten with Alice,' Helen continued, heaping more cake and cream onto her fork.

Ruth was surprised at herself for not doing the same. Normally, more than likely, she would have devoured the cake by now, but she just felt no stomach for it. 'I'm very pleased for her – but what to become of them when we are back in England?' Ruth nibbled her cake.

Helen nodded gravely, agreeing. She was obviously worried for Alice. Just as Ruth got a decent amount of cake nearly at her mouth, a voice at her elbow made her start.

'Excuse me. Do excuse me.' She smiled, prim in a tight box hat and neat gloves clutching a notepad with a gold pen. 'But there is conversation around the café that you are Emirau Island survivors?'

Ruth wiped her mouth on the napkin and glanced at Helen.

She was doing the same and answered, 'That's right.'

The lady stood up straighter and nodded. Then she raised her hand and beckoned someone else, saying, 'It's true!'

A man came rushing over with a camera that started flashing in their eyes.

'What was it like on board the raider? I heard they locked you below deck with no food and drink. Is that right? Left to stand and sit in your own filth?'

She spat the last question out vehemently. Ruth and Helen sat gobsmacked.

The lady continued. 'I heard that the captain tossed people overboard if they couldn't stand up. I heard the guards beat people with sticks. Did you get beaten? Did you know people thrown overboard?'

The questions weren't stopping; the camera wasn't stopping.

'Is it true that the island was a secret home to a resistance group who tricked the Germans to land there? Do you have names of these people?'

All the time, the camera was flashing; it seemed like hours, but it was probably only a matter of thirty seconds before the café manager came bowling over and bellowed at the reporters to leave them alone.

He kept yelling after them. 'I've got your names and numbers! You're barred for life! Miscreants!'

Helen and Ruth were still sitting in shock.

Helen looked at the café manager and burst into tears. 'It was as bad as they're saying.'

Ruth added dumbly, 'They got our pictures. Everyone is going to think we made it up.'

The café manager introduced himself as Bill and assured them that he, personally, would go and demand the camera film. 'I will also bring you more cake and make sure that you're safe here. I am sorry this happened to you.'

He walked away, and Ruth could see him slicing more cake behind the counter. She looked back at Helen, who was still teary eyed.

'It's OK, Helen. What does it matter? We know the truth. Let's use the postcards to tell home we are safe and well and heading their way.'

Helen smiled weakly and nodded. Ruth wrote on one that had a grand view of the whole harbour on it. It was hard not to pour her whole heart out onto the tiny piece of card, but it was also hard to know where to start, what to say. She flipped the card back and forth while she thought. Bill brought the cake, and they thanked him. This time, she ate.

They had been at the café for well over two hours, but they were reluctant to leave the shelter that Bill had created for them. The other patrons had looked on in sympathy and had become nodding and smiling reassurances but gave them their space.

Helen had written furiously on both postcards and numbered the sides one to four. 'I wrote on the front too. It just kept spilling out.'

'Is it to your parents?'

Helen nodded.

'I have written to mine, but I assume they will be in touch with yours and can be more informed.'

Helen nodded again. 'Who is the other one for then?'

Ruth was coy.

Helen smirked. 'Don't say it's for Filip. What a waste. I doubt he even gave you the right address.'

Ruth was offended and huffed, turning her back on Helen, and looked out the window to the busy street. She saw Alice and Frank coming towards them and waved. Alice looked so happy; it really was wonderful to see. Ruth's heart was heavy but pleased at the same time. Maybe it was too much cake in the end. They pulled up two more chairs, and Bill was immediately there with tea and cake for Alice and Frank.

'My dear girl!' Bill exclaimed. 'You have no foot!'

Alice giggled. 'No, I know.'

Bill looked apologetic but didn't say anything more.

Ruth was still huffy at Helen, but she tried to enjoy the conversation around the table. The postcard wasn't for Filip. She thought about Geoffrey every day and had written to the RAF contact he had given her all that time ago in New Zealand. Now, after months at sea and on a remote island, they were only a stone's throw away from where they had left off. Ruth felt like she could enjoy Sydney; it felt like a comfortable hustle and bustle which she preferred to the hectic nature of the inner London streets.

Frank suggested, 'A walk around the harbour front and take some tourist photos?'

He was eager to please, and Ruth suspected he was keen to see some boats and planes. They agreed and said a fond farewell to Bill and thanked him immensely. Ruth took note of his address and the café name, Café Rosa. They walked arm in arm again. Ruth didn't want to be huffy anymore; the effort it took was not worth it, especially when Helen had no idea. The street was full of men in uniforms, mostly navy, but a few were different. They were all very chipper and loud. Some of them were barely out of their school uniforms; they were so young. Ruth hoped they stayed happy and stationed here away from any action.

Chapter 25

Ruth was sick of meandering around, and her feet hurt. Frank had been talking to everyone and taking photos, making them pose with him. Ruth was fed up, and she could tell Helen was well over it, and Alice was trying to keep a brave face, but her stamina was fast running out too.

'May we sit down, please, Frank?' Alice said, pleading a bit.

'My love, oh, I'm sorry, look at you! I got too overexcited.' He looked around at where they were. 'Let's get to the main road, and I'll flag down a taxi for us. I'm so sorry.' He looked at Helen and Ruth. 'Forgive me. I am too eager when it comes to the armed forces.' He genuinely meant it.

They forgave him.

'We don't have the money for a taxi. If I just sit for ten minutes, we can walk back.'

Frank shook his head, kissed her lightly on the cheek, whispered something in her ear that made her giggle, and said, 'No, no, not at all. My entourage of princesses do not walk!'

The taxi pulled up, and they piled in; Frank sat in the front and laughed the whole way back to the hotel. Alice grinned from ear to ear, and Helen laid her head on Ruth's shoulder; it had been a good day in the grand scheme of things.

After supper, they were heading back to their room when Alice announced, 'I'm going out with Frank tonight. Just us. Help me to find something to wear!'

Helen squealed.

'Don't make a fuss, Helen. Don't.' Alice was smiling. 'But please make a fuss. I'm giddy with excitement.'

They tittered and tattered and truly fussed over Alice. In the end, she looked sparkling – with her hair done, makeup neat as a pin thanks to Helen, and a mashup of all their pieces of clothing.

Alice sat down on the end of the bed. She looked pensive and worried. 'I'm going to be alone with him.' Then she giggled. 'I'll be OK, won't I?'

Helen looked at Ruth.

Ruth shrugged. Did she mean safety wise? 'You're safe with Frank.'

Alice was tearing up.

'Don't smudge your makeup,' Helen said a bit sharply. 'I worked hard on that.'

'Sorry. It's just that he lives here, I live miles away, and the bloody never-ending war.' She sobbed.

Helen rolled her eyes but let her cry on her shoulder. It was dreadfully unfair.

'We still have two more days,' Ruth suggested hopefully. She thought that might be a reassurance to make the most of them, but Alice wept even harder.

Ruth was exhausted. They'd planned to go back out to sightsee some more tomorrow. Frank had assured them no boats or planes this time, but Ruth just wanted to stay in bed all day. That would be a complete treat. Helen was pottering about, getting ready to go to bed, and Ruth was already under the soft and luxurious covers. After what they had been used to, anything would have been marvellous. She snuggled down and closed her eyes.

'You know, that postcard wasn't for Filip,' she murmured.

'Oh?' Helen replied, uncaring.

'Just thought you should know.'

'Mmm,' Helen replied with only half a reassurance that she believed Ruth.

It didn't matter, really, but she desired nothing more than to forget that dreadful man, and the last thing she wanted was her friend to think she was still mourning his betrayal. She sometimes wondered what became of the men on the ship. Most of them were very fine men, and some were quite ancient. She sent a silent thought and hope out to the world that they were all OK, including Filip. She didn't wish him that much ill will, just a bit of discomfort.

'Ruth, Ruth, *Ruth!*'

The shouting in her ear was mixed with her dream. She was in the middle of nowhere, unfamiliar and lost; she couldn't tell where the voice was coming from. She woke up more but forgot where she was; the room was not familiar at all. The yelling was panicked; it was Helen.

'What? I'm awake. What is it?'

Helen was white. 'Alice hasn't been home.'

The permanent knot in her stomach, clenched from months of unknown, seemed to rise up and strangle her. What time was it? Maybe she had gone for a walk, but her bed was not disturbed at all. The little clock next to the bed said just past eight. *Oh dear.* They had assured her she would be OK with Frank, convinced themselves too, and just gone to bed without a care while their friend was at the mercy of a stranger.

'Get dressed,' Ruth suggested, 'quickly, and we can go out and look.'

Where? She had no idea, but it was something. Ruth had a sudden memory of the time she thought Alice was dead in a ditch and the panic attack it caused. She breathed hard. *It won't happen again. We've been through worse now.* She was reassuring herself in her head.

They were ready and racing down the hallway. A porter tried to ask if they needed anything, but they bowled past him like a cartoon whirlwind and left him spinning in their wake. Left or right – it didn't really matter. They went left. They couldn't run along shouting her name, but they were running for some reason.

Helen pulled back. 'Stop. We need to think.' She was panting. 'Shouldn't we go and find a restaurant close by and ask if they'd been in last night? Then do the same down the other side of the street?'

Ruth agreed. 'You're right. Wouldn't have been able to walk far if they didn't catch a taxi.'

The first restaurant was closed. They decided they wouldn't have gone in there as it didn't look romantic enough. Ruth managed to see the humour in their logic, panicked as they were. On the opposite side of the road was a likely looking place, but it was also closed. They crossed back over the road, which was surprisingly busy for early in the morning, and they heard shouting. They stopped in the middle to let bikes pass and a milk van, and a decrepit-looking policeman came up to greet them on the other side.

'That was very dangerous, young ladies.' He was older than the oldest person in the world; what was he going to do about it if anything did happen?

'Sorry,' Helen said politely. 'We won't do it again. Have a good day.'

They walked back down the road giggling; it was rude. They felt like naughty schoolgirls.

'He could have helped us,' Helen said.

'Did you see how old he was? Not a chance,' Ruth replied.

They were somehow not as panicked after their laugh over the old policeman. They were walking now, and Ruth was sorry they had no money and that it was too early in the morning. Some of the clothes shops looked very inviting. She pulled back on Helen's elbow in front of one shop window, and as she gazed longingly at the clothes, a familiar person came into view in the reflection.

Ruth turned around and yelled, making Helen jump and stumble, 'Alice! Where have you been?'

Alice was grinning, and Frank was grinning, but they both looked like they hadn't slept.

'Let's go back to the hotel for breakfast,' Alice said, calm and cool as a cucumber.

Ruth was a little bit angry at her, but she didn't say anything.

'Where have you been?' Helen repeated. 'We were so worried. We were looking for you.'

'Well, not very hard, by the looks.' Alice smiled even bigger and said, 'We will tell you at breakfast. Come on. I'm starving,' and she and Frank were linked arm and arm with crutch and fair-galloped down the road.

Helen said, 'They've had a lot of practice at that, by the looks.'

Ruth agreed. *A handsome couple indeed.* Her stomach was also calling for breakfast, so they hurried after them.

Helen dropped her fork in surprise. It landed with a clatter and a mess of scrambled eggs on the tablecloth. Ruth couldn't work out why she felt sad and elated all at the same time and just sat silently, staring at Alice and Frank. They stared back.

'Are either of you going to say anything?' Alice asked indignantly. 'I tell you the biggest news of my life, and you're both silent.'

Ruth started. 'Of course, of course . . .' She tailed off and started again. 'I'm so very happy for you. This is amazing.' She was truly pleased.

Helen picked up her fork and started eating again. 'What's amazing?' she asked.

Alice made a little cry-squeal, upset at Helen responding to the news of her and Frank's engagement.

'The ceremony is this afternoon? We leave tonight. It's not possible.' Helen was cross, and Ruth couldn't understand why.

Alice started to cry.

Frank explained, 'It's quite possible. We want you both there. It would mean the world to us.'

Ruth grinned; it was thrilling, a wedding to plan and execute in just a few hours.

Frank looked at his watch. 'I must go and make a few phone calls. I will be back in the lobby in two hours with everything that you will need.'

He scribbled on the back of an envelope and handed it to Alice. 'This is my sister-in-law's name and address. I will call her to expect you. I know she will have a wonderful dress for you.' He kissed her hand and then her cheek. 'See you soon, ladies. Have a good morning.' He left swiftly.

'Well, I don't care what you two want to do. I'm going to get my wedding dress. Frank gave me money, and I intend to spend it.'

Helen was looking down at her plate, but Ruth replied, 'I want to come. I'm so very thrilled for you. This is so exciting.'

Helen lifted her head, looked at Alice. 'Me too.' She had a sad smile.

'I'm sorry, Helen. I know it's painful. I don't expect you to be happy for me, but it will mean everything to me to have your approval.'

Ruth was holding her breath, but Helen smiled weakly and said, 'Of course, you have my approval. You don't need it, but you have it. The three of us together. Plus Frank. Poor Frank will have his work cut out. Does he know it's three for the price of one?'

Alice giggled, but Ruth thought it was actually quite true. They had become one another's worlds; it would be hard for anyone to come in, let alone a strange man.

The taxi took them all the way out to the suburbs – wooden houses with deep verandas and big gardens, straight roads with them lined on each side. Ruth thought it was odd that they had so much space but the houses were crammed right next to each other. They were pretty, and the backdrop of tall, tall trees was very picturesque. She imagined living in one of her own as the taxi pulled up outside. She couldn't picture who she was living with. *Possibly alone. Maybe Helen and me alone together. The maybe widow and the spinster.*

A plump and excited-looking woman came running out of the house. She threw her arms around Alice and exclaimed, 'So wonderful to meet you, darling, darling Alice!' She looked over Alice's shoulder, still excitedly yelling, 'You must be Helen and Ruth! It's so very exciting to meet you all! Frank has told me everything and nothing!' She leant into the taxi and said, 'No need to wait. I will run them back, thank you.'

Ruth had visions of her running them over; she was so excited.

'We don't have much time,' she said as she slapped the back of the car on its way. 'I have a great dress if you love it. If you love it, I'll take it in for you.'

They walked up the path and in through the open door. The corridor was dark, but it opened out to a bright kitchen and side room at the back. The house was a complete mess, not dirty, just things absolutely everywhere.

'Sit down, sit down. There really is no time to waste. Wait there.'

They moved piles of books and material off the end of the sofa and sat squeezed together.

'What's her name?' Helen hissed at Alice.

'Lucy. She's Frank's elder brother's wife.'

Ruth giggled. 'She's lovely.'

True to her word, Lucy came up with a lovely cream dress that she adjusted so quickly and so perfectly, you would have thought it had been tailor-made for Alice.

Alice was grinning from ear to ear, and Lucy kept repeating, 'This is going to be such a happy union.' Ruth believed it too.

Lucy turned to Helen and Ruth, who were still sitting on the crowded sofa. 'Can you please go into the back garden and pick low-hanging gum tree branches and some of the red bottle brushes? I will quickly make a bouquet for Alice. There's also some sweet-smelling jasmine out there too.'

She handed Ruth some big scissors and opened the back door. Helen and Ruth obediently went outside. They heard Lucy say, 'I want to have a sister-to-sister chat with you . . .' before the door closed. Helen looked as bemused as Ruth felt. They looked around the garden.

'I know what jasmine is,' said Ruth.

They looked down the side of the house and found the jasmine growing along the fence line, but they had no idea what a gum or a bottle brush looked like.

'Well, after all we've been through, it's a couple of plants that's going to be the end of us,' Helen said after they had been out there for quite some time.

They decided on some green foliage that had nice long leaves and the silver coin–looking leaves of the tall trees. Quite what Lucy was going to do to make these look like a wedding bouquet was beyond them.

'Well and truly stumped.'

Ruth agreed. They giggled. It was nice to be in cahoots with Helen again.

Lucy trimmed and arranged their garden clippings into a fine little flowing bouquet that elegantly swept over Alice's hands. She tied it with the off cuts of the hemmed dress, and it looked absolutely perfect. Who was this magical woman in a cluttered house on the outskirts of Sydney?

The whole thing was so bizarre feeling, so surreal, and it got even more so when Lucy said, 'Right. To the truck! Everyone in!'

Lucy was in the driver's seat. Alice squeezed in next and then Helen and then Ruth, who had to lean so far out to shut the door, she almost fell out. The truck was so noisy, they couldn't talk and so bumpy, they had to concentrate to hold one another down from bouncing through the windscreen. Lucy was in a hurry. It was an urgent matter – time wasn't on their side – but Ruth was nervous they wouldn't make it at all. Alice looked so sweet in her dress; they'd all got a lot skinnier over the months, and Ruth really saw the effects in her friends. The three of them were together – and now this wedding to be excited about.

Hopefully, they would have a bit of time to do their hair and makeup. She still had the lovely little lipstick tucked in any outfit with a pocket. Today its weight was a comfort in her blazer pocket. She had taken the little jacket from the last of the clothes at the island shop. It was tight on her – must have been a young girl's. She had originally liked the little embroidered pansy on the breast pocket, but then she couldn't put it down. She'd had a dreadful feeling that if she didn't take it to look after, the original owner would meet some terrible fate. She'd also thought within an instant that they may already be dead, and at that point, she couldn't bring herself to put the jacket down at all. She felt she owed it to the girl, whom she had never met. She could feel the lipstick pressed against her thigh and Helen's. Each time they turned a corner, it dug in more. A lipstick was easily misplaced, but a blazer that came in a whole, unclaimed suitcase – that was a different story.

'What's the time?' Ruth yelled over the roar of the truck, but Lucy didn't hear her.

They pulled up outside the hotel, and the concierge on the forecourt gave them a sceptical glance.

When they all piled out, he realised who they were and what was happening, and he said grandly, 'Ladies, if you'd follow me, please, your room is waiting for you.'

Lucy called from the driver's window, 'I'll be back for the wedding part!'

They shouted, 'Thank you!' over the top of the engine noise that was even louder outside the truck than in, but she had rumbled off.

'Right this way, ladies.'

They were swept through the front lobby up in the lift to the eighth floor. When the lift doors opened, the view of the harbour through a large window directly opposite was amazing. Ruth wished she had a photographic memory. Along the corridor, the concierge opened a grand room and let them past first. Alice squealed in delight, and Helen and Ruth just stood in amazement at the opulence of it all.

'I'll knock on the door when they are ready for you downstairs.'

They thanked him and turned back into the room.

'Look! Champagne!' Helen grabbed it and popped the cork immediately. 'Oh, Alice! *Who* are you marrying? This is wonderful.' She poured them each an overflowing glass and threw hers back almost to empty.

Alice stood at the full-length mirror with the big window next to her. Even if everything was normal, she would have looked beautiful, but somehow, on this day, after everything, she looked like a movie star.

'Let's get your hair and makeup done. Our bags have been moved. Look!'

There they were, neatly stacked by the door. Ruth felt embarrassed; her belongings had been all over the bed and floor. *Careless.*

They'd had a glass and a half of champagne each and were happily chattering away when the knock came at the door.

'Ladies, if you would come out and follow me, please?' the muffled voice said.

Alice took a deep breath in and beamed at them. She was really doing this. *What utter madness – but so romantic.*

The concierge beamed back at her and said, 'Beautiful, beautiful bride.' Then looking at the bouquet Ruth was holding, he said, 'Aha. Lovely. Jasmine for purity, beauty, and love. Perfect.'

Ruth thought it odd to put so much meaning into a flower they had scavenged from the garden only hours before, but the sentiment was nice. She imagined him talking to his plants in a big greenhouse; he seemed like the grandfather type to talk to plants.

Helen pushed her from behind. 'What are you waiting for?'

Ruth scurried after Alice, who was racing on her crutches, eager to be at the altar. Lucy met them in the lift. She was transformed. Her flyaway hair was in ringlets and pinned to the side of her head. Her makeup was modern; her bright red lips were flawless. She was like a different person in a silky powder-blue dress with a swish-able skirt.

'Let's do this, kiddos.' She was genuinely excited.

Chapter 26

'I don't mean to sound rude, my love, but can you walk on your bung leg?' Lucy asked.

Alice was silent. The lift ride seemed to be taking a long time.

'I'm sorry, hun.' Lucy was sorry she had asked. 'Only we were thinking that you'd like to be walked down the aisle by Ruth and Helen.'

Alice smiled wistfully. 'OK, yes. I can do that.'

'Good girl.' Lucy was cheered again.

The lift opened behind the stairs in the lobby, but when they turned the corner, the whole entrance had been transformed. Ruth gasped; it was truly magnificent. Frank stood beaming at the end of the aisle by the front desk. There were garlands of beautiful flowers right across the desk and down the aisle. Frank was standing with another man who couldn't be anyone else but his brother. They were identical except for the fact that Frank had black hair and his brother's was salt-and-pepper grey. There were no chairs, but the hotel staff were standing like guests on either side of the aisle. Ruth took Alice's good side so she could hold her bouquet in front of her. Helen adjusted herself to brace Alice on the other side, and they walked. The wedding march started playing, and they realised there was a small chamber orchestra. Alice was shaking. Ruth and Helen were crying; it really was beautiful.

Alice stood without crutches the whole ceremony. Frank held her hands the entire way through. Everyone clapped so hard when they were announced husband and wife, and they all cheered and hooted when Frank scooped Alice up in his arms and danced her back down the aisle. Ruth couldn't stop smiling. She felt so happy for Alice; it seemed like something out of a dream.

The six of them all piled into the hotel bar for celebration drinks. Ruth was starving, but there was only flowing alcohol to keep the wolf from the door. Their excited chatter and laughing managed to clear out the bar except for a table of sailors and young women who joined them in the festivities. They didn't need much encouragement, especially when Frank said it was all on him.

Helen whispered at Ruth, 'Do you think his family is wealthy?'

It wasn't as quiet as she'd hoped, and Lucy overheard. She tapped her finger to the side of her nose and nodded, eyebrows raised.

Ruth wondered what would make a family so wealthy. 'Are they wealthy enough to get us food? I'm really hungry,' Ruth blurted.

This made Alice laugh and laugh. Everyone was laughing, but Ruth was indignant.

'I'm so hungry, I can't go on.'

Frank patted her on the back and called over her shoulder, 'Can we please be served our entrées?'

Everyone ate, including the table of wedding crashers.

Ruth was spinning. The hotel bar was still a cacophony of wedding celebrations, and more people had shown up. Alice was having a wonderful time, which meant everything to Ruth, and Helen even seemed to be enjoying herself very much. Ruth was delighted but also rather woozy. She sat down at the bar and smiled weakly at the bartender.

He smiled back. 'Bit worse for wears there, are you? I'll make you a pick-me-up, shall I?'

Ruth clutched her stomach and shook her head.

'Aha. OK.' He laughed a rumble laugh that came from his portly belly. 'A soda and lime coming up. The bubbles will make you feel better.'

She sipped through the mountain of ice in the glass and watched the festivities.

Lucy came and sat by her. 'OK there, girl?'

Ruth nodded and smiled. 'Bit tired. Sore feet.'

'Ah,' Lucy said knowingly. She grinned at Ruth. 'Lovely, just lovely. Cracking.'

Ruth felt like she had known Lucy for years, and so the next question, fuelled by alcohol, came out before she could stop it. 'Kingsford-Ross sounds like royalty. Are Frank and his brother Australian royalty? Is that the same as the British royal family?'

Lucy almost fell off the seat laughing. Ruth was embarrassed.

'It's true, the family is wealthy – but not royal, no.' Lucy was still laughing a bit. 'Imagine me as royalty. I'd be exiled. Mind you, you probably thought I already had been by the state of my house.' She started laughing again, but Ruth felt rather silly.

'Well, can I ask about the money then, or is that rude?' She normally wouldn't have asked, but she was so curious at what Alice had married into.

'It was gold. The Australian gold rush with their great-grandparents.

Then that turned into large investments until their father owned a hardware shop and a greengrocer's. He met their mother's family through their rich "goings-on"' – she said it rather sarcastically – 'and married into old money on her side.'

Lucy was wistful, far away, retelling a family story. Ruth wished she wasn't so woozy; she was interested and wanted to remember.

'The boys have never wanted for anything. They embraced it, but both worked in the hardware shop as soon as they could. You'll not meet more generous men.' She continued, seemingly without breath. 'Me? I would have wanted out of it so fast. Money makes me uncomfortable for some reason. I do owe my parents a lot for such a positive upbringing regardless, but the simple life's for me and Doug.' Lucy took a breath. 'Frank has a big house. He has staff to keep his gardens and a housekeeper. I'm glad he has a wife to fill it now. That's so lovely, isn't it?'

Ruth's heart missed a beat. She was going to have to leave Alice here, wasn't she? It was all too much for her, and she got up fast. The room started spinning, and she plopped back down.

'Easy does it,' Lucy slurred.

'I'm going to bed, I think.'

Ruth went to find Alice and Helen in the big crowd that had formed on the little wooden square of a dance floor. She gave Alice a huge hug, and Helen came up behind her so Alice was in the middle of a big bear hug.

'Thank you, my two best people in the world. Thank you.'

'You're a beautiful bride. See you in the morning, beautiful bride.'

Ruth hugged her again and tottered down past the reception desk to their room. She realised she hadn't done a stick of packing. They had to be back on board the ship in the morning.

Chapter 27

'What on earth were you doing with all our clothes last night, Ruth?'

Ruth's head hurt so much, and she couldn't open her left eye very well. 'I have no idea. I think I thought I was packing.'

Helen giggled. 'Silly drunken goose. At least we don't have to be on the ship until the afternoon.'

Ruth wasn't so sure, but she felt she couldn't be a reliable source of information at this point in time. Ruth groaned and lay back down on the pile of things on her bed.

Helen did the same. 'I wonder how the newlyweds are.'

Alice and Frank had obviously spent the night in the luxury room that they had got ready in. Ruth was remembering the remnants of the end of the night, the conversation she was having with Lucy. The pile of clothes on Alice's bed suddenly groaned loudly and sat up. Helen and Ruth screamed out in shock and then started to giggle as a bedraggled Lucy appeared from under everything.

'What on earth are you doing here?' Ruth was still laughing.

Lucy laughed too. 'Well, I was in a right state, wasn't I? With a brother-in-law and husband who provided bottomless bubbles . . .'

This made the three of them giggle again.

'Alice brought me down here. You girls were snoring like troopers.'

It was so nice to laugh; it was so nice to not be worried, scared, and sad all the time.

'Oh no!' Helen jumped to her feet. 'Are you sure it's embarking this evening, Ruth?'

'No? You were the one who said that. I think it's this morning!'

'Quick. Run to the front desk. I'm in my night clothes!' Helen was scrambling.

'So am I. Why should I go?' Ruth said crossly, throwing her things in her case without a care in the world for creases.

'You should go, madam, because you are dressed.'

Helen was laughing again, and Ruth looked down and saw she was indeed still dressed in the clothes from the wedding. Now she was laughing too, and Lucy was just making groaning, grunting laugh noises. She was in no fit state to go. So with her head pounding but laughter in her heart, she rushed down the corridor.

The porter at the desk looked at her just as she imagined he would – somewhat amused, somewhat cross, and mostly just shameful embarrassment at the mess of fluster in front of him. He calmly said, 'No need to worry, miss. The coach will come for you at seven in the evening.'

She thanked him but turned back; a cheeky idea had come to her. 'By the way, could we please have coffee and cake for three sent to our room? Please charge it to the Kingsford-Ross and company account.'

She smiled sweetly, but the porter still gave her a suspicious look. 'Certainly, miss. Right away.'

She felt like she was a naughty schoolgirl but hoped it would work all the same. After all, there was a Kingsford-Ross in their room, just not the one.

They were more relaxed knowing they had the whole day. They were enjoying wallowing in their post-drunken haze when the room service knocked on the door.

'Coffee and cake as requested, ladies. Mr Kingsford-Ross was most obliging for what he assumed was Ms Lucy's orders?' He was smirking at the cheekiness but not angry.

They gleefully took the tray and thanked him.

'Did you do this?'

Ruth nodded. Lucy was impressed. They went back to their beds and enjoyed a good hour of gossip and lazing about. It was an amazing feeling, and Ruth was genuinely feeling so happy, but there were niggling feelings of sadness and regret. She wanted to squash them and enjoy the time, but they ate away at the edges of the happiness.

'There's a faraway look on your face, darl,' Lucy said, interested and concerned at the same time. 'A penny for your thoughts, as they say?'

Ruth smiled. 'I'm just thinking how brief this wonderful time has been and how long the harrowing times were.'

Lucy smiled and patted her knee.

'I don't want to go on that boat without our Alice,' Helen said suddenly, surprising them.

'We need to get dressed and go knock them up then, don't we?' Lucy exclaimed, slapping her hand on the bed as a call to action.

Alice answered the door in a beautiful silk flowing dressing gown with embroidered flowers all over it. It really was lovely, and she looked lovely and so happy. Ruth's heart panged. She wanted desperately to be happy. It didn't mean that she wanted what Alice had; she just wanted to be happy like Alice was. She was pleased for her friend and felt rotten for being envious. She gave Alice a big hug.

'You're right into the hugging at the moment, Ruth. You still drunk?' She was laughing, but it was a serious question.

'No, silly. Just happy to see you so happy and want to hold on to you for as long as possible, seeing as you're staying and we go tonight.'

Alice's face dropped. 'Oh, that's right.'

Helen ran and hugged her this time, head on her shoulder like a child would bury their head on their mother's shoulder.

'Oh, do stop it, you two!' Alice said. She was upset herself but didn't want the fuss.

Frank came through the door in a cheese-cutter hat and a newspaper tucked under his arm. It was odd to see him out of uniform, and it made him look like an errand boy. 'Good morning, ladies, and . . .' He smirked and looked at Lucy. 'And gentleman.'

She pushed him playfully. 'Darling, we were thinking we could all go and do something splendid before Helen and Ruth have to get on the ship.' She was calling for Frank's suggestion.

They went back to pack and left their cases with the lobby assistant for the day. Everyone was still being most obliging. They waited in the lobby for the rest of the Kingsford-Ross party. Ruth was being a snob, and she knew it, but it was so much fun to know a real-life millionaire. Lucy had gone quickly to meet a friend. Ruth had marvelled at her ability to throw on last night's clothes and run her fingers through her hair without a care or second thought as to what she looked like.

Frank and Alice were leisurely getting ready, so Helen and Ruth sat on the big full sofa in the lobby, linked arms and thighs pressed together like Siamese twins – the two of them and weeks at sea again. They sat in silence, looking out at the street. They knew what the other was thinking. They wouldn't let each other go. They'd make it home.

Lucy came bustling along the footpath and waved at them gleefully through the window. She beckoned them out. They waited on the street for the other two. It was nice to be part of a city again. Ruth was so conflicted, desperate to get home but feeling like she couldn't wrench herself away from Alice. *Australia is very far away.* Helen was much quieter than normal, but Ruth thought it pointless to fill in silence with unnecessary chatter, so she linked arms again and answered Lucy's questions and nodded along to her talking. Eventually, the newlyweds met them, and Frank led the way down the street. They did have a most enjoyable time.

'Sydney is a great place for tourists, even in the middle of a war.' Frank was proud of his city.

Ruth agreed. Even though her feet hurt and her eyes were heavy with exhaustion, she had pushed on through the day and all the walking. They were in the art gallery tea shop, and Frank had insisted on buying Ruth more postcards. She was thumbing through them, trying to decide which one to send her mother and if she should send again to Geoffrey. She obviously didn't expect to hear back from him, and he had her home address anyway. However, she was concerned that he might think she was a nuisance to send all the letters and cards to him. She decided she didn't care and would send him a casual line or two on the back of some interesting Aboriginal art that he might like.

'We should be getting you ladies back to the hotel soon.' Frank looked at his watch. 'More or less now, I'm afraid.'

The pit in Ruth's tummy opened up; she started to cry.

'Come on now. None of that.' Alice was tearing up as well.

Frank said to Lucy, 'Did you drive the truck in?'

Lucy nodded. 'The valet has it.' She laughed out loud.

'Let's drive everyone down to the dock, and that way, we can wave you off,' Frank suggested.

They all agreed.

Alice squeezed next to Lucy driving, with Helen and Ruth next to her. They were all laughing at Frank in the back like a dog with all the luggage. Alice had given Helen and Ruth a lot of her clothes, so they were leaving with even more than they'd left England with. Ruth wore the green jacket. It was making her feel brave. She was hot, but it didn't matter. It was the green coat.

It was very hard to get out of the truck. It was very hard to let go of Alice. They said a fond farewell and thank-you to Lucy and Frank. Alice was in good hands – but what of them? The thought of miles of open water for weeks on end made Ruth sick. She gulped back howls, but big plopping tears ran down her cheeks. The docks were busy, and there were some familiar faces who had been with them through the thin and the thinner times. Helen clutched hard on her hand; Ruth was holding back tears so hard that she could hear her heart thudding in her ears.

They inched closer to the gang plank, their farewell party inching along with them until the bitter end. Walking up the gang plank was hard with such a heavy heart. When they reached the top, they scrambled for a place to look over the rails. Alice had her hand up to her mouth, shouting something, but it was lost in all the other noise. They looked small standing down there.

There was a brass band on board and a brass band on the docks. It was a dreadful cacophony. Ruth was already feeling scatter-brained, and the beat made her already racing heart thump in time. *Concentrate on something else.* She looked down at the three little figures, barely distinguishable from the rest of the crowd. Alice was waving a handkerchief and was still trying to shout out. There was no hope of hearing her. Ruth just waved back, ridiculous arm movements which meant nothing and just made her look deranged.

Helen still had her arm tightly locked in her other arm. She was beginning to lose feeling in her fingers. Helen hadn't really said much all day, and now they were on the boat, she was even more silent. Her eyes were hollow, and she just stood looking down. For all they had been through, for all the times before they left, Alice and Helen had become very close. It was different from Ruth and Helen's friendship, something which Ruth would sorely miss. This realisation made her even more upset.

'Us two,' she whispered right into Helen's ear so she knew she would hear.

'Us two,' Helen repeated. She smiled thinly and looked down again, gave a little wave and sighed heavily.

Pulling away from the docks gave rise to more frenzied band music, and there was even confetti. Ruth's heart couldn't take it; she wished she had hugged Alice at least once more, thanked Lucy and Frank at least once more. *Just stayed.*

She was longing for one of Cook's roasts. 'How did she get those potatoes so crispy?'

Helen laughed out loud. 'What are you on about, girl?'

Ruth realised she must have said it out loud, embarrassed but pleased that Helen was laughing. 'I was thinking about home.'

Helen hugged hard and repeated, 'Home. Home time now.'

Epilogue

It's the day of my great aunt Helen's funeral. I'm sad, but by all accounts, she had a good life. Of course, she's not an aunt by marriage or blood; she just thought of my mum as a niece. She was always around at my gran's place, like family, so I knew her well. It's sad when anyone dies, but today I think my gran is very upset. She and Great Aunt Helen went through a lot in the war together. My gran spoke more than Helen but not by much.

They both talked a lot about their friend Alice, however. A few years ago, they had even flown together to see her and her husband, Frank, in Sydney. I remember because it was the millennium, and Grandad had worried himself silly that all electronics would collapse, and they'd be stuck there. Aunt Helen had said they were used to long boat trips home, if that was the case. I don't think it reassured him at all. He stayed with us while Gran was away for a whole month, and every day he'd forget the time difference and ring them in the middle of the night.

Grandad Geoffrey is not my grandfather by blood either, but he's the only grandad I've known. He's my gran's second husband and father to my uncle Horse. Don't ask why his nickname is Horse; nobody knows, and I don't think anyone knows his real name either. My mum is quite a few years older than her brother, and she says it's because he was always horsing around, but Uncle just winks at anyone who asks. I suppose he has his father's goofy sense of humour. Even though I'm 16, almost 17, he still thinks it's hilarious to pinch my nose and pretend he stole it. Grandad is similar, and his laugh booms out at anything. I'm glad my gran still has him.

I'm glad my gran has Grandad Geoffrey, full stop. He was in the RAF in the war, and Gran met him on the boat going to New Zealand. Even though my gran wrote to him any chance she got, they never saw each other again until years after the war, years after Gran had been married, had a child and been widowed. Grandad had been shot down over Germany and had been taken in and hidden for the whole war by a farmer and his family in a remote part of the Rhine Valley. That is a whole other story for another time. He obviously made it out safely and spent the next few years recovering, thinking about my gran.

It's so romantic. My gran had been writing even when she was a POW on a German raider ship and couldn't post them. Apparently, Frank still teases that my gran owes him a lot of wasted money for postage because when they had absolutely nothing in Sydney, he paid. I think that my gran had also posted a couple of her drawings from New Zealand before the fated *Rangitane* journey. I know the one she sent her parents, they framed and hung in the hallway. Either way, none of them ever reached Grandad Geoffrey. When he returned home and his squadron knew he was alive, he had just supposed that Gran simply forgot him, but he never forgot her. Meanwhile, my gran married a returned soldier from the village, father to my mother, but sadly, he died from complications after surgery to remove shrapnel. I don't know much about him; I suppose I should try to find out. My mum remembers it being just her and Gran and Helen for a long while but calls Grandad Geoffrey Dad.

It wasn't until 1951, I think. Don't hold me to that, but apparently, a large envelope appeared on Gran's parents' doorstep with 'RAF' stamped all over it. It was everything Gran had ever sent Grandad Geoffrey, with an official letter explaining that he had been missing in action, assumed captured and now assumed dead. With it was a letter of apology that they had not been able to deliver the contents, so they were returned to sender. Gran decided to try and find out what had happened to Geoffrey, and with her father's connections to the newspaper and Helen's help, they tracked him down. They thought they were looking up a 'how' and 'where' he was killed, but they found him alive and well in his family home. The package had taken six years, sent straight after the war ended, to arrive at Gran. The connection was instant again, and the rest is a fairy tale existence in this very village. I wish that romantic things like Alice and Frank and Gran and Grandad happened nowadays.

My mum is also very sad today; she often talks about growing up with Great Aunt Helen around and the fun and cheekiness she'd bring as opposed to my gran, who could be quite serious and stern seeming at times. On the day we found out Helen had died, Mum, Gran, and I went round to the 'master's mansion'. Gran always called it that even though it was quite an old, ramshackle house at the back of what used to be the family fruit shop, but it has always been some kind of odd takeaway place in my lifetime. We were sitting at the kitchen table, and Mum was saying we really ought to make the funeral arrangements, but Gran was reminiscing about a time a couple of years after the war, when Alice and Frank had come to stay. Gran said they had been sitting around this very table with Helen's parents, Gran's parents, and their Cook, all laughing at Frank telling long-winded stories. Gran said it was particularly memorable that day because a lady called Trudi was there too. Apparently, Gran and Alice boarded with her before they had left to New Zealand. Gran said it was extremely odd for her but good she had joined.

My gran has helped me pick out an outfit for Helen's funeral. She said it would please her to know that I had put in the effort to be stylish as well as sad. My gran loves outfits; one green coat of hers, I covet, and she said I can have it when I'm older. She said there's no point in writing it into her will for me because she intends to live forever – that is, as she always says, 'if I remain not quite close enough to London to be exciting but near enough for the need to have black-out curtains'.

Printed in Australia
Ingram Content Group Australia Pty Ltd
AUHW020605060923
383264AU00001B/2